In Sherman's Path

J. F. Spieles

Royal Fireworks Press
Unionville, NY

In Sherman's Path
By Jeffrey Spieles

For Mom and Dad

Thank you for shining your love,
wisdom, and guidance into my life,
and for helping me find my path.

Jeffrey Spieles is a native of Wauseon, Ohio. He is a graduate of the University of Dayton and holds an M.A. in Education from The Ohio State University. His personal interests include acting, traveling, sports, and the outdoors. Mr. Spieles currently lives in Englewood, Ohio, and teaches fifth grade for Northmont City Schools. *In Sherman's Path* is his first novel.

Royal Fireworks Press
41 First Avenue, PO Box 399
Unionville, NY 10988-0399
(845) 726-4444
FAX: (845) 726-3824
email: mail@rfwp.com
website: rfwp.com

ISBN: 978-0-89824-859-3

Printed and bound in the United States of America on acid-free, recycled paper using vegetable-based inks and environmentally-friendly cover coatings by the Royal Fireworks Printing Co. of Unionville, New York.

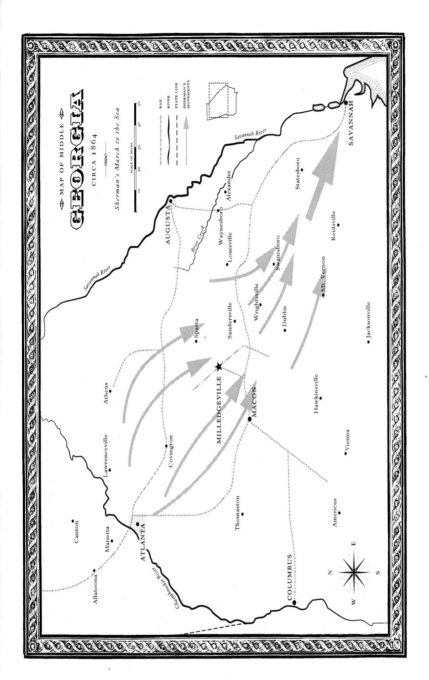

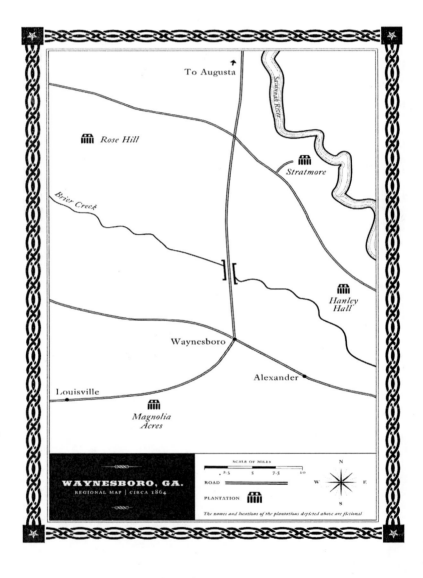

To Augusta

Savannah River

Rose Hill

Stratmore

Brier Creek

Hanley Hall

Waynesboro

Alexander

Louisville

Magnolia Acres

SCALE OF MILES

2·5   5   7·5   10

ROAD

PLANTATION

N   W   E   S

WAYNESBORO, GA.
REGIONAL MAP | CIRCA 1864

The names and locations of the plantations depicted above are fictional

By autumn of 1864, the Civil War had been raging for more than three years. The Confederate Army had suffered major defeats at Gettysburg and Vicksburg. Lincoln had issued the Emancipation Proclamation. The Union blockade of the Eastern Seaboard strangled Southern trade and made supplies scarce.

Still, the people of the South were tenacious and fought with courage and passion. With the odds mounting against them, their spirit seemed to be the source of their strength.

Then on September 1, 1864, the Confederate Army evacuated Atlanta following a month-long siege. The victorious Union general sent a telegraph to President Abraham Lincoln: "Atlanta is ours, and fairly won."

On September 8, that very same general rode into the city and took up headquarters. His name was William Tecumseh Sherman.

General Sherman and his troops occupied Atlanta for two and a half months. During that time, he laid plans for an offensive specifically designed for a singular purpose: to crush the spirit of the Southern people.

Sherman proposed a plan for total war that came to be known as *The March to the Sea*. He intended to march his army from Atlanta to Savannah, passing through the heart of Georgia and destroying everything in his path. He blurred the distinction between military and civilian targets. He resolved to bring the horrors of war to the doorstep of anyone blocking his progress, and he chillingly declared, "I can make the march and make Georgia howl!"

On November 15, 1864, Sherman's troops burned sections of Atlanta to the ground. On that same date, he began moving his army of 62,000 men eastward. The March to the Sea had begun.

Militarily, it was a risky operation. Sherman's army was entering enemy territory with no communication or supply lines of any kind. They cut all of the railroad lines in and around Atlanta—lines which only months before they had fought so hard to protect—so that the Confederates could not use them to their advantage.

To feed his troops, Sherman gave standing orders that permitted his men to roam the countryside and take whatever provisions they needed. These roaming bands of soldiers came to be known as Sherman's "bummers," and it was not long before some bummers helped themselves to much more than just the food that they needed. Stories of Sherman's bummers soon struck fear into the hearts of all Southerners who found themselves in their path.

The voices that he thought were dead were talking in his head again.

"Them Yanks won't git ye!"

Crack! Rifle fire splintered the night.

In an instant he was face down on the ground, hugging the earth so that his panicky gasps brought into his nose the pungent smell of rotting leaves. Unwanted images of battle swam behind his pinched eyelids.

"The'll be butchered!"

Crack!

Sweat beaded on his temples. Clay-smeared fingernails clawed at the ground, tore at the earth, begging it to open and offer him safety.

Crack! Crack!

He was certain he heard a ball whiz over his head. He lost control of himself and felt the crotch of his pants become wet.

While the stream trickled to a stop, a breath that was hot and moist spread across his neck and down his ratty shirt. Hairy nostrils nuzzled him, prickling his skin.

The feel of his horse caused the boy to open his eyes and look back at her. Her ears were up, but she was not spooked. She shifted nervously but did not bolt.

Seeing his horse react with a good deal more courage than himself, he suppressed his own impulse to run.

"Easy, now. Jist take it easy."

He spoke at her but to himself.

Gallivanter pawed at the ground and pulled away from him, retreating toward the spindly tree to which she was tied.

"Aw, c'mon, son! Move it!"

He shook his head, desperately trying to silence the haunting voices. With deliberate effort, he slowed his breathing. He extracted his left hand from its imprint and wiped at the chilly sweat. A hint of calm and a trace of reason returned.

Guns still argued with one another, but the popping indicated small arms. The noises were retreating into the distance.

Though not fully convinced that all was safe, the boy drew himself to his knees and peered from behind a wavy wall of weeds. Occasional muzzle flashes dotted the night. For a long time, he watched and waited. Gradually, the flashes disappeared, and the distant noises ceased.

He slumped back into the thicket, ashamed and embarrassed. With his head in his hands, he mused at his own cowardice. He had pissed himself at the sound of gunfire that was probably just a skirmish in one of the plantation's fields. What was the matter with him?

He looked at Gallivanter. She simply snorted, pulled up some grass, and seemed to roll her eyes at him as she chewed.

"Must be some action afoot," he said aloud, trying to find his voice again. "We's pretty close to Waynesboro. Mebbe Wheeler's boys are givin' it to them Yanks."

Remembering the strict words from his boss, he knew that time was precious. Clearly, the Federals were in the area. If he didn't act now, the Yanks would beat him to it.

He had come to do a job, and he meant to see it through, no matter how harrowing it might be. He had made that resolve once before, but this time he intended to hold true to it.

Picking up a burlap sack and a hooded lantern that sat next to him, he whispered to the horse. "Well, Gal. I cain't lay here in the weeds all night. You jist sit tight now. I'll be by in a bit."

She swished her tail, which swiped against the tongue of the small wooden cart harnessed to her.

The boy rose and waded through the flimsy weeds that were his only cover. He emerged on the plantation's grounds and squinted through the darkness at the big house. Clouds swallowed the November moon, turning the outbuildings into charcoal shapes without form. There was still no sign of anybody.

Not wanting to be in the open longer than necessary, the boy quickly made for the house. The burlap sack swish-swished against his britches. The closer he got, the more he could make out the building's details.

The place reminded him of his boss' house. It was a two-story brick structure with an impressive colonnade and verandah. Three dormers poked their angled heads into the sky. Beyond them, nearer the roof's peak, two rectangular chimneys faced each other.

There was an aura of elegance about the house, and as he arrived at the front door, he speculated on the riches he might find within. It was wealth that the thieving Yanks would love to get their hands on. He was there to prevent that. He would save what he could before the looting bluebellies arrived.

But before him now was a moment that required extreme caution. Despite his long stakeout and everything that his boss had assured him, he did not know for certain if the home was deserted. His intentions, no matter how noble in his own mind, could easily be misconstrued. His explanation, no matter how sensible, could not be uttered faster than the drop of a revolver's hammer.

Intimidating double doors loomed before him. Hands shaking, he tried the knob. As expected, it was locked. It was probably also barricaded from the inside.

He put down his sack and lantern and picked up a sturdy branch that had fallen from one of the many oaks that lined the lane. Gripping it tightly, he stepped close to the enormous window adjacent to the front door.

He took two practice swings, ax-like. Then he slipped the burlap sack over his head to protect his face from flying glass. Under the sack he closed his eyes, took a deep breath, and then let it fly with the mightiest swing that he could muster.

Crash! Even though he knew it was coming, the shattering sound startled him. As the branch pushed through the glass he let go of it. It left his fingers and flew into the house. A second loud crash followed the first, and the boy crouched low as shards cascaded all around him. It seemed forever before the tinkling and colliding debris finally stopped.

The boy remained motionless. He was listening. Surely such a racket would bring forth anyone who might be inside, but he heard nothing.

He rose slowly and removed the sack. He was surprised at how much damage he had caused. He had knocked out the window's lower portion and the upper part had come crashing down after. The window was now a gaping mouth with pointy glass teeth still clinging to the edges, and this was his entryway.

He grabbed the lantern and straddled the window frame. Swinging through, he parted the drapery and found himself in the dining room. Now certain that the house was deserted, the boy lifted the lantern's hood and cast a puddle of light on the floor.

Glass fragments strewn across the marble floor caught his eye. The oak branch lay near the fireplace. As he had suspected, the door had been reinforced with two boards nailed across the inside.

The dining table was in the center. An elegant chandelier dangled above it, and it looked to be made of brass, or maybe even gold. Enchanting as that was, the table displayed items that were within easier reach: two silver candlestick holders.

Their highly polished surfaces winked as he approached. He grabbed the one nearest him and examined it. This single candlestick holder, he thought to himself, was probably the most expensive object he had ever touched in his life. He turned it over in his hands, staring at the shiny piece. Then he stashed it and its partner into his sack. With a muffled clink, they became the night's first collection.

The boy's boss had told him that a Mr. Brewer owned Rose Hill Plantation, and that he had a wife and three small children. It was reasonable to assume, his boss had said, that Brewer would flee when the Yankees approached Waynesboro. Not that Brewer was a gutless man. On the contrary, he would likely face death rather than see his lands in the hands of Northern troops. But he had to consider more than himself and his land. He had to think of his family's safety, and it was unthinkable to let them remain in the path of an advancing enemy.

His boss had been right. As he collected valuables from the house's various rooms, the boy saw no evidence that the family had been there for at least several days. Now assured that he would never be discovered, he concentrated all of his energy on bagging precious items to accompany the candlesticks. Moving from the dining room into the sitting room, he collected a porcelain tea set, two fancy oil lamps, and a silver serving tray. In the pantry he helped himself to several more candlestick holders and a vast array of fine china pieces.

With his burlap sack growing heavy, the boy went back to the dining room and carefully set it down. He slipped through the window and ran back to the thicket where Gal was still tied. He quickly untied the horse and led her, along with the cart that she pulled, to the house's first floor verandah. After looping Gal's rope around one of the columns, the boy retrieved the sack and carefully emptied the contents into the straw-lined cart.

With that done, the boy reentered the house. Using a back staircase he had discovered in the pantry, he made his way upstairs. He passed through the balcony, which offered a dark view of the property behind the house. Then he entered the parlor.

Here, the boy's eyes widened at the riches that the lantern light revealed. An ornate astral lamp occupied the center table. A wooden clock with gold trim was perched upon the mantelpiece. Atop the piano sat two hand-painted piano baby statues made of bisque. The boy quickly bagged all of these, but then stopped when he noticed what hung upon the walls.

There were three magnificent paintings, all of them depicting people whom he supposed were Brewer family members. Though he had no experience in judging such things, the boy felt that the portraits surely must be the works of masters. But the canvases were nothing compared to what held them. All three frames were made of gold.

Quickly, the boy pulled a chair near the wall where one of the paintings hung. The image alarmed him. It was a portrait of a man in a black suit with a severe look upon his face. The eyes were accusing, seeming to note every detail of the boy's thievery.

"He wouldn't look so durn mad if he knew what I'm doin' it fer," the boy whispered to himself. Even so, he shuddered as he lifted it off the wall and laid it on the floor, face down so that the eyes would not follow him. He likewise removed the two other paintings, one of a sophisticated looking woman and the other of a small child.

The paintings were large and heavy. He could not manage them and the sack at the same time, so he took the paintings down to the cart and then returned upstairs to retrieve the sack. After picking up the bag, he quickly scanned the other upstairs rooms. There were no valuables, but in one of the bedrooms a full-length mirror drew his attention.

He paused long enough to study the way he looked: tousled black hair, dirty britches, streaked face, lips drawn into a tense line that seldom relaxed. He stepped nearer the mirror and gazed more deeply into his own eyes, searching for the sassy gleam that had once been alight in them, the glint that declared he could bend the whole world over his knee and give it a licking.

But there was no longer such a flame within him. No, it had been altogether snuffed out. The world, it turned out, had been more than a match for him. His appearance now betrayed the deep-rooted anxiety he carried after having seen too much in his twelve years. He glanced at the dark spot that still lingered on his pants. With a deep sigh of self-loathing, he turned abruptly away.

Hefting the sack onto his back, he trudged out of the bedroom, through the adjoining dressing room, and back onto the balcony. The night air had cooled considerably, and he felt goose bumps rise.

He had not taken two steps when he became aware of something else that made his neck hair stand up. He hooded the lantern and collapsed on the floor behind one of the columns. With the sack in his lap, he tried to make himself narrow enough to hide. Head tucked down so that strands of burlap irritated his chin, he listened over the sounds of his own breathing, praying it had only been his imagination.

It was all too real. From across the backyard, in the open space between the slave quarters and the smokehouse, came the muffled voices of men. They spoke to one another in hushed tones, but from his curled-up position on the second floor the boy could tell that they were coming closer. Soon, he could make out some of the words that they were saying.

"…horses in the stables…"

"Naw, …meat…maybe some corn."

"…smokehouse first…"

There were three distinct voices, and all three had accents that gave them away as Yankee soldiers. They were bummers who had come to raid the plantation.

He gulped hard. He wanted to remain hidden, but he knew that if the soldiers should walk around to the front of the house, they would discover Gallivanter and the cart. They would then search for him, and when they found him…well, he didn't want to think of that. Though his mind raced, it seemed that he had only one option. He had to somehow reach Gal and ride away before they were wise to his presence.

A loud clank made him hug the sack tighter. It was the sound of wood on metal, and a second clank sounded quickly after the first. Desperate to see what the Yanks were up to, the boy carefully turned his head and leaned so that he could see around the pillar and across the backyard.

It was easy for him to spot the bummers. They had a lantern of their own, and it created a pool of light where they stood near the smokehouse. All three were in full uniform, and in the shadowy night their rifles looked like menacing black rods. One of them lifted his rifle high into the air and brought the butt end down on the smokehouse door latch. The clank matched the sounds he had heard moments before.

The third blow must have been successful, for soon the smokehouse door was thrust open and all three soldiers piled inside, taking the lantern with them.

The boy recognized his chance. He scrambled to his feet, and with the sack and lantern he scurried across the balcony and through the door that led to the back stairs.

Once again indoors, he paused at the top of the steps to unhood his lantern so that he could see where he was going. A flurry of questions whirled. *What if there were more than just the three soldiers he had seen? What if an entire company was already out front? What if they had found Gal?* These thoughts made him tremble, but he did not see how his plan could be any different. It would not take them long to clean out the smokehouse, and then they would come into the house. He could not tarry.

Down the steps he plunged, taking them two at a time. He emerged in the pantry, and he held his lantern high to light the way. But as he did so, he heard a shout that froze him in his tracks.

"Hey! A light! There's a light on in the house!"

Only then did he realize that he had held his lantern next to one of the large pantry windows. A soldier must have come out of the smokehouse and seen it through the glass. They were coming for sure. There was nothing left to do but sprint.

The boy bolted through the sitting room and made the tight turn into the dining room, tipping over a chair. He tried to stop quickly when he reached the broken-out window, but he slipped on some of the loose glass shards. He fell, dropping his lantern and landing hard on his side. The bag's contents clanged as they jarred against him. He moaned, but he knew that staying down even for a minute might be the end of him. The boy struggled to his feet and hoisted the sack out the window. He straddled the frame and followed quickly after, leaving the extinguished lantern behind.

Gal greeted him with a whinny. But it was a nervous kind of whinny for she, like the boy, could now hear the Yankee bummers shouting to each other as they came around the side of the house.

The boy heaved the sack into the cart, forgetting to be delicate. But he did not care. He was acting on instinct, like a threatened animal preparing to fight or to flee. Except the boy, even if he had been armed, knew that he could not stand and fight. He thought only of running.

With a hard flick and a yank, the boy untied Gal. Leading her a few feet into the lawn, he crossed around to her side, snugged his foot into the stirrup, and swung himself into the saddle. As he gathered the reins, he stole a glance over his shoulder and saw two of the bummers tear around the corner of the house.

He did not wait to see any more. With a loud *Yah!* and a firm kick into Gal's side, he spurred his steed forward. If Gal needed any extra coaxing, it came when one of the bummers discharged his rifle. The exploding gunshot sent Gal into a mad dash across the plantation lawn, momentarily throwing the boy off balance in the saddle. He recovered his wits and control of the horse just as a second rifle shot rang out. The boy heard the ball thud into a tree as he streaked by, and he clung to his horse and prayed that she could outstrip the danger.

Gal did not let him down. In the time that it took for the Yankees to reload their weapons, she was already across the lawn and out to the road. He reined her hard to the right, and she turned so sharply that the cart was almost upset. But as Gal fell into a strong gallop, the cart righted itself and all three of them, horse, boy, and cart full of boodle, streaked safely into the night.

Henry Akinson never had a place to call home. His mother had died when he was seven. His father worked on the railroad and was frequently gone for long stretches of time. Following his mother's death, Henry, who was an only child, was sent to live with his aunt and uncle on their small farm outside of Macon, Georgia.

The adjustment was difficult at first, but with time his experience on the farm turned into one of his few happy childhood memories. His aunt became a second mother to him, and his uncle lavished him with attention. Under his guidance, Henry learned how to ride as well as most boys in the county, and he learned how to shoot as well as most men. They spent hours together near the fence row taking target practice. *"Exhale... aim...squeeze"* his uncle always said. And almost every time, Henry hit the target dead on.

But when the war between the North and the South broke out in April 1861, those happy days on the farm came to an end. Henry's uncle was among the first to enlist in the Confederate Army. It pained Henry to see his uncle leave, but he understood that sometimes a man has to stand up for a cause that he believes in.

This left his aunt to care for him and the five other children while trying to run the farm on her own. She made a valiant effort, but in the end it proved to be too much. Henry and the three youngest children were sent to an orphanage in Macon. It was supposed to be temporary, just until his uncle returned from the war. Yet in 1862, word came that he had been killed at the Battle of Antietam. Temporarily had turned into indefinitely.

For Henry, time wore on at a snail's pace. He hated the orphanage and yearned to be free of it, but he knew that once he was outside of its walls he would have no place to go. But then, in the early autumn of 1864, chilling news swept across Georgia that distressed Henry and yet offered him a chance for freedom. Union General William T. Sherman had occupied Atlanta, and Southern leaders had put out a call for all men and boys strong enough to bear arms to come to the defense of Georgia and drive Sherman out.

Like many young southern boys, Henry had followed the war news for years. He dreamed of fighting for the Confederacy. He knew he could shoot as well, probably even better, than anybody else. He asked the headmaster for permission to join the Confederate troops, but he was denied on the grounds that he was too young.

During the three years that he had lived at the orphanage, there were many issues on which he and the headmaster did not see eye to eye. This was to be the last. That very night, Henry gathered the few belongings that he had, waited until everyone was asleep, and then slipped secretly out the back door. It was September 10, 1864. He was twelve years old, alone, and heading off to war. But he didn't feel that he was leaving home, for he never really had one to begin with.

Henry left knowing neither where he was going nor what he was getting himself into. Relying on the kindness of strangers for food, shelter, and direction, he wandered northwest for two weeks, covering some 100 miles, until he found himself in Cobb County, Georgia. He skirted the city for fear of being detained by the Federals and was now just north of occupied Atlanta.

Henry learned through hearsay that General John Bell Hood's Confederate Army was in this area and that Hood planned a campaign to cut the Federal supply lines upon which General Sherman's army relied. After questioning the locals and doing some searching, Henry discovered a detachment of Hood's army commanded by General Alexander P. Stewart. He walked straight to the general's tent and offered his services.

By this point in the war, the Confederate Army was desperate for troops. Many of the men in their ranks were either too old or too young for action, but out of necessity they were pressed into service. Henry was assigned a position in Stewart's corps that was under the command of General Samuel French. When asked if he knew how to handle a gun, Henry boldly described himself as an expert marksman.

The corps, however, was so low on supplies that they had no gun to give him. Instead, he was assigned to a regiment where he served as messenger, ammunition bearer, and personal assistant to the sergeant. His duties included relaying messages between the officers and, during action, keeping the men supplied with rounds. He was also at the sergeant's beck and call for any other odd jobs that their circumstances required.

It was not long before Henry's division was called upon. In early October, Stewart's men advanced northwest and attacked several small Union garrisons in hopes of breaking the Federal supply line. The Rebels won victories at Big Shanty, Moon's Station, and Acworth, but these small battles were fought with relative ease. In total, no more than 500 Yankees had defended the three positions. However, despite the minor Rebel victories, the Union supply line remained intact. It would take a more decisive engagement to break it.

A rail line connecting Atlanta and Chattanooga, one that was vital for supplying Sherman's army of 62,000, ran just east of a town called Cartersville. The tracks passed through Allatoona Pass, a deep gorge that had been cut into the mountainous terrain. To protect this crucial link in his supply line, Sherman ordered a division of his men, led by Major General John Corse, to move on Allatoona Pass and to reinforce the Union garrison stationed there.

On October 4, Corse left his post in Rome, Georgia, and began traveling to Allatoona Pass. On that very same day, Stewart ordered General French to march on Allatoona Pass, destroy the Federal rail line, and burn a nearby bridge.

The Yankees approached from the west.

The Rebels approached from the east.

The race to Allatoona Pass was on, and Henry's regiment was right in the thick of it.

A Federal garrison of about 1,000 men already occupied the small earthen forts perched atop the ridge that protected the pass. The larger of the two, shaped like a star, stood on the western portion of the ridge while a smaller one occupied the eastern peak. A deep chasm separated the two, at the bottom of which ran the prized railroad tracks. The two small fortifications were joined by a wooden plank bridge that was laid from one precipice to the other and spanned the chasm.

Having traveled through the night, Corse and his men arrived at Allatoona Pass at 1:00 a.m. on October 5. The number of Yankee troops now swelled to 2,000, and they quickly worked to dig outer defenses and to reinforce the earthworks. At three o'clock in the morning, General French's Confederate force arrived. In the darkness, they surrounded the Federal fortifications and took up positions for attack. Numbering 3,000, the Rebels outnumbered the Yankees, but unfortunately they had lost the race for position by two hours. If Allatoona Pass was to be taken, the Confederates would have to storm the Union forts.

At sunrise, Henry was able to get a better sense of his regiment's position. They were along a route called the Alabama Road on the southwestern side of Allatoona Pass. As far as Henry could tell, one Confederate regiment was in place ahead of his own. Facing them was a Yankee redoubt, a temporary defensive position consisting of trenches. Beyond that, perched on the ridge overlooking the pass, was the larger, westernmost side of the Federal forts.

It had been a long night of marching, but Henry's eyes were wide. This was to be his regiment's first action since he joined them. He longed for a weapon, but he was still unarmed. He stood dutifully by the ammunition case. Every man already had forty rounds, but Henry knew that they could run out quickly if the engagement lasted a while. It was his job to keep them resupplied.

At 8:30 a.m., General French sent a message to General Corse, demanding his surrender. Corse did not dignify the demand with a response. Two more hours of uneasy tension passed until finally, at 10:30 a.m., the Rebels began their assault.

The regiment ahead of Henry's advanced on the Yankee redoubt, but they were repelled by devastating Federal fire. From his place, Henry saw the distant forms of men falling at an alarming rate under the intense hail of grapeshot and cannister. So many weapons were discharged at once that the view before him became a smoky haze. The deafening noise, incessant popping and booming and crackling, beat its way into Henry's brain, and he could not shut it out. His hands flew to his ears, his shaking fingers vibrated against his scalp. He wanted to turn his back to what was unfolding before him, but at that moment his sergeant came by, hustling to the front of his regiment.

Above the roar, the sergeant yelled in Henry's direction. "We're going forward! You stay put until we take that trench, then bring up fresh ammo!"

The sergeant did not wait to see if Henry understood the order. Henry only stared back at him, watching him as he began leading his men at the quickstep toward the Yankee entrenchment. They were soon lost to Henry's senses amid a swirling tempest of smoke and noise and heat.

Henry stood beside the ammunition box for what seemed like an eternity, not knowing what to do. His regiment had disappeared into the hungry jaws of the battle and had not emerged. He was frozen, uncertain, scared.

Suddenly he felt himself being jostled from behind. It was a sergeant from the regiment behind his own. He spoke directly into Henry's ear, "Our boys have taken that trench! We're moving up! Bring that ammo case and come with me!"

Henry grabbed the heavy box and tottered forward. Soon he began hearing balls whizzing through the air around him, and men in front of him and beside him fell to the ground. Henry's hands were so sweaty that he dropped the box twice, causing the men behind him to stumble and curse at him. Henry wanted to shout back at them, that it wasn't his fault, that he didn't know what to do, and that he couldn't even remember why he had wanted to come here. But his words were only in his mind as he struggled with the case and finally toppled with it down into the overrun trench.

Henry recovered from his tumble and glanced wildly about him. He was now in the redoubt that the Yankees had held only minutes before. Ahead, the Federals fell back to the star fort which overlooked Allatoona Pass. Breathless, Henry at last managed words.

"We…we won."

A grizzled veteran heard him and said in reply, "Naw, son. We ain't won. We ain't even started yet. We gotta take that fort."

Henry was incredulous. It seemed to him that he had been on the battlefield for a year, but the chaos was only beginning. The Rebels regrouped in the trench, and Henry began to recognize some of the men from his own regiment. But his eyes were quickly drawn away from them to the dead bodies draped on the slopes like rag dolls strewn about a child's playroom. He took one step and stumbled over a corpse, landing face to face with a Yankee who had caught one in the head. Henry felt his abdomen spasm, and then he vomited all over the dead man's blue uniform.

He lay there, face down and retching, until a strong hand pulled him to his feet. It was his sergeant.

"You made it up. Good. Open that case, and resupply our boys. Then come find me before we charge that fort." With that, he disappeared into the roiling confusion of men who were trying to stay low in the trench and find their regiments.

Suppressing his fear as best he could, Henry dragged the box toward some of the faces that he recognized. He opened it and began handing out rounds to the men who came to him. It didn't seem like he had been at his job more than a few minutes when the sergeant reappeared and barked at him.

"There you are! I told you to come find me. We're gonna storm that fort, and I need you up here! Here…" He reached into the box and withdrew strapped leather pouches that were packed full of ammunition. These he draped over Henry's shoulders and chest.

"Come on now!"

Henry followed him to the northeastern side of the trench, the side facing the fort. All around him, crouched against the sloping dirt walls, were Rebels ready to spring forth and charge. The sergeant pulled Henry up to the top edge of the trench and forced him to peer over it.

"See that ravine up yonder? It's the only approach to that Yank fort. We're gonna rush up and take 'em right now. Once we do that, you gotta get up there lickety-split with them fresh rounds. If we stay in that ravine too long, we'll get pinned down, and I ain't gotta tell ya boy, we'll be sittin' ducks. Once you get up there, we can move forward to the fort. You keep your eyes on me. I'll motion for you. You got it?"

Henry's mind was swimming. He saw the sergeant talking, his eyes pinched with intensity, and his jaw working as he formed the words, but what he said was too fast, too confusing. The booming, bone-jarring gunfire fractured the sergeant's speech into disconnected phrases. Henry didn't know what to do. He wanted to crawl away from this madness and hide. He wanted to bury his face and never look up again. He wanted the sergeant to shrink away and disappear.

He shook Henry. "Hey! I said you got it?"

Henry nodded.

He just wanted the sergeant to go away.

In another moment, the Rebs were up and over the trench wall. At least five that Henry could see fell backward, dead the very instant they stuck their heads above the earthly protection. The others scrambled forward, randomly crumpling into heaps as minie balls poured down on them from the walls of the Yankee fort.

Henry pressed his nose against the dirt and raised his head just enough for his eyes to peer over the edge. He saw the men from his regiment running forward, becoming smaller, darting in and out of smoky clouds as they advanced on the fort. Then, suddenly, they began dropping from view, like clothespins falling into a cup. They had reached the ravine and were hitting the deck.

Henry watched intently. His sergeant appeared through the smoke and waved frantically.

The time was now.

But instead of vaulting the wall and sprinting forward, Henry turned his back to the dirt and slid downward into a crouch, his arms wrapped tightly around his stomach.

A soldier standing beside him, not much older than Henry himself, urged him. "C'mon. They need ammo up 'ar. We'll cover ye. Them Yanks won't git ye."

Still Henry sat doubled over, motionless.

An older veteran sized up what was happening. He grabbed Henry by the shirt collar and yanked him to his feet. "Dang it, boy! Get that ammo up thar! Soon's they run out, they'll be butchered!"

Henry only stared vacantly back at him. He was frozen.

The gruff veteran grabbed Henry by the waist and hoisted him over the trench wall. "Do it! They're all gonna die!"

Henry landed face down on the ground in front of the trench. He felt and heard balls thudding in the dirt all around him. Not knowing how, he rose to his feet.

Ahead, he saw his sergeant screaming and waving his hands wildly. He cupped his hands to his mouth and screamed something that Henry could not hear above the roar.

Behind him in the trench, men shouted at him to do his duty.

"Get up thar!"

"Aw, c'mon, son! Move it!"

"Somebody else get that ammo off 'im and run it forward!"

Henry raised his eyes to the Federal fort. There he saw Yankees leaning over the edge of their earthworks, taking close aim, and firing into the ravine.

In the ravine, he saw appendages flailing about. He no longer saw his sergeant.

It was too much for Henry. Right where he stood, he stripped the ammunition pouches from his body and dropped them on the ground.

"What are you doing!?"

He turned and leapt back into the trench, wriggling free from the men who tried to grab him. Gaining the other side of the redoubt, he scrambled over the earthen wall and tore across the open ground, sprinting for the Alabama Road and then beyond it, all the fear and anxiety within him channeled into an energy that carried him faster than he had ever run in his life. Even when the sounds of battle had faded far behind him, he did not stop.

Henry Akinson ran from the Battle of Allatoona Pass. But he would soon discover that no matter how far or fast he went, he could not drive the memory of it from his mind.

"Them Yanks won't git ye!"

"Aw, c'mon, son! Move it!"

Those voices again. Henry looked over his shoulder for the hundredth time, but there was no one there.

He faced forward again and shifted in the saddle as Gallivanter turned off the main road and headed down the lane leading to Stratmore Plantation. In the waning night, the impressive hedge along the property line was like a solid wall, the great divider between the world within and the world without. Passing through the gate, Henry allowed himself some measure of relief. No one had seen him on the road; the soldiers had not followed.

Henry found himself underneath the overarching oak boughs that lined the way to the big house. Looking up through the branches, Henry noted that the first inkling of dawn had changed the eastern sky to a lighter shade of gray. He permitted his tense shoulders to relax slightly. It would soon be morning. The tumultuous night was behind him.

Gal slightly hastened her step, for after a harrowing night of strange roads, frightening gunshots, and a desperate escape, now at last she was on familiar soil. Indeed, Henry might have dropped the reins entirely and let Gal guide herself past the big house and into the stable, so familiar was she with the plantation grounds.

For a moment, Henry was jealous of his horse. Of course, she was not really his horse at all. Gal belonged to Henry's boss and Stratmore Plantation's owner, Mr. Templeton. Still, during the few weeks that he had been at Stratmore, tending the stables and doing other odd jobs, Henry had developed a bond with Gal and liked to think of her as his own. He was jealous because now, as they made their way up the lane, Gal knew that she was home. Henry, on the other hand, felt neither the comfort nor the warmth of a homecoming. True, he had only lived here a short time. Like when he moved to his aunt and uncle's farm, it would take a while to feel like home. But deep down, Henry could find no reason to believe this place should ever become anything more than just another stopover on his road to who-knows-where. But at least it was shelter.

By the time Gal rounded the bend in the lane, the early morning sky had brightened enough for Henry to make out some detail in the vague shapes before him. The oak trees parted their branches. Like a slowly opening curtain, they revealed Stratmore Plantation's big house. Like the house at Rose Hill, which Henry had observed through the murky shadows of the past night, the house at Stratmore was proud and elegant. Even after several weeks, it still filled Henry with a sense of awe, for his humble beginnings seldom afforded him a chance to view a place of such grandeur. Now he was living at one.

Henry mused at the turns his life had taken over the course of the past month. After the horror of Allatoona Pass, he had been a lost and wandering soul. Out of stubborn pride, he refused to go back to the orphanage. That chapter of his life was over, and on the night that he ran away he swore to himself that he would never return.

Yet he knew that he could never return to his regiment, either. They would likely brand him a coward or maybe even shoot him for desertion under fire. The specter of a death sentence hung over him like a black cloud, but even if he were somehow granted a pardon, he knew that he could still never go back. He would never be able to look those men in the eye. He bore personal responsibility for those troops who had been killed in the ravine, and his mind was haunted by the recurring vision of their arms and legs flailing under the cascade of Federal fire. No, his army days were over. A gutless wretch like himself did not deserve to be called a soldier.

And so, he had wandered. As he had done when he traveled from Macon to Cobb County, he relied on kindly country folk for food and sometimes shelter. Most often he performed an odd job here or there in return for a meal, and then moved on and bedded down under some trees or, if he was lucky, in someone's barn. But always, he kept drifting.

As the war news trickled across the state, he had heard that the Confederate attack at Allatoona Pass had failed. The Rebels had assaulted the western fort four times, each time coming within 100 yards of taking it, but ultimately they had been repelled. General Sherman's supply line had remained intact.

New, horrifying rumors began to spread about Sherman's plans to sweep across the state, taking the war to women and children. As the rumor circulated, Georgians became increasingly wary about whom they allowed into their homes or on their property. Some made plans to move away or abandon their houses altogether. Many women, whose husbands were in the army, began to fret over how they would protect their children and property should the Federals come marching. As October turned into November, it became more difficult for Henry to survive on the charity of those who had to put their own welfare first.

And then, by chance, Henry met Mr. Lewis Templeton. He had wandered into the town of Waynesboro, some 150 miles east and south of Atlanta, and he began asking the shop owners in town if they had any odd jobs that he could perform in exchange for a meal. Mr. Templeton had been in town conducting business that day, and he had overheard Henry's inquiries. He approached Henry, introduced himself, and informed Henry that he owned a large plantation northeast of town along the Savannah River. Times were hard, Mr. Templeton explained, and he was in need of a laborer to help him keep up his property. He told Henry up front that he would not be paid for his services, but that he would be compensated with food and a place to sleep. Henry eagerly agreed to these terms and accompanied Mr. Templeton back to his plantation.

In time, Henry explained to Mr. Templeton the circumstances of his upbringing and how he had become a drifter. He even told him, with no small amount of shame, what had happened at Allatoona Pass. Mr. Templeton absorbed it all in a most thoughtful and stern manner. Desertion under fire, he explained, was indeed a severe charge and was most often punishable by death. He went on to say that he was a respectable citizen and was not in the habit of harboring deserters. This made Henry uncomfortable.

However, Templeton added that as long as Henry performed his chores and faithfully carried out whatever orders he was given, he saw no reason why he should have to turn Henry in. An understanding was established, and Henry dutifully went to work for his new boss.

Now, as Gal plodded forward, and the cart trundled after, Henry noticed that a light was on in the sitting room. He figured that Mr. Templeton had sat up during the night, awaiting the boy's return. Henry unconsciously glanced behind to make certain that the goods he had acquired were safe. Mr. Templeton was a grim man, and he had strictly admonished Henry that the mission was to remain a secret. Even though Henry felt that the Yanks had not discovered what he had really been doing, he was still uneasy about reporting back to Mr. Templeton. Something about the man put Henry on edge, and he never wanted to find out what would happen if he let him down.

Mr. Lewis Templeton sat slumped and drowsing in the sitting room of his fine Southern mansion, a frock coat draped over the back of his rocker and his boots standing obediently straight on the floor beside him. On a nearby table, an oil lamp burned with a steady yellow flame. A half-full bottle of brandy and an empty snifter cast short, stubby shadows.

Even in sleep, Templeton's face was austere. His high forehead was seemingly supported by ever-present tension in his cheeks. His hair, mustache, and beard formed the gray fringes of a face punctuated by a dash of a mouth, a straight line that appeared more apt to frown than smile. Made fuller by the beard, the man's jaw was square and firm. Now, as his head tilted to one side of the rocker, his lips parted slightly, allowing a sleeping-sigh to escape.

Atop his white linen shirt, a key that was attached to a chain around his neck rested on his chest, and it rose and fell as his breathing resumed the rhythm of slumber. His gray woolen pant leg wavered as his right leg twitched slightly.

Henry was correct in his estimation that Mr. Templeton was a harsh man. Before the war, he was a prominent businessman who had earned for himself a reputation of being calculating and impersonal. He single-mindedly pursued profit, at times resorting to ruthless means to get what he wanted. And while such personality traits did not win him many close friends, they served him well in his business dealings.

After several successful ventures as a young man, Mr. Templeton gained enough wealth to purchase Stratmore Plantation, located fifteen miles to the northeast of Waynesboro, Georgia. He quickly put his business savvy to work in Georgia's plantation economy, capitalizing on his land's location on the Savannah River. Cultivating cotton as his chief crop, Templeton ginned and baled his product before loading it onto flatboats and sending it down the river to the city of Savannah, where brokers sold it to English merchants for a tidy sum.

As it became clear that he was riding his cotton boats to financial success, Mr. Templeton swiftly became one of the most eligible bachelors in the South. He eventually married a young woman from Atlanta. After bearing him only one son, however, she died of yellow fever. Awash in the pain of her departure, Templeton further immersed himself in his work, making it the sole focus of his energy. After several years of turning high profits, Templeton purchased more land and, unfortunately for those poor souls who found themselves under his ownership, more slaves.

Though he depended upon their labor to fuel his business, Templeton loathed his slaves. He considered them creatures so far beneath himself that they did not deserve any amount of respect, and so he treated them cruelly and made no secret of his disdain for them.

Harsh treatment of his slaves aside—and it was so easily pushed aside—it was not long before Templeton became one of the wealthiest plantation owners in Georgia. Though friendship is perhaps too intimate a term, he shared mutual respect and admiration with other area planters who enjoyed social and financial standing equal to his own, among them William Hanley, Jonathan Graves, and Cyrus Brewer.

For Mr. Lewis Templeton, then in his early fifties, the world seemed laid out for him on a silver platter. But life, it seems, has an uncanny way of shifting just when it seems everything has gotten comfortable.

On January 18, 1861, Georgia seceded from the Union.

On April 12 of that same year, the Civil War began.

From the very moment that it arrived, the war put a strangle-hold on all that Mr. Templeton held dear. Soon after the attack on Fort Sumter, his son Robert enlisted in the Confederate Army. Now, Lewis Templeton was not a man who had ever gotten truly close with anyone, even his wife. But if there was someone with whom he felt a deeper connection, it was his son. Robert helped to manage the plantation and shared with his father a keen business intelligence. When the time was right, Templeton planned to turn the entire operation over to him. So when Robert left, Templeton felt that a vital part of the life he had built, and the cornerstone for its future growth, had just been pulled away. And though Robert's departure created a painful void, so much more agonizing was the fact that during the three years he had been away, Robert had not sent one letter to his father.

Then came the blockade. As part of its strategy to win the war, the North had positioned war-ships all along the Southern coastline, effectively halting Southern trade. The upshot for Mr. Templeton was devastatingly simple: no longer could he get his product to market. His income evaporated, and yet the expenses of running the plantation remained. After two years Templeton had to sell some of his land, auction off many of his slaves, and dismiss his overseers and other white men who had worked under him for wages. His beloved Stratmore-on-the-Savannah, as he referred to it in its glory days, had been reduced to a shadow of its former self.

Then came the Emancipation. As news of the signing slowly trickled south, slaves everywhere felt their spirits rise, for now a Northern victory would bring to an end their forced servitude. Like many others, those slaves who remained on Lewis Templeton's plantation began to run away, taking their chances on making it to Northern soil.

With no overseers left to help him, Templeton could do little more than keep a close eye on his slaves. On one occasion, he discovered a plot for a nighttime escape that several of them had arranged. Templeton loaded his gun and waited in the shadows for the would-be runaways to try crossing his property line. Sure enough, they crossed, and many of them kept going even after the gunshot. But one black man fell dead with Templeton's bullet lodged in his head.

Templeton had hoped that the shooting would deter others from taking flight, but it did not. It was impossible for him to keep constant vigil, and he knew that with each passing day there were fewer and fewer slaves living in the jumble of shacks that they, for so many years, had called home. And so it went until only three of them remained.

By 1864, Lewis Templeton, like so many landowners in the South, had witnessed the destruction of a lifestyle he had known since he was a babe in the cradle. He was penniless, his position in society was meaningless, and his beloved plantation was in ruin. His son was missing and, for the first time in his life, he felt utterly alone. Everything had collapsed, and it seemed that there could be no injury or insult worse than those that had already been dealt to him.

Then came Sherman.

After occupying the city of Atlanta for ten weeks, General Sherman received orders to move out. When he had arrived, Atlanta was a flourishing city with industry and businesses built around principal railroad lines. When he departed, it was a smoldering heap of ash.

On the night of November 15, 1864, the city was put to the torch. Factories, railroad depots, shops, and homes were burned to the ground. Federal troops set fire to everything that the retreating Confederates had left standing. Railroad tracks were ripped up, slave markets destroyed, and crops burned. And as horrific as this scene of wholesale destruction was, it was only the beginning of what Sherman had in mind.

He moved his troops out of Atlanta in two columns, heading southeast across the state of Georgia. His ultimate goal was to reach the Atlantic Ocean and capture the city of Savannah. But along the way, Sherman vowed to blast the Southern countryside with total war, smashing into oblivion anything that the Southerners needed to wage resistance. He gave his men standing orders to steal food, rip up railroad tracks, and burn crops and bridges. Moving slowly and methodically, the two branches of Sherman's army moved forward, cutting a swath of destruction sixty miles wide.

On the night of November 26, a cavalry division from Sherman's army camped just outside of Waynesboro.

Sherman was at Templeton's doorstep.

Templeton could hear him knocking.

Tap! Tap! Tap!

Templeton grimaced in his sleep, as if memories of all that had gone awry in his life came back to him in his dreams. He stirred, shifting his weight in the rocking chair.

Tap! Tap! Tap!

Templeton slowly became aware of the noise. He shook away the heavy veil of sleep. Inhaling suddenly, he snapped open his eyes and sat forward in the rocking chair, his hands poised on the armrests ready to push himself to his feet.

Tap! Tap! Tap!

Outside one of the sitting room windows, a silhouetted figure rapped lightly upon the glass. What surrounded the figure was not the deep dark of night, but rather a muted gray. It was nearly dawn. The boy had returned.

Quickly, Templeton leaned down and pulled on his boots. Then he stood and stretched, his back lightly cracking as he did so. Long had he sat awaiting the boy's return before sleep had overcome him. Now at last he would see if the deed had been properly done. He picked up his frock coat, passed through the dining room, and opened the front door.

The early dawn's chilly air greeted him, and as Templeton stepped onto the verandah, he slipped on the coat. Before him in the lane stood Gallivanter, the cart still attached to her. Then, from the corner of his eye, he saw the boy approaching, walking across the verandah from the window at which he had been tapping.

Henry stopped in front of Templeton. He looked past the rigid face, over his shoulder, and only made eye contact with quick, sideways glances. Templeton intimidated him terribly. Henry felt the plantation owner's eyes boring through him, probing him for information. Templeton slowly adjusted the buttons on his frock, covering the pendulous key that hung from his neck. Henry wanted to speak up, but he could only shuffle his feet.

Finally, Templeton broke the silence. "Well, boy, am I to stand here all morning waiting for you to find your tongue?"

"No, sir," Henry stammered.

"Then give account of yourself," Templeton bluntly demanded.

Henry met Templeton's eyes for a brief moment and then looked away. Those eyes seemed powerful enough to see directly through him. An unbidden thought crossed his mind. What if Templeton saw the stain on his britches? Henry shuffled sideways, turning toward Gal and the cart, trying to shield embarrassment. He cleared his throat and finally found his voice.

"I...I done what you asked, sir." With a feeble gesture toward the cart he added, "From Mr. Brewer's place. I took all's I could."

After getting the words out, Henry threw another look askance at Mr. Templeton's face, and he thought he saw there something resembling a glimmer of satisfaction.

"Well, then," said Templeton, "why don't you show me what you've got." He turned and walked toward the cart. Henry followed after.

The first thing that Templeton removed was the burlap sack. Placing it on the grass, he reached inside and pulled out the astral lamp. Even in the gray pre-dawn light, it looked shiny and impressive.

"Here's a nice piece," muttered Templeton as he examined the lamp, then carefully set it down on the grass. "What more is in here?"

Again rummaging through the sack, he produced the wooden clock with gold trim and the two piano baby statues. One statue's head had been broken off.

Templeton shot an accusing glance at Henry. "A bit careless with this one, I see."

Henry wanted to explain about his desperate escape from the bummers, why he had been forced to so roughly handle the sack, but Templeton had already turned his back to him and was sifting through the cart's remaining contents.

Henry was suddenly sick with worry that during his rough ride away from Brewer's plantation more of the valuables had been broken. He had not thought to check the condition of his cargo before showing it to his boss. Any further broken pieces would be an unpleasant surprise to both of them.

His heart sank as Templeton pulled out several broken fragments of china. Templeton said nothing, but the ire in his eyes and the force with which he tossed aside the broken bits caused Henry to fidget.

But then Templeton noticed something that greatly eased his expression. A glittering, golden corner peeked at him from under a layer of straw, and as Templeton brushed the straw aside and removed the entire frame, he forgot the anger that had bubbled up a moment ago.

Henry breathed an audible sigh of relief as Templeton eagerly withdrew the other two frames, the silver candlestick holders, the oil lamps, the silver serving tray, and the many pieces of the porcelain tea set, all of which amazingly remained intact. As Templeton more closely examined all of the items, the rising sun finally topped the trees. The morning light allowed all of the objects to reflect their brilliance. In all, only one piano baby and three pieces of china had been damaged. Henry stood speechless, waiting for Mr. Templeton to pass judgment.

For a long time, Templeton stroked his beard and thoughtfully gazed upon the items spread about him, as if making mental calculations. Then he turned abruptly to Henry.

Without smiling, he said, "I must say that you've satisfied my expectation. A bit reckless, perhaps, and next time I'll expect fewer damaged goods. But for the first time out, this is acceptable."

Henry was amazed. During the few weeks that he had been at Stratmore, he had cleaned the stables and tended the horses, repaired rotting planks on the dock, and had kept the grounds. But today was the first time that Mr. Templeton expressed to him something that at least resembled appreciation. Henry smiled inwardly, thinking that perhaps he had gotten on Templeton's good side. But to Templeton himself, all he could manage was a meek, "Thank you, sir."

"Help me reload these. We'll take them down to the storehouse."

"Yes, sir."

Henry helped him put the items back into the cart, and then he walked alongside as Mr. Templeton led Gal down a path that wound around the western side of the big house. Once they came around the corner, the ginning house came into view. Beyond it, separated from the plantation's inner grounds by a split-rail fence, sprawled the western section of Stratmore's once abundant cotton fields. The land, now lying fallow and filled with weeds, stretched as far as Henry could see. No bales of cotton had come from that field, or any of the others, for two years. Mr. Templeton gazed briefly out at the field as they passed by, and Henry saw that it pained him.

They walked for a while in silence, but as they approached the vegetable garden Mr. Templeton spoke.

"Was my prediction about Mr. Brewer correct?"

"Yes, sir," Henry answered, speaking with more confidence now after having pleased Mr. Templeton. "The house looked like it'd been empty fer a spell."

Templeton nodded, as if he already knew that he had been right.

"Mr. Brewer informed me some weeks ago that he intended to relocate his family to Valdosta. Have his properties been damaged?"

"No, sir. Everything seemed fine and dandy when I got there. But…" Henry trailed off.

"But what?"

"Well, sir, there was some skirmishin' out on one of his fields. And some Yankee bummers, they come up to the house jist as me and Gal was leavin'."

"Did you see them damage anything?"

"Yes, sir. Broke into the smokehouse and prob'ly did more after me and Gal skeedadled."

At this, Templeton scowled. Then he stopped walking and eyed Henry severely. "Did they see you? Did they see what you were doing?"

"They sall my backside as we rode off…popped a couple shots at us…but they didn't see my face. I was done cleanin' the place out afore they come after me."

"You're certain you were not followed?"

Henry shook his head vigorously. "Naw, sir. I checked three or four times. Ain't nobody followed us."

Satisfied with the certainty in Henry's voice, Templeton walked on. He was, however, clearly disturbed by the news that Yankee troops had raided Brewer's plantation.

"Curse that Sherman!" he suddenly swore. "Military targets are not enough for him! Railroad tracks wrecked, crops burned, private property looted and vandalized!"

Templeton appeared to be talking to himself, his narrowed eyes focused on the ground before him, his words forced through his clenched teeth. He turned and focused his heated gaze upon Henry.

"But mark me, boy. The day will come when that butcher and his bluebelly pig soldiers are driven from this land. The South will be scrubbed clean of their filth. Our people who have been forced away will return to rebuild."

Templeton fell silent for a moment, allowing the gravity of his prediction to sink in. Henry was surprised when he spoke again. It was the most he had ever heard Templeton say at one time.

"These invaders are trying to break our spirits, to rob us not only of our wealth but of our very identity as well." Here he looked at the boy more sharply than ever. "We must not allow it. We must preserve all that we can. We must keep out of thieving Union hands all the precious items that remind us of who we are, of what we once had, and of what we shall have again. And for those who cannot protect their own, like Mr. Brewer, we must do it for them. Upon their return, we shall give back to them what is rightfully theirs."

As Templeton spoke, it occurred to Henry that "we" meant the two of them. He was shocked that Mr. Templeton viewed him as a partner. He felt elevated, like he had just assumed a higher status. The sensation was entirely new for him, and it felt good.

"I'm the first to admit," Templeton continued after musing for a moment, "that I haven't been the most selfless of neighbors. But this is war upon our very way of life, and there is honor in doing what I can to preserve it, not only for myself, but also for my fellow countrymen."

Again he stopped walking and eyed Henry. This time Henry met his gaze with solid contact. *Honor.* The word resonated with him, a long hungered-for badge of which he had never yet proven himself worthy. Before him now was another chance.

"Do you understand what I'm saying, boy?"

Henry nodded.

"You are my right hand in this endeavor. Will you help me see it through?"

Again Henry nodded, his chest inflated with pride. "I will, sir."

Templeton nodded at him affirmatively, and then they walked on. Finally, Henry felt that he had an opportunity to do something honorable for his country.

It was a chance for redemption.

By this time, they had walked past the plantation's vegetable garden, a sizable plot of land that, unlike the cotton fields, was cultivated and well tended. Since the beginning of the war, the garden had become more important to the daily life on the plantation. It provided much of the food that found its way onto Mr. Templeton's dinner plate. Tended by the few slaves who remained at Stratmore, the garden had yielded a rich harvest. Yet now, during the waning weeks of autumn, it was time for the garden to be cleared in preparation for winter.

Except it was not yet cleared. Mr. Templeton had assigned the task to Reuben, a slave boy who lived with his mother and sister. They were the only three slaves who still remained at Stratmore. Since his arrival, Henry had seen Reuben about the property, but he had never spoken to him. He appeared to be about Henry's age. On more than one occasion, Henry had heard Mr. Templeton instructing Reuben to clear the garden and to repair the fence that separated it from the slave quarters. Now, as he and Henry passed by on their way to the storehouse, Mr. Templeton's critical eyes did not fail to note that the jobs were still not completed, and Reuben was nowhere to be seen.

The slave quarters, which were nothing more than a collection of ramshackle cabins, lay just beyond the fence that needed mending. Most of the buildings were abandoned, but smoke from a morning cook fire could clearly be seen rising from the cabin that lay nearest the western cotton field. It was hard for Henry to be sure, but he thought he heard the distant cries of a baby over the clip-clop of Gal's hooves. He tried to listen harder, but Mr. Templeton's coldly spoken words drew his attention.

"Looks like that lazy slave boy decided to have a leisurely morning when there's work yet to be done. I suppose I'll have to give him a lesson in obedience."

Henry was not even the one in trouble, but he still felt scared by the way that Mr. Templeton spoke those words. The cries, if he had not imagined them in the first place, had now stopped, but as Henry looked once more at the cabin with the smoke rising from it, he could not help but think that, before the day was done, more wailing might fill the air.

They arrived at the back edge of the plantation's property, which was the very bank of the Savannah River. Templeton led Gal up to the doors of a large storehouse and tied her lead rope to a fence railing. During the height of the plantation's productivity, the storehouse had been crammed full of cotton bales awaiting their trip down the river. Just to the east of the storehouse doors, beneath drooping tree branches festooned with Spanish moss, a wide dock jutted into the river. It was here that the flatboats would be tied up while Templeton's slaves loaded them with bales. But all that had come to an end as the war dragged on. The storehouse now sat empty, and the flatboats had all been sold off. Now only a small rowboat was tethered to one of the pilings. It bobbed idly with the moving current.

Lifting the chain from around his neck, Templeton used the key to unlock the storehouse. The bales that used to be stored inside that building were the lifeblood of his entire operation, and so he kept the key to it, the only key, on a chain which he wore around his neck, and took security in knowing that the key was always near to his heart. Now, after swinging the doors wide, he replaced the chain. He and Henry then carefully transferred all of the valuables from the cart into the storehouse.

As they worked, Henry summoned up the courage to ask Mr. Templeton a question that had been nagging at his mind. "Sir, I been thinkin'. I mean, if them Yanks take Waynesboro and theys bummers all about raidin' plantations and sich, what's to stop 'em from comin' here? I mean, theys only about fifteen mile off."

Mr. Templeton gingerly propped one of the gold frames against the storehouse wall and draped gauze netting over it for protection. Then he straightened and addressed Henry.

"Well, boy, that's been a concern of mine for a fortnight. I suppose there's no guarantee that the bummers or Sherman himself won't make their way here, but I have a strong feeling that they won't. If Sherman takes Waynesboro, then I do believe he'll turn southeast, away from us. Sherman has his eyes on the sea, and the port of Savannah is too fine a prize for him to pass up. No, boy, I don't believe they'll come this way. We are on the outermost edge of his wake."

Templeton's answer both relieved Henry and gave him butterflies. It did make sense for Sherman to turn southeast, and it was nice to be somewhat assured that Stratmore would remain a safe haven. But the part that made him nervous was the realization that, in order to keep the riches from other plantations out of enemy hands, he would have to venture further into Sherman's path.

"Now then," said Templeton as the last of the goods were placed in the storehouse and the door was again locked, "you take Gal on up to the stables. Unhitch the cart, feed and water her, rub her down. Clean out the whole stable while you're up there. I have other matters that need my attention."

This order was a letdown to Henry. Though he usually enjoyed working in the stables, he was by now feeling very tired after a long, sleepless night filled with intense activity. He had hoped that Mr. Templeton would allow him to rest. But disappointed though he was, he dared not show his feelings, especially after hearing Templeton's comments about Reuben's unfinished duties.

Untying Gal's lead rope and turning her toward the stables, he said to Templeton, "Yes, sir."

But Templeton did not respond. He was heading toward the slave quarters.

Henry led Gal across the back yard, past the privies, which were well concealed by trees, and the kitchen yard that was situated well opposite the privies. In days past, the kitchen yard had been a place of constant activity. It contained the smokehouse, the well, the dairy, the icehouse, and water troughs. It was here that house slaves toiled from before sunrise to well after sunset preparing all the meals that the master and his family required. As the plantation's population had declined, so too did the bustle in the kitchen yard. But of course it did not cease altogether, for Mr. Templeton, and now Henry, still needed to eat.

As he rounded the corner of the kitchen yard where the dairy was situated, Henry heard Violet, the only remaining house slave, preparing breakfast for her master. As with all other matters, Mr. Templeton expected his meals to be on time and in accordance with his particular tastes. Having worked at Stratmore all of her life, Violet knew all too well the consequences of not pleasing her master, and so she now hustled to have breakfast prepared on time.

The middle-aged woman's skilled hands flew over her utensils, performing the well-choreographed routine that years of daily rehearsal had made automatic. Henry caught a glimpse of her as she went to the well and deftly drew a bucket of water. She was a sturdy woman with arms and hands as toned as they were dexterous. Typically, a light blue bonnet covered her hair, sitting atop a face that was round and defined with high cheekbones. She generally wore a determined expression that warned the world not to get between her and the job that she had to accomplish. Still, there were times when her face could soften, and a pleasing, white-toothed smile could bring forth a dimple on her right cheek.

Now, as breakfast time drew near, Violet's face was set in determination mode. Having drawn the bucket, she stepped quickly back toward the kitchen, causing her pink dress and white apron to ripple. She caught sight of Henry and acknowledged his presence with a half-nod of her head before setting down the bucket and carrying a tray through the servant's doorway into the big house.

Henry did not return the gesture. He simply continued leading Gal to the stables. He had seen Violet everyday since his arrival at the plantation, but he had never spoken a word to her. He knew only that she was Reuben's mother and that she was a good cook. That was all he needed to know and all that he cared to know. After all, he was not one of them.

The circumstances of Henry's upbringing did not bring him into contact with many slaves though he had sometimes seen them in and around Macon. He derived most of his views from other whites. Not that he was ever taught anything directly. No, the messages were never made quite so obviously. Just the same, the meaning was loud and clear, and he saw it reinforced time and again. It was a belief, an attitude so pervasive that Henry had adopted it without ever questioning, without ever wondering why.

And just what did he learn from it all?

That slaves are property, not people.

That they are ignorant and inclined to laziness without a master's forcible hand to keep them on task.

And he learned that he, poor and lowly as he was, still held claim to a higher status just because he was white.

So he had been taught, and so he believed.

Outside the stables, Henry unhitched the cart that had followed Gal's every step for going on twelve hours. Glad to be rid of it, Gal sauntered into her stall and immediately set to eating and drinking what Henry provided for her. He was about to brush her and rub her down when he heard the sounds of a distant commotion. Brush still in hand, he stepped out of the stable to see what was the matter.

The sound of an angry voice rose and fell across the property. It came from the slave quarters. He knew that he was hearing the confrontation between Reuben and Mr. Templeton, but the ferocity of Templeton's shouting startled him. Curiosity got the best of him, and he wanted to see what was going on. The low buildings in the kitchen yard obscured his view, so he walked to the corner of the dairy and peered around it.

What he saw made his heartbeat quicken and his palms go sweaty. Reuben and Mr. Templeton stood face-to-face at the end of the dusty path that led back into the slave quarters. Templeton was railing at the slave boy, every once in a while gesturing toward the garden and the fence that Reuben had failed to maintain.

But it was not Templeton's ranting that made Henry so enthralled with the scene. Rather, it was Reuben and the way that he held himself as he took his master's onslaught of scathing remarks. Reuben did not back away. He did not turn his face aside nor did he fidget. He stood solidly before Templeton, feet and shoulders square, arms crossed in defiance, chin raised so that he looked his master straight in the eye.

Henry was incredulous. Even from his far away position, Templeton's barking made Henry want to run and hide. But Reuben stood firm and held his ground...until he took his audacity a step too far.

From the distance at which he stood it was difficult for Henry to discern the exact words. However, it appeared that

Templeton hollered a question at Reuben and, to Henry's surprise, Reuben brazenly shouted an answer in reply. This was followed by a moment of eerie silence, after which Templeton pointed a finger at Reuben and probably whispered a threat. That's when Reuben made his regrettable move. He took a step toward Templeton and pushed his pointed finger aside.

That movement was like the falling stone that triggered an avalanche. Templeton swung with his right hand and delivered a blow to Reuben's chin. The boy, as daring as he had been, was no match for Templeton's full-grown strength, and he immediately collapsed onto the grass. Templeton watched him writhe for a moment, and then he stepped forward and delivered a sharp kick into Reuben's stomach. On the ground, Reuben folded himself into a kidney shape and absorbed the blow. Then, as Reuben clutched his stomach and tried to regain his breath, Templeton took a whip from his belt and flaunted it in the air above the moaning boy.

"No!"

The cry came so sharply and so close to Henry that he jumped when he heard it. Amidst the clamor, he had forgotten that Violet was working in the kitchen yard. He turned to see her emerging from the servants' doorway, exiting the big house and stepping back into the kitchen yard. She came outside just in time to see the first lash tear into her son's back. The crack was so sharp that Henry jumped again.

"No!" Violet cried once more, and this time her exclamation was high-pitched and drawn-out by her sobs. The whip rose and fell again. She ran some distance into the backyard and then, like a slowly melting wax figure, she sank to her knees and buried her face into her apron. Her sobs were accompaniment to the whip's cracks and Reuben's cries. Her abdomen shook, and her breaths came in great howling gasps. She was powerless to stop what was unfolding before her.

Henry watched until it was over. Templeton laid on fifteen lashes before he straightened, wiped his brow, and backed away from Reuben's crumpled form. Even from where he stood peering around the corner of the dairy, Henry could see the blood seeping through the back of Reuben's shirt. Templeton gathered in the cords of his whip, turned, and made his way to the big house. Passing Violet on the lawn, he said in an eerily calm tone, "My breakfast had better be on time, or you'll share his fate."

Then he disappeared into the house, and Violet, still shaking terribly, rose to her feet, turned away from Reuben, and went inside to feed the man who had just beaten her son.

Henry delayed a moment longer. Once again the baby's crying could be heard faintly, and Henry watched unblinkingly as Reuben rolled himself over, got up on all fours, and began crawling slowly back toward the cabin from which the baby wailed.

Henry turned away and walked back to the stable, shaking his head and trying to make sense of what he had just witnessed. There were many truths about his own life that he wished could be different, but he was thankful for one truth that could not be changed.

"Thank Gawd I'm no slave," he muttered to himself.

That evening, Henry found himself seated in the dining room with Mr. Templeton. He did not feel well. Not once during the day had Mr. Templeton allowed him a respite. After Henry had cleaned the stable, Mr. Templeton set him to work on mending the fence and clearing the garden, jobs that the now injured Reuben would not be able to complete. By now Henry was so fatigued that his muscles ached, and he longed to lay his head on the table and shut his eyes.

Besides physical exhaustion, he could not erase from his memory the image of Reuben being whipped and beaten, left to crawl away like a licked dog. Nor could he forget Violet's helpless expression as she had been forced to turn away from her wounded son. The mournful baby's crying underscored it all, and Henry could not get it out of his mind.

He did not condemn Templeton's actions. Templeton was the master, and he had dealt with a disobedient slave in the way that he saw fit. It was entirely within his rights to do so. Still, the events strangely discomfited Henry, and he struggled to make sense of his feelings.

There was still another reason for discomfort as he sat at Mr. Templeton's fine dining table. It was the first time that Templeton had asked Henry to share supper with him, and Henry felt nervous in this new situation. He had always taken his meals in the pantry, eating various leftovers that Violet had set out for him. But tonight he would be served as if he were an aristocratic gentleman, and he had never felt more out of place. No experience from the farm or his days in the orphanage had done much to refine his manners, and he dreaded appearing a lout before the man whose presence alone intimidated him.

Mr. Templeton sat opposite Henry, a somber look upon his face. The table between them was set with fine china, waiting for the food to be served. The flames on the many-candled chandelier above their heads danced according to the will of unseen air currents. Templeton sat back and stared for long moments at the blazing wicks, his eyebrows furrowed. Hidden by his bushy beard, his lips were pulled tight as if he were pondering an unfortunate situation. The room was too quiet, and Henry began to wonder if Templeton had forgotten about his presence. Something about the man's demeanor told him that it wouldn't be wise to speak unless directed to do so, so the boy remained silent.

Mr. Templeton's reverie was at last broken when Violet entered the dining room. Having come from the pantry, she carried two large platters, one full of smoked ham and the other with biscuits. These she placed on the serving sideboards, and then she returned from whence she came to bring the remainder of the food. Henry tried to get a look at her face, but her familiar blue bonnet seemed pulled lower than usual, and she kept her gaze fixed on the floor. Templeton watched her leave the room, and then he turned his attention to Henry, whose mouth had started watering as soon as the smell of the ham had reached his nostrils.

"I received some news today," Templeton said, still not easing his expression. "A former business associate of mine from Waynesboro stopped by this afternoon. He informed me of some fierce cavalry clashes that have taken place just outside of town. He reported hot fighting between Joe Wheeler and an advance company from Sherman's column, a cavalry unit commanded by a man named Kilpatrick. This associate of mine was making his way to Augusta when he became mixed up in some of the skirmishing on the road. He said he was lucky to escape with his life."

News of battle turned Henry's thoughts away from his fatigue and hunger. "Did he say if Wheeler whooped them Yanks?"

"It appears that Wheeler has managed to hold them at bay. He surprised the Federals last night and was able to push them back. Today the Yankee cavalry rode through town and caused some damage, but Wheeler drove them out and pushed them south. Waynesboro has not yet been taken. Even so, Sherman has tens of thousands of troops marching behind his cavalry. Wheeler will be no match for them." Templeton narrowed his eyes, either in anger toward Wheeler's inability to protect the town or else in pure hatred toward Sherman.

Henry knew that Major General Joe Wheeler was a Confederate cavalry officer under the command of General Hood. Many Georgians had looked to Wheeler to stop Sherman's advance, but after a skirmish at Sandersville, Wheeler's tiny unit had been forced time and again to fall back before Sherman's oncoming horde. The news was alarming. Templeton seemed resigned to the idea that Waynesboro would be occupied, which meant that a sizeable Union force was now virtually on Stratmore's doorstep.

Henry remembered the previous night's events. The gunfire that had so spooked him at Rose Hill Plantation must have been the sounds of Wheeler's men engaging Kilpatrick. The bummers he encountered must have strayed from their unit.

Violet returned bearing the reminder of the food: cornbread, black-eyed peas, and greens. As she filled the plates from the sideboard, first Templeton's and then Henry's, Templeton spoke on about Sherman's march.

"He razed Atlanta, laid waste to our capital in Milledgeville, and now threatens to take Waynesboro, with countless other towns and villages having already fallen before him along the way. Surely a man so bent on inflicting pain and suffering deserves death."

At this comment Violet, from her place near the sideboard, raised her head and eyed Templeton accusingly before dropping her gaze once more. Templeton did not notice, but Henry clearly saw the smolder in the slave woman's eyes. She walked hurriedly from the room.

"This turn of events makes our endeavor all the more urgent," continued Templeton as he and Henry began to eat, Henry taking great care to use the proper utensils and to chew with his mouth closed. "As the Yankee infantry approaches Waynesboro, they will begin to forage farther and farther. It's the only way they'll be able to feed their troops. Word has it that Sherman has upwards of 60,000 men. That means bummers will be raiding plantations, starting with those nearest the town. If we are to preserve what we can from their thieving hands, we must act quickly."

Henry now understood why he had been called to have supper with his boss. He was getting his next assignment.

Templeton chewed a piece of meat, the muscles in his cheeks bulging as his jaw worked. All the while his calculating eyes bore down on Henry, so much so that the uncomfortable boy squirmed and looked away as he nibbled at his own piece of cornbread.

Mr. Templeton motioned toward him with his fork as he spoke on. "Magnolia Acres is a plantation owned by a Mr. Jonathan Graves. He is a gentleman who greatly assisted me when I acquired my flatboats. He enlisted soon after First Manassas, and the last I heard was that he was with A.P. Stewart's Army of Tennessee. His wife, Amelia, and her two children have been living at Magnolia Acres since he departed for war. I do not wish to see their personal valuables taken by the Yankees."

Violet entered the dining room again, checking to see if Mr. Templeton or Henry needed anything more from the sideboards. At a motion from Templeton, she served him another piece of ham. She then retreated and began gathering some of the serving platters to be taken back to the kitchen.

"Your ride to Magnolia Acres will be longer than your ride to Rose Hill. You will cross Brier Creek and ride south, passing through town. Once south of town, you will take the road west toward Louisville. Magnolia Acres is some fifteen miles south-west of Waynesboro. If you ride into Louisville, you will know that you've gone too far. As before, you will take Gallivanter and the cart. I will allow you one day to rest. Then, we must be wary of the Federal cavalry. If the news that I hear is accurate, they are presently camped near the road you must take. I'll not send you until I know the way is safe. There is too great a risk of losing the valuables. Is that clear?"

"Yes, sir."

Templeton reached into the inner pocket of his frock coat and produced an envelope. He held it up, and in the candlelight Henry saw the wax seal.

"I have here a letter that I've written to Mrs. Graves. In it I have expressed to her my interest in her safety, as well as that of her children and her husband's estate. I've explained my willingness to remove her personal valuables from her property and to store them here at Stratmore, under lock and key, so that they will not be stolen by the enemy. I have further explained to her that you are my agent who is to collect whatever valuables that she desires to have protected. I've signed this letter myself. Mrs. Graves knows me to be a man of my word, and she should not give you any trouble once she knows the purpose of your mission. Present this letter to her when you arrive." Templeton placed the envelope on the table and pushed it with his long arm toward Henry.

From his wandering across the Georgia countryside, Henry knew that many plantations were being managed by women whose husbands had gone off to war. Though some were stoic, even defiant, in the face of Sherman's approach, Henry knew that many more were frightened beyond words about what Sherman's bummers might do to them, their children, and their property. Without anyone to defend them, their fates were left to the whims of Yankee soldiers.

Henry reached across the long dining table to retrieve the letter that Templeton had pushed toward him. Henry's arms, however, were not long enough so he leaned awkwardly forward. His fingers closed on the envelope, but when he sat back in his chair he did so too quickly. His elbow bumped a long-stemmed glass of water. With wide eyes, Henry watched the glass totter for a moment, and then plunge off the edge of the table and hit the floor, bursting into a hundred pieces.

The sound of breaking glass was alarming, but more disquieting was the silence that followed the crash. Henry had pinched his eyes, and he kept them pinched as he waited for the angry scolding that was sure to come from Mr. Templeton. Hoping to make up for his blunder and possibly lessen his punishment, Henry clambered to the floor and began picking up bits of glass.

At last, Templeton spoke.

"Stop it."

The man's calm tone shocked him. Expecting to be berated for his clumsy act, Henry instead saw in Templeton's face an expression of pardon. Henry sat back down in his chair. Still clutched in his fingers were the two glass fragments that he had picked up.

Templeton now looked away from Henry toward the sideboards.

"Violet."

Henry had almost forgotten about Violet, so quietly had she been standing near the wall. At her master's call, she now stepped forward.

"Yes, Massa."

"Clean this mess on the floor."

Violet replaced the platters that she had gathered from the sideboard and walked to where the broken glass was strewn on the floor. Before stooping to pick up a single shard, she stared at Henry straight in the eyes. She did not say a word, but her expression sent a message that Henry heard loud and clear, "It's yo mess, little white boy. You clean it."

Then something happened inside of Henry that he had never felt before. His skin became hot, and all at once he felt indignant, though he struggled to understand why. After all, it was his mess. But somehow in his mind, that was no longer the point. Templeton had told her to do it. He was the master. He had the power. That was it. It was a question of power.

He returned Violet's stare, and then became aware that Templeton's gaze was bearing down on him too, as if scrutinizing Henry to see how he would react. Violet shifted her weight and put her hands on her hips, once again speaking without talking, "Well?"

Then, almost without realizing what he was doing, Henry flung the two shards forcefully to the floor at Violet's feet. Looking her straight in the eyes, he said, "Do it."

Immediately, a lump formed in his throat. Never in all of his life had he dared to speak to an adult that way. There were plenty of times at the orphanage that he had challenged the headmaster, but nothing like this. His own audacity shocked him. On the farm or at the orphanage, that kind of back talk would have earned him a licking for sure. He quickly looked at Templeton, not knowing what kind of reaction his words would draw from the man.

Mr. Templeton sat back in his chair and gave Henry a half nod, the nearest expression he had to approval.

Meanwhile, Violet stood with her hands on her hips for a few moments longer. Then, breaking her pose as she bent toward the floor, she said, "Yes, Massa Henry." Those were her words, but her expression seemed to say, "Boy, you oughta be ashamed o' yoself."

But her expression did not register with him. He only heard her words: Massa Henry. Once again, he felt elevated. Lowly as he was, he knew now that he was not the lowest. On the contrary, he was the right-hand agent of a wealthy planter working to protect his homeland. Templeton had placed his faith and trust in him, and Templeton was a man who knew how to take charge. Henry's mind whirled back to the whipping, and now he seemed to understand. When you want things done, you have to demand it. And if your demand is not heeded, there must be a consequence. That's how it is when you're the master.

Henry and Mr. Templeton finished their meal in silence. The only sounds they heard were the occasional clinks and the swish of a broom as Violet cleaned up the broken glass.

That night, Henry was shown more evidence that he was gaining favor with Mr. Templeton. Instead of being sent to sleep in the vacant overseer's cabin, as had been the routine for the past couple of weeks, Mr. Templeton invited him to sleep in the big house. Henry was further amazed to discover that he was to occupy Robert's bedroom, a room that had remained empty ever since Mr. Templeton's beloved son had ridden off to war. But in truth, Henry was now so tired that he didn't much care if he had been told to go sleep in the water trough. He had been up for nearly thirty-six hours, and he just wanted some rest. He was grateful that Mr. Templeton would allow him to wait a day, maybe more, before going on his next mission.

His slumber, however, was delayed a few minutes longer, for just as Mr. Templeton was about to take him upstairs and show him to the room, there was a knock at the front door. Mr. Templeton answered it as Henry hung back near the entrance to the dining room.

Mr. Templeton opened the door, and a rider stood on the verandah. Henry could see the outline of his horse tethered behind him. At first Henry thought he was a military man, maybe from Joe Wheeler's cavalry, and he became tense. But he relaxed again when he saw by the man's dress that he was just a messenger. "From Mr. Hathaway," he said as he handed a small envelope to Mr. Templeton.

Templeton broke the seal and read the message right there in the doorway. After musing for a moment, he said to the messenger, "Tell Mr. Hathaway that his plan is agreeable and that I shall be ready for him when he arrives."

The rider nodded curtly, mounted his horse, and disappeared into the night.

Mr. Templeton placed the message in the inside pocket of his frock coat, closed the door, and turned once more to Henry. "Now then, let me show you to the room."

There were not any personal items of Robert's left in the bedroom. In fact, other than a four-post bed, a bureau, a chair, and a washstand, the room was quite plain. But it was the bed that Henry gazed at longingly, and as soon as Mr. Templeton left Henry flopped down on the mattress, every muscle in his body grateful for the chance to relax. As he drifted off to sleep, Henry absently noted that there were two windows in the room. One faced the stables, and he hoped that Gal was resting easy in her stall.

The other faced the slave quarters, and from that direction Henry heard crying again. But that was nothing more than a minor annoyance to him; the concerns of those people were not his to think about. Before long, the crying was lost to his ears, for he had fallen fast asleep.

Mrs. Amelia Graves was a proud, strong-willed woman. When her husband rode off to war in 1861, she felt certain about two things. The first was that the Confederacy would prevail and that her husband would return safely to her. The second was that through sheer determination she would keep Magnolia Acres running until he came home. She had no control over the war's outcome, but the control of Magnolia Acres started and stopped with her.

And take control she did. She retained a fair number of slaves, enough to keep one cotton field productive. Though it was difficult to sell, she stored her cotton in the hopes that it could be sold after the war's conclusion. She worked with her own hands to keep all of the buildings in good repair. She made clothing for her children, kept them on track with their studies, and kept food on the table. Whatever hard circumstances the war brought upon her, nothing seemed too formidable for Mrs. Graves to overcome.

Still, as the long years of war unfolded and took their toll on the Deep South, even Mrs. Graves had to admit in her own heart that the situation was growing bleaker by the month. She had not heard from her husband recently. The defeats at Gettysburg and Vicksburg had been serious blows to the South, and the news of Atlanta's burning had further demoralized the people of Georgia. Then Sherman began his march, and awful reports began reaching the ears of Mrs. Graves and other women who had taken over their lands in the absence of their husbands. Stories of robbery, pillaging, burning, and all kinds of vandalism circulated daily. Fear increased as Sherman neared. Mrs. Graves began carrying a pistol in the folds of her dress, for she never knew when the blue-bellied bummers might break down her door. Now they were upon her; only a thin line of Joe Wheeler's cavalry separated Waynesboro from the advancing Yankees.

On the morning of December 1, 1864, Mrs. Graves found herself doing something she never imagined she would have to do. On the back edge of her property, she knelt on the ground near a fence row that separated the slave quarters from the garden. As a couple of her faithful slaves loosened the dirt around the fence posts, she wrapped some of her family's small but precious items in bundles of cloth. One bundle contained the family table silver, another contained gold coins, and a third contained three of her husband's most expensive watches. When the posts were removed, she would bury her treasures at the bottoms of the holes and then have the posts replaced. This, she hoped, would be effective enough to keep her valuables out of sight until the plundering Yankees had moved on.

She was just about to place the first bundle in the ground when she was startled by a horse whinny behind her. She scrambled to her feet and spun around, her hand feeling for the pistol. She expected to see blue-coated Federal soldiers advancing on her. Instead, she saw a small boy riding a horse and pulling a cart.

At dawn on December 1, Henry saddled Gal, hitched up the cart, and departed for Magnolia Acres. He left while it was still dark, for Mr. Templeton expected him home by nightfall, and he had a long day of riding ahead.

Crossing the bridge over Brier Creek, he rode south into Waynesboro. The sun emerged, spilling its rays on the collection of homes, stores, churches, and the railroad depot that comprised the tiny town. It was the first time that Henry had been to town since the day he had met Mr. Templeton, and as he rode through the quiet streets, he noted with alarm the vandalism evident on so many of the buildings.

A few days earlier on November 27, Kilpatrick's Federal cavalry had ridden into town and caused significant damage before being driven to the south by Joe Wheeler's men. Windows had been broken, buildings burned, and train cars had been destroyed. At this early hour the streets were deserted, but Henry wondered how many citizens were afraid to leave their homes even at midday. They could never be certain if, or when, the Yankee cavalry would strike again. Henry's heart was heavy knowing that so many people, normal folks like him, were forced to live in fear. Still, the Confederate flag waved proudly from the top of the town hall. Waynesboro had not fallen to Sherman yet.

Henry continued through town, to the south. Here, he turned west and picked up the road toward Louisville. According to Mr. Templeton, Magnolia Acres was about fifteen miles ahead. So far his morning ride had been chilly, but peaceful enough. He hoped that it would stay that way.

Henry was much more at ease in approaching Magnolia Acres than he had been at Rose Hill. For one thing, it was daytime. Since Mrs. Graves still lived on the property, there would be no need to break in as he had been forced to do at Mr. Brewer's place, and therefore no need to wait for the cover of darkness. Then, too, he had Mr. Templeton's letter tucked safely in his coat pocket. There was comfort in knowing that Templeton's own written word would erase all suspicion that might otherwise cloud his activities.

Still, Henry could not totally dispel from his mind the constant worry about Yankee cavalry. Though there had been no news of skirmishes for the past couple of days and Mr. Templeton had deemed it safe to send him, rumor had it that Kilpatrick and his mounted troops were resting in Louisville. Henry was uneasy about coming so near to that town. Worst of all, he was afraid that he might miss Magnolia Acres and ride too far west, landing smack in the middle of the Yankee camp. To avoid such a disastrous mistake, he slowed Gal from a canter to a walk and carefully scanned the roadside for the lane that would lead him to the plantation house. Soon enough he found it, and he breathed a sigh of relief.

Turning up the lane to the big house, Henry noted smoke rising from the kitchen yard and some activity near one of the barns. A herd of goats stood clumped together, and chickens stalked about the barnyard. These modest signs clearly indicated that Magnolia Acres had not been abandoned. However, Henry was surprised when his knock at the door was not answered. He re-mounted Gal and decided to ride around to the kitchen yard to inquire about Mrs. Graves.

He found a frightened looking slave girl looking after Mrs. Graves' children. Without saying a word to him, she answered his query by pointing toward the fence row at the back of the property. There, in the distance, Henry saw a woman in a fine dress kneeling before the fence while several slaves worked beside her with shovels. This, he assumed, was Mrs. Graves. Henry spurred Gal to a walk and made his way to the fence row.

Gal whinnied as Henry approached, and this noise brought Mrs. Graves to her feet. She came toward him, her strides quick and choppy beneath her dress. When she was close enough, Henry saw that her eyes were squinted and her chin jutted forward, a countenance clearly etched with suspicion and defiance. Her expression alarmed him. He stopped Gal, and as she came alongside the horse he tried to greet her in a way that showed he meant no harm.

"Mornin' ma'am. I's jist ridin' on back here ta…"

"Get down from that horse!" The woman's words were sharp, angry, and authoritative. She instantly made Henry forget whatever nerve he thought he had developed when it came to holding his own against adults. In spite of himself, he fidgeted in the saddle. This was not the greeting that he had expected.

"Ma'am, I ain't lookin' fer no…"

"I said get down from that horse!" This time when she spoke, her temper reminded Henry of steam escaping from a pot. Then, to his utter astonishment, she pulled a pistol from the folds of her dress and pointed it at his head.

Henry threw his hands up in the air and then froze still as a statue. *Was this woman crazy?* He was now so scared that he was afraid to blink.

"I'm going to count to three," hissed Mrs. Graves, "and if you're not down from that horse by the time I'm done, I'm going to pull this trigger. Don't test me."

She needn't have made that final admonishment. Henry had already made up his mind that she was a woman not to be tested. Before she got to two, he had dismounted Gal and was standing on the ground facing her, his arms still straight up in the air.

Still brandishing her weapon, she questioned Henry tersely. "What's your name?"

"Please ma'am, I…it's Henry. Henry Akinson."

"Akinson?" she repeated. "You're not from Waynesboro."

"No ma'am."

"What are you doing trespassing on my property?"

"I din't mean to do no tresspassin' ma'am. I come here on account of Mr. Templeton sent me."

"Templeton? Lewis Templeton?" At the mention of Templeton's name, Mrs. Graves relaxed her expression slightly.

"Yes, ma'am. He writ you a letter. It's in my coat pocket…" Henry made a motion to retrieve the letter, but he froze again when Mrs. Graves flaunted her pistol once more. She stepped forward. With her free hand, she reached inside Henry's coat and removed the envelope. Then, retreating a couple of steps but still keeping her weapon trained on Henry, she broke the seal and removed the paper. She took her eyes off him just long enough to read the lines that Templeton had written.

November 27, 1864

Dearest Mrs. Graves,

It is my most sincere hope that this letter finds you, your children, and your estate safe during this most trying time. I am certain that I do not have to recount to you the details of General Sherman's approach. I fear that you are all too aware of the perils that his advance brings for you, myself, and all of our Southern countrymen. It is because I do not wish to see our properties, indeed our very lifestyle, laid waste by the Northern aggressors that I take my pen in hand and write to you.

Through what can only be described as an act of Providence, it appears that the Federal columns will pass well south of Stratmore. For this I am most grateful, yet my heart bleeds for those of you whose lands lie directly in Sherman's path. As an act of charity and patriotism, I am offering you the chance to transfer your valuables and family treasure to my estate, where they will be kept under lock and key and protected until the filth of these thieving invaders can be scrubbed from our soil. At which time, your most precious items will be returned to you. I ask no compensation for this service; I offer it only as an outreach to my neighbors and fellow countrymen during this period of fear and uncertainty.

For many years, your husband and I conducted business together. Let my honest dealings with him be the seal with which I now make this promise to you.

Should you decide to avail yourself of my services, the bearer of this letter will conduct the transfer. He is my own agent in whom I have placed my trust. I vouch for him to complete the work with expediency and honesty.

In closing, I exhort you to take this opportunity while it is before you. Take no stock in the mercy that the Federals supposedly show to civilians. They will steal from you if given the chance.

Yours in service,

Lewis Templeton

When she finished reading, Mrs. Graves lowered the letter and the pistol. When she looked at Henry again, her expression had softened somewhat, although the furrows of concern around her eyebrows appeared to be permanent. Henry did not know what Templeton had written about him, but he surmised that the words had greatly altered her attitude toward him. He slowly lowered his arms, and Mrs. Graves allowed him to do so.

"Well, young man. It seems I owe you an apology. But you must understand that a person can't be too careful. With each passing day, there are fewer folks around here who can be trusted."

Henry swallowed with relief. "Yes, ma'am."

Then, speaking almost as much to herself as to Henry, Mrs. Graves continued. "So, Lewis Templeton is showing some compassion for his neighbors. Well, now, there's a switch. I didn't think that man felt pity for anyone or anything.

"Jonathan…that's my husband…Jonathan always used to tell me that Lewis Templeton was the most ruthless businessman in all of Georgia. He always got what he wanted, and it didn't matter to him whom he trampled in the process. Still, Jonathan said he always dealt honestly with those who were on his side and didn't try to cross him. Of course, you ought to know that if you've been working for him any amount of time."

At this, Henry only nodded.

"They got along well, they did. Respected each other. Jonathan helped Mr. Templeton acquire his flatboats for quite a bargain, and Lewis always said he felt indebted to him. Maybe this is his way of paying us back."

Mrs. Graves sighed and looked mournfully up to the heavens. "Times like these, I do wish he was here to tell me what to do. But he's not, and a decision needs to be made."

Henry, along with the slaves standing back at the fence row, stood quietly while she deliberated.

At length, Mrs. Graves said, "I think Jonathan would trust him, and so will I. Lord knows we don't have many options." Then, gesturing to the fence row, she added, "Anyway, it's better than some hole in the ground. Come along now…what did you say your name was?"

"Henry, ma'am."

"Yes, well, come along Henry. Time is not on our side."

For the next hour, Henry was busy helping Mrs. Graves load the cart with all the items that she held dear. Along with the table silver, the gold coins, and the watches, they added a looking-glass, a violin, antique silver trays, and an ivory vase. All of these items were hidden in the cart under a thick mat of straw. When the packing was complete, she turned to Henry with a renewed look of suspicion.

"You know that Mr. Templeton vouched for you in his letter, don't you?"

Truthfully, Henry had not read the letter. But he replied, "Yes, ma'am."

"What assurance can you give me that you'll deliver these items honestly to Mr. Templeton?"

Henry thought for a moment and then said, "On'y my word of honor as a Southerner, ma'am."

She stepped close to him and looked him square in the eye. "See that you keep your word."

Henry then mounted Gal and spurred her on, the little wagon following behind as Mrs. Graves watched them disappear down the lane.

Mrs. Graves returned to her house and called her children to the study. A girl nine years of age and a boy of six came to her, and she began to help them with the day's lessons. Although the children did not detect it, Mrs. Graves' mind was certainly not focused on reading or arithmetic. She second-guessed herself, wondering if she had made the right decision to send her valuables with Templeton's boy. Of course, she knew better than to put all of her eggs in one basket; she had not turned over all of her valuables to Henry. She had kept some items hidden in the house, figuring she had a better chance of retaining some of her wealth by dividing it. Still she fretted incessantly. In times like these, she knew that there was no such thing as guaranteed safety, no matter what Templeton assured her.

Her thoughts were interrupted by the sound that she had been dreading for weeks. Drums. The steady, relentless cadence that accompanied marching soldiers.

The slave girl from the kitchen yard burst into the study. "Mrs. Graves! They's soljas a-comin' up de lane!"

Amelia Graves stood up, pulling the pistol from her dress. "Camilla. Willie. Stay close to me."

The children obeyed and followed their mother to the verandah. Peeking out from behind her dress, they saw blue-uniformed soldiers coming down the lane. One of them was on horseback, and many more were on foot. All of them were armed. Beyond them, out on the road, she could see a long blue column of men snaking its way to the east.

Mrs. Graves displayed the pistol in front of her, her eyes steely with defiance.

The mounted soldier halted just before the verandah. Several of the foot soldiers separated from the group, hustling around the side of the big house toward the back property. Mrs. Graves followed them with her eyes, but she did not budge from her position. The children were shaking and tucked themselves in closer behind their mother.

Without dismounting, the rider spoke. "Ma'am, I have to ask you to step clear of the house."

"This is my home, and I'm not leaving. You have no right to be here. Get off my property."

"We have no intention to harm you or the children. Lower that pistol and step clear. We don't want trouble."

"Cowards! You Yankees bring war to women and children, but you say you don't want trouble? You've sorely underestimated my resolve to defend my land. Now, I'll ask you again to get off my property before I put a bullet in your head."

At that moment, a tumult erupted from the side of the big house. The bummers who had previously dashed toward the back property now emerged. They were leading two cows and a string of goats. Between them they carried six chickens.

At the sight of this, Mrs. Graves moved in their direction and shouted at the bummers, "You leave those animals be! That's all I have left to feed my children!"

Distracted by the sight of her livestock being taken away, Mrs. Graves did not see the Yankee soldier who rushed her from her blindside. He wrenched the pistol away from her, and another soldier grabbed her by the waist and physically removed her from the verandah.

"Get your hands off me! You have no right!"

The children cried and ran to their mother as she was deposited near an oak tree in the front lawn. Two soldiers stepped forward to guard her, their guns leveled. She made a lunge toward the house, but they forced her back.

"We don't mean to be rough, ma'am, but we can't have you in the way. It's for your own protection."

Mrs. Graves could only scowl at him as her livestock disappeared from view.

The Yankee trooper grinned. "Boys, go see what's inside."

Finally getting the order that they had been craving, the remainder of the bummers stormed into the house. Mrs. Graves sank to her knees and sobbed into her dress as she listened to the sounds of the ransacking within: doors opened and slammed, windows broken, furniture overturned. Like locusts, the bummers swarmed through the house and across the plantation grounds. Looting and plundering, they took anything they wanted. Everything else was reduced to a heap of debris.

Still held at gunpoint, Mrs. Graves saw the bummers emerge from the house and carry her belongings away down the lane. They stole all that she had tried to conceal in the house: an Italian harp, more gold coins, a silver tea set, and fine crystal.

She screamed at them. "You can't! That's private property!"

She tried again to rise to her feet and to run after them, but again the soldiers guarding her forced her back down.

More bummers came around from the back property. Having cleaned out the smokehouse, they carried large hams spiked on their bayonets.

Then, as quickly as they had swarmed in, they swarmed back out again, moving down the lane and catching up with the column that had passed on the roadway.

One of the men guarding Mrs. Graves spoke to the mounted trooper. "All out, sir."

"Very well," he replied. "Prepare to fire the house and the outbuildings."

"NO!" Mrs. Graves wailed. "You devils! You CAN"T! This is my home!"

But even as she screamed, Federal troops hurled torches through the broken-out windows. The barns, kitchen, and smokehouse were also put to the torch.

As the flames climbed high, the heat became so intense that Mrs. Graves and her children were forced to retreat further. Black smoke blotted out the sun, and between their sobs they choked on the acrid air. On her knees with her head in her hands, the once defiant Mrs. Graves now assumed the posture of one defeated.

Seeing that she was now thoroughly subdued, the two guards fell away and retreated down the lane.

The mounted trooper was the last to leave the scene. He walked his horse over to the spot where Mrs. Graves knelt in the grass, her children clinging to her on either side.

"Well," he said tersely, "what do you think of your secession now?"

Then he turned his horse sharply and rode away.

It was early afternoon by the time Henry was on the road heading back toward Stratmore. He was pleased with the way his morning had turned out. Aside from having a pistol waved in his face, this assignment had been much less harrowing than his ordeal at Rose Hill. He was grateful for Mr. Templeton's foresight to write the letter, otherwise things might have turned out very differently. Now he was intent on remaining true to his word and delivering Mrs. Graves' valuables to Mr. Templeton.

But as the miles rolled past, the quiet countryside lulled him. A tall stand of trees and scraggly brambles bordered the road to his right, but a wide open meadow fell away to his left, climbing until it disappeared over a ridge. Henry relaxed in the saddle, allowed his mind to wander, and absently began to sing a tune he learned at the orphanage.

> Travelin' 'cross the countryside
> Where'er I choose to roam
> My hoss will al'ays lead me
> Straight back to my sweet home
> And even if I travel
> 'Cross crik or mountain or plain
> I know my steady companion
> Will get me home again
>
> Once I was a-ridin'
> The long road to Savannah's sea
> When an old…

Henry's voice trailed off, and Gal's ears pricked up. He pulled up on her reins and stopped her. Something was different. The quiet that had reigned before he started singing was not the same. A couple of moments fled before Henry realized what he was hearing. Rumbling. The pounding of galloping hooves. And it was coming from just around a bend in the road ahead.

No sooner had Henry recognized the sound when a unit of men on horseback galloped into view. Through the dust that they kicked up, Henry saw that they wore Confederate gray and bore the stars and bars. *Wheeler's men!* But Henry's relief that they were not Yankees lasted only a second, for there were so many of them that they occupied the entire road. He and Gal were directly in their path, and they were galloping so hard that they could not stop. If he and Gal did not move, they would be trampled.

"Uh-oh, Gal! We got some trouble!"

Knowing that the stand of trees to his right afforded him no place to escape, Henry pulled the reins hard to his left, toward the meadow. Gal responded willingly, for she too saw the cavalry horses bearing down on her. She veered sharply to the left, so sharply that Henry feared the cart would be upset. It balanced on one wheel for a second, but it remained upright. Gal put forth a burst of speed which sent her, Henry, and the cart clear of the road and into the meadow's low grass, and not a moment too soon. As Gal continued running forward up the ridge, Henry looked back over his shoulder to see the cavalry troops rushing past, a blur of hooves and dust and uniforms that all seemed to swirl together.

Suddenly, above the horses' din, a bugle call rang out. Henry's heart leapt into his throat, for the call did not come from the road. Instead, it sounded from the top of the ridge, the very spot toward which Gal galloped. He snapped his head around to look forward, just in time to see the blue-uniformed riders of the Yankee cavalry charging over the top of the ridge, down toward the road.

It was an ambush. The Yanks had been waiting behind that ridge to charge the Confederates when they came past on the road. Now Henry was caught directly in between.

A Rebel yell rose up from the graybacks on the road as they turned to face their assailants, but it was soon drowned out by gunfire. Henry saw the puffs of smoke and muzzle flares from repeating rifles as the mounted Federals cascaded down the ridge, firing as they came. He heard balls whizzing through the air all around him, one of them lodging in the cart with a crackling thud. Pistols sounded off behind him, too, as the Rebels returned the fire.

Desperate for her rider to steer her out of this madness, the terrified Gal ran forward at a full gallop but whinnied and shied. Henry found himself unable to react, the terror of the moment having shocked him into a state of paralysis. Ahead of him he saw men falling dead, screaming, toppling from their saddles, and crashing to the ground. Horses, too, crumpled into fleshy heaps and were trampled by those who rushed from behind. He saw the men draw their sabers, anticipating collision with the Rebels charging upward behind him.

His mind flashed back to Allatoona Pass.

The voices spoke.

"The'll be butchered!"

"Them Yanks won't git ye!"

"Do it! They're all gonna die!"

"Butchered!"

"Aw, c'mon, son! Move it!"

"All gonna die! …All gonna die!"

Henry let go of the reins. The onrushing wave of Yankee cavalry engulfed him. A Federal trooper bore down on Henry and raised his saber.

Gallivanter was not a war horse, but she possessed the natural instincts to preserve her own safety and that of her rider. Just before the Federal stampede overwhelmed her, she cut sharply to her right. Though the cart impeded her, she evaded collision with the front riders. The swiftness and strength of her motion snapped the cart's right wheel from the axle, but Gal continued to drag it behind. The movement jerked the benumbed Henry in his saddle, causing the Yankee trooper's saber to miss its mark. It sliced the brim of Henry's hat.

In a desperate effort to get clear the area, Gal made a beeline across the open meadow. The cart now dragged behind her, the broken axle carving a deep groove into the sod until it hit a large rock. With a horrible jolt, the tethers gave way. Gal, now separated from the cart, streaked across the meadow seeking safety in the distant tree line. But the brave horse no longer bore her rider, for the jostle had thrown Henry from the saddle.

Impact knocked the wind out of Henry, but it also reawakened his senses to the imminent danger. He stayed still on the ground, feigning death so that a Federal trooper would not see the need to ride over and finish him off. As he lay there, he listened to the clamor of the cavalry clash. Shots crackled, men screamed and shouted, horses' hooves thudded and pranced, saber blades rang against one another. But as the moments wore on, Henry perceived that the commotion was growing more distant. The tide of the struggle was moving away from him.

Henry waited a while longer, and then slowly turned his head toward the direction of the fight. Indeed, the battle had now carried all the way back to the road. Wheeler's men had been overwhelmed and were now retreating eastward. The Yankees rallied in pursuit. The uproar that had shattered the stillness of the countryside now faded away down the road.

But not all was silent. All around him, Henry heard the cries, moans, and pleas of wounded men; the gut wrenching snorts and whinnies of horses that floundered with broken bones. With this miserable overture rising everywhere around him, Henry crawled toward the cart.

It was broken beyond repair. He quickly scanned the field, but amid the battle debris he could not spot the missing wheel. Not that it mattered; the axle was completely splintered. Of more immediate concern to Henry were the valuables' whereabouts. The cart remained upright, though the front had been driven into the sod and it tilted to the right.

The contents and the layer of straw meant to conceal and protect them had shifted. Some of the items poked their noses through the displaced stems, and Henry quickly accounted for the table silver and the watches, still bundled in the cloth. The looking-glass had been shattered, and a jagged crack ran across the back of the violin. The silver trays and the ivory vase were intact, but the bundle of gold coins was nowhere to be found. Henry frantically sorted through the straw, but to no avail.

Upset, he sat on the ground. Disappointment and failure reared their ugly heads. Mr. Templeton had expected no more damaged goods. Upon his word of honor, he had assured Mrs. Graves that her valuables would be protected. On both counts, he had failed. In anger, he snatched his hat from his head and slapped it against the side of the cart. Only then did he see the slash in the brim. If it had not been for Gal, that slash would have been through his skull.

Gal! Suddenly panicky, Henry scrambled to his feet. He had no idea where Gal was! His last glimpse was of her streaking off toward the tree line. He had to find her. Without thinking, he replaced his hat and ran to the top of the ridge to get a better view of the distant woods.

When he reached the crest and gazed across the meadow, he breathed a sigh of relief. She was not far off, standing in waving grass that reached to her flanks. Her head was lowered, and she was grazing when Henry whistled. She pulled up attentively, but did not move. Henry was afraid she was still spooked and would not come. Too, he had only been around her for a few weeks and was not sure he could call her in with just a whistle. But she surprised him. As if deciding that she had no better place to go, she trotted toward him with head tossing and tail swishing. Within moments, they were reunited. There on top of the ridge, Henry hugged her neck and ran his fingers through her mane. Then he took the reins and led her back to the broken cart.

They had not gone far when they heard a moan so agonizing and pitiable that it could not be ignored. They picked their way across the field to find the source. A Confederate soldier was lying on his side, his knees pulled up to his stomach. His right arm was extended across the grass, his left hand held something which he clutched to his chest. Henry could tell from the matted grass stretching out behind him that this man had crawled, or rather pulled, himself for some distance. Drawing closer, Henry saw a bloody, gaping chest wound. Against it, the man had pressed a wad of cloth in hopes of stopping the bleeding.

But it was hopeless. By the time Henry knelt beside him, the soldier was dead. His lifeless eyes stared vacantly back at Henry. He thought back to the dead Yankee he had seen at Allatoona Pass, and again a wave of nausea passed over him.

Tears welled up in his eyes, but he knew that he could not stay. He had to complete his task. He reached out to close the dead man's eyes and to fold his right arm across his chest, giving him at least some sense of repose. In so doing, he looked at the bloody wad of cloth. This was what the soldier must have crawled for in his last, agonizing moments of life.

Henry was about to turn away when something dawned on him. He took a closer look at the cloth, which was now so saturated with blood it was hardly recognizable. Gagging, he pried it from the dead man's hand and laid it open on the grass. There inside, smeared with blood but otherwise safe, were Mrs. Graves' gold coins.

Henry cast another tearful glance at the dead man. Many would have fought and killed for that amount of treasure. This man spent the final minutes of his life clawing for the cloth, hoping that it would preserve him. He never had any idea what lay inside.

Sniffling and wiping his eyes, Henry became aware of a new sound. He looked away from the fallen soldier and cast his gaze westward down the road, the direction from which he had departed Magnolia Acres. He was still high enough on the ridge to view the road about two miles distant. There he saw mounted riders, followed by several rows of troops marching to a drumbeat, the sound that had caught his attention. It was the Yankee infantry. They were marching eastward behind their cavalry, probably bound for Waynesboro. Henry had to move quickly before they spotted him, but before he moved he noted a tall column of black smoke rising in the west.

Henry refolded the bloody cloth and walked Gal back to the broken cart. There, he placed all he could carry on top of the silver serving trays: the table silver, the watches, the coins, and the ivory vase. Then, carrying the trays like a butler leaving the scene of a gruesome dinner party, he hustled down the ridge back to the road, leading Gal as he went. Making sure that the Federals were still far enough off, he crossed the road to the opposite side where trees and brambles grew. He stashed the valuables in the ditch, concealing them as best he could with twigs and grass. Then, he and Gal took cover behind a thick stand of trees. They would hide there until the infantry passed.

The Federal infantry turned out to be a full brigade, and it took a while for them to pass the spot where Henry and Gal waited. The march was halted momentarily when they reached the site of the clash. Through the trees, Henry watched as medical wagons were brought forward and driven into the meadow, up the ridge where most of the men had fallen.

After the ambulance wagons had been dispatched, the troops on the road moved out. They filed by in what seemed like an endless parade of wiry, dirty men with shaggy hair that had not been cut for weeks. Their uniforms were tattered. Henry was aghast that Federal officers would permit their men to be so disheveled, but then he remembered that these were Sherman's men. They had been in the heart of Georgia for some time now with no supply lines to refresh them. They had been living off the land.

Once again Henry glanced at the smoke curling upward in the western sky. Deep dread overcame him as he realized that it was rising from the area of Magnolia Acres. His face flushed with anger as he glared once more at the passing Yankees.

These were the invaders who were ravaging the Georgia countryside, and it was against their thievery that Mr. Templeton was trying to protect his neighbors. As Henry watched, he began to see evidence of the bummer's work. At the rear of the passing brigade came a long string of cattle, followed by wagons full of goods that had been taken from homes along the way. A noisy bunch of chickens occupied one cart, and a string of goats marched stubbornly along the road's berm. Several soldiers carried hams that had been skewered on their bayonets. Henry could not make out all of the items in the wagons, but he thought he saw the top portion of a harp leaning cockeyed against a corner. It seemed like a strange thing for them to steal, but Henry reasoned that they would most likely sell it and pocket the money. His contempt for them intensified as their parade of plunder vanished eastward down the road.

But now something was happening that shifted his attention. At the very rear of the column, a small detachment of men stopped while the rest marched ahead. They unloaded shovels and picks from two small, mule-drawn carts. The soldier who appeared to be in charge gave sharp, snappy orders. He had a beard that came to such a point at his chin that it looked like a spike. Henry could not make out the words that Spiky Beard was saying, but he soon figured out what the men were doing. They took their digging tools into the meadow and up the ridge. They were going to bury the dead.

Henry's eyes bulged when he realized the chance that was before him. The two empty carts had been left by the roadside, and nobody was guarding them!

Henry forced himself to be patient. He waited until the men were well up on the ridge and busy with their loathsome task before he and Gal slipped from their hiding place and moved onto the road.

"Shhhhh, Gal," he whispered. "We gotta do this real quiet like."

Henry stole silently up to one of the mules, who seemed completely indifferent to everything around it. It did not even raise a hint of suspicion when Henry removed the harness from it and attached it to Gal. Pleased that this had been accomplished so quietly, Henry led Gal across the road to the place in the ditch where he had stashed the valuables. Minutes seemed like hours as Henry worked to remove the branches and brambles that hid the treasure. Finally, he located all of the items and loaded them into the cart.

When he glanced up toward the ridge to see if the men were still working on the graves, he could not believe his eyes. To his horror, Henry saw that the mule he had unhitched from the cart had decided to go for a walk—right up the ridge where the men were working! While Henry looked on, the mule ambled past the grave site where Spiky Beard himself was digging. Spiky Beard looked at the mule, did a double take, scanned the road, and then looked straight at Henry.

"Son of a gun! That boy is stealing our cart!"

Henry swung into the saddle as quickly as he could. Gal seemed to understand the need for speed and required no coaxing. She was off at a canter with the wagon rolling behind. By this time, Spiky Beard had recovered his gun and fired a shot. The bullet did not come close, but the shot sent Gal into a full gallop. Soon Spiky Beard and his grave digging companions were left well behind.

Henry and Gal were heading northeast, but he knew they could not keep to the road for very long. Soon they would ride up on the rear of the Yankee infantry. So Henry slowed Gal to a walk and guided her off the road and into a field. They would have to find their way back to Stratmore by cutting cross country, but Henry did not care. He was eager to have this mission behind him.

Casting a look backward, he again eyed the smoke column that was every bit as dark and menacing as it had been before. If Magnolia Acres was burning, Henry at least took comfort in knowing that Mrs. Graves' valuables were safe in his cart. Once the Yankees had moved on, her precious items would be returned to her, a starting point from which she could rebuild her life. Mr. Templeton would make certain of that.

In the darkness of Robert's bedroom, Henry's day finally wound down. He lay wide awake in Robert's bed. He could not tune out the day's events. He had made his way back to Stratmore without further incident, though he had worried ceaselessly that he was being followed. Cutting cross country had enabled him to elude the Federal troops, but it had also made his progress slow. It had been very late in the evening when he finally returned, and due to his tardiness, Mr. Templeton had greeted him sternly. The man's mood did not improve when Henry showed him the few items in the cart. Clearly, he had been expecting more from Magnolia Acres.

Stumbling over his words, Henry had recounted the cavalry clash, the broken cart, and his reason for stealing the Yankee wagon. He told of the troop movements that he had witnessed and the smoke he had seen rising from the direction of Magnolia Acres. Mr. Templeton absorbed all of this with keen attention but the muscles on his face flexed with bitter disappointment. Only the gold coins, still folded in the bloody cloth, seemed to ease his expression. Henry noticed that after unwrapping and examining them, Mr. Templeton had slipped them into his own pocket rather than placing them back in the wagon with the other items.

Though he very much wanted to avoid the issue, Henry felt compelled to explain about the broken violin and the shattered looking glass. He knew that when Mrs. Graves came to reclaim her items, she would expect to find these along with the others. He felt it was best to explain now rather than waiting for the subject to come up later. The news of these lost items further soured Mr. Templeton's humor.

In the end, Henry helped him lock the valuables in the storehouse. Then Templeton dismissed him to stable Gal and turn in for the night. Henry departed from his boss with a heavy heart, for despite all of his efforts to do his best, he knew he had let him down.

Now he lay in bed desiring nothing more than a restful sleep, but each time he closed his eyes, his overactive mind spun up disturbing images: Templeton's eyes glowering at him...the flash of the saber as it sliced his hat...the haunting white face of the dead Yank...the column of black smoke coiling like a snake. And with all of these there emerged in Henry's gut a loathsome mix of guilt and shame, for he knew that, once again, he had frozen. He tried not to think about it; attempted to drown it with thoughts of the day's activity, but here in the stillness of the night, he was forced to admit it. When the Yankee cavalry had descended upon him, he had frozen like a gutless wretch, just like he had done at Allatoona Pass. It was only because of Gal that he had survived at all. A common farm animal had more bravery than he! This, along with knowing that he had fallen short of Mr. Templeton's high hopes, made him feel so bad about himself that he wished, just for a fleeting moment, that the Yankee's saber had found its mark. At least then he would no longer have to face the truth: that he was really a spineless coward.

What had happened to him? Where was the nerve that had emboldened him enough to run away from the orphanage and join the army? Where was the courage he'd had when he ran messages for the Confederate officers? After Allatoona, these qualities had retreated deep within, had been buried beneath so much fear and anxiety that he could not coax them up. And without courage, how could he ever deserve to be called a man?

Disturbed by his own dark thoughts, Henry rolled out of bed and staggered toward the wash stand. A splash of chilly water upon his face took his breath away. Stray droplets ran down his cheeks, fell away and formed beads on the white marble table top. They were joined there by droplets of his own tears, for as much as he knew that he should not have such thoughts about himself, he could find no reason to think otherwise when he looked in the mirror.

The water's chill hung with him. He pulled the itchy blanket about his shoulders and paced the room, first toward the door, then back toward the window. He wept quietly and longed for someone to talk to, but only the ticking hall clock answered his stifled sobs.

He stopped in front of the window. The draft reached for him and, as with prying fingers, slid beneath the blanket, sending another chill from head to toe. He placed a hand on the pane. The glass, too, was cold to the touch. In the darkness beyond, Henry made out the shape of the stable. He thought of Gal and at once longed to be with her, stroking her warm, strong neck. Pulling away from the glass, he stopped his snuffling and resolved to go down to her. Gal would listen to him without judgment. She had been there. She understood.

Henry quickly tossed aside the blanket and put on his old, tattered britches. Noiselessly, he opened the bedroom door and then paused. The hallway clock, ticking ever onward, produced the only sound. He looked at the hands. At this late hour, Henry was certain that Mr. Templeton had retired for the night.

Sneaking out was an art that Henry had perfected at the orphanage. Many times he and his mates had slipped away, under the headmaster's nose, to get into mischief. Now, however, the risk was greater. While he never had much respect for the headmaster, he downright feared Mr. Templeton. Henry knew the man was already disappointed with him, and he did not want to discover the penalty for someone caught sneaking about the house.

Through the hall, softly down the rear stairs, and stealthily into the pantry, Henry sneaked through the servants' entrance and found himself outdoors in the kitchen yard. The night air was chilly and sent a wave of goose bumps over him, but he folded his arms close to himself and began making his way toward the stable.

The outbuildings loomed in front of him, and he quickened his step, eager to be with Gal and out of the cold. But he had not gone far when two things happened at once that froze him in his tracks.

First, the baby's crying pierced the quiet night. The mournful sounds rose and fell, coming in waves across the expansive property. They stirred up within Henry the same heartbreaking pity he had felt when he heard the wounded men's desperate moans. Too, the cries were mysterious, for as often as he had heard them he still had never seen the baby. Nor did he know what caused it such distress.

But it was a mystery that he did not have long to ponder, for the second thing that stopped Henry filled him with fear and dread every bit as much as the baby's cries had moved him to pity. Far off, on the riverbank that formed the northeast ridge of the property, he saw a light.

It was a lantern light, he had no doubt. And it was moving along the riverbank, bobbing and swaying slightly as its unseen owner moved toward the dock and, beyond that, the storehouse which held the treasures.

Bummers!

Henry's knees went weak, and his stomach did a flip-flop as he crouched low to the ground. He shook his head in disbelief. He must have looked over his shoulder a thousand times last evening to be sure he had not been followed, but obviously he had not been careful enough. The Yanks were here, literally in his own backyard, and they were snooping dangerously close to the treasure. How could he have been so stupid! He had led them right to it, and when Templeton found out...well...there was no telling what he would do.

Glancing back at the house, Henry noticed that there were no lights on. Perhaps Mr. Templeton was still asleep, unaware of the Yankee trespassers. Henry figured that, in order to save his own hide, he would have to scare off the bummers before they did any damage, and he would have to do it before Mr. Templeton found out that they were even here.

The baby's crying slowly evaporated into the night air, as did Henry's thoughts of visiting Gal. This sudden emergency made him forget why he had come outside in the first place. His mind was whirling, searching for some strategy to spook the bummers away. He fixed his eyes on the lantern. It still bobbed and moved along the riverbank, but it was no closer to the storehouse.

As quickly as possible, Henry stole behind the stable, and from there he crept behind the barn. This brought him within earshot of the lantern-bearer, but he did not hear any conversation. Was it possible that the bummer was alone? Henry did not think this was likely. Sherman's bummers usually worked in packs. Probably this man had companions somewhere in hiding, waiting for his signal.

Concealed behind the barn, Henry was very close to the river. Peering around the corner, he saw the dock. Just beyond it was the dark impression of the storehouse. The lantern light now appeared to be still, resting on the dock. In the light that spilled across the water, Henry saw the silhouette of the one who had been carrying it. He was short, and much to Henry's surprise the man was actually standing up to his knees in the river, holding very still. Then, after a time, the shadowy figure slowly waded back toward the dock, rippling the water as he went.

After standing statue-still for some minutes more, the figure retrieved the lantern, turned, and began wading downstream... toward Henry's hiding place.

Henry pulled his head behind the corner of the barn. He heard water sloshing as the shadowy figure pushed his way slowly through the shallows, each movement louder than the last as the distance between Henry and the river-walker shrank. Henry's cheek rested against the barn's coarse wooden siding, splinters spiking his skin like miniature bayonets.

Slish-slosh.

His heart thudded in his chest.

Slish-slosh.

The pool of lantern light slid into view.

Slish-slosh.

The man was nearly upon him. Henry had to decide what to do. He considered leaping out from behind the barn to surprise the soldier, but he knew such a move would be rash. The Yank was probably armed, and Henry was not. He figured his best hope was to slip quietly back to the house and alert Mr. Templeton, never mind what consequence he'd have to pay for leading the bummers here. He was just about to retreat when he realized that the slish-slosh sounds had stopped. Unable to curb his curiosity, Henry pushed his nose beyond the corner of the barn, just far enough for his eyes to peer around.

What he saw surprised him. The river-walker was standing still in the stagnant water along the shore, a shadowy mass among slender reeds. The lantern bathed him in just enough light to reveal torn and tattered trousers rolled up to the knees, a dirty over-shirt, and a flimsy hat. There was no blue uniform, no rifle slung across his shoulder, no kepi upon his head. With a surge of relief, Henry realized that this was no Yankee soldier. This river-walker was not even a man. It was a boy who appeared to be about Henry's own height. He shifted the lantern, and the light fell briefly across his face and neck.

Black skin.

It was Reuben.

Henry jerked his head back. He had expected a bummer, perhaps even an entire company of them. That would have been explicable, even logical.

But Reuben?

What was he doing, skulking about the plantation so late on a cold night, up to his knees in the river? What purpose could have brought him out of his cabin, risking Templeton's wrath?

Slish-slosh.

The sound came again, and this time it dredged up a distant memory. Long ago he had heard it said that slaves intentionally walked through rivers and streams when they were running away. The water masked their scent and made it more difficult for the slave hunters' dogs to track them.

Slish-slosh.

Henry's eyes narrowed. *So that's it*, he thought to himself. *That slave boy's makin' a break for it. Well, I ain't no bloodhound, but I got a nose fer figgerin' when a slave's up to no good.*

He realized that this situation presented a welcome opportunity. How better to assuage Templeton's disappointment than to prevent one of his slaves from escaping? Why, such an accomplishment would put him back in the man's good graces for sure.

Emboldened by this chance for redemption, Henry stood up. He recalled the encounter with Violet in the dining room, how he had made a command and she had done it. He remembered the power he had felt and how much he had liked it.

Before he really knew what he was doing, he jumped out from behind the barn and strode with authority to the river's edge.

"Hey, boy!" he shouted with a voice that cracked like a rifle report in the otherwise quiet night. "What you think you doin'?"

Reuben's head snapped up. The water rippled around his ankles as he stepped backward. In one motion, he hooded his lantern and turned to flee, but in his haste he dropped something from his other hand. Henry heard it splash, but he could not see what it was.

Reuben muttered a curse. Turning again, he unhooded the lantern. Frantically, he looked about for the object that he had dropped. Locating it, he plunged his hand into the water and retrieved what looked to be a mason jar. He straightened, and then looked hard for a few moments into the darkness. Unhooding the lantern even further, he held the light up and cast it in Henry's direction.

The bright light momentarily blinded Henry, and he shielded his eyes.

"Dang," came Reuben's voice from the river. "Thought you was Temp'ton."

Henry squinted in his direction. With the light in his eyes, he could no longer see Reuben's outline. "I asked you what you was doin', boy."

Reuben stood still for a few moments. Then he waded to the water's edge, stepped onto the shore, and stood toe-to-toe with the white boy.

Reuben held the light up to Henry's face for almost a minute before lowering it and looking at him directly.

"Who you callin' boy?"

Henry studied Reuben carefully. Up close, he was much taller. Intense eyes, ringed with white that shone in the lantern light, glared down at him. Henry returned the gaze shortly, but then found that he had to break it off.

Reuben's jaw line was square and strong, his lips pressed together in a straight line. A scar above his right eyebrow leered from beneath the sloping, floppy hat. His shoulders were broad. His biceps bulged. Even as Henry stood before him, he felt the boldness leaking out of him.

"I know what you's about, b-boy," said Henry, desperately hoping that his words would mask his mounting intimidation. "You was runnin'."

"I's tellin' you agin. Don't call me boy."

"But you was runnin', wasn't ya?"

At this, Reuben merely grunted. He knelt down, placing the lantern on the ground in front of him. Then, reaching for his left leg, he ran his fingers over the skin exposed beneath his rolled trousers. In the harsh light, Henry noticed a dark blob protruding from Reuben's calf. Placing thumb and forefinger on either side of it, Reuben pinched and pulled. The dark thing detached from his leg, and with a wince Reuben straightened and eyed Henry once more. He raised his hand and held it directly in front of Henry's nose. Trapped between his fingers was a writhing and slimy leech.

"You tink I be runnin'? What you gonna do 'bout it? Gonna run off 'n tell yo man Temp'ton? You's sucked up tighter to him den dis lich in my black skin."

He squeezed the leech tighter. Making sucking noises, he made like he was going to put it on Henry's cheek. Henry turned aside and retreated a step, prompting a snicker from Reuben.

When Henry looked again, he saw Reuben bend over and put the leech in the mason jar where it wriggled about with several companions.

Reuben then hoisted the lantern, directed the light into Henry's eyes, and took another step closer to him. With a biting voice, he said, "You tink you knows what I's about? You don't know nuttin what I's about. You betta shut yo lip and don't go runnin' to yo man Temp'ton."

By now, Henry's confidence had all but collapsed. Still, from somewhere inside of him, his voice bubbled up. "You ain't nothin' but a runaway slave."

Reuben's eyes and nostrils flared at this. He stepped forward, pushed Henry hard in the chest, and hissed, "Don't you never call me dat! If you tink I's runnin', why don't you do sompin' 'bout it? Why don't you do sompin' 'bout it right now, white boy?"

He pushed Henry again.

Anger boiled up in Henry, the steam of it rising within him, turning his cheeks red and hot. He was not going to be pushed around by some slave boy.

"You lazy cuss! Touch me agin, and I'll make sure Templeton whips you extra good and hard!"

"Yeah," Reuben retorted. "You run off and tell Temp'ton like he's yo mammy. Go on! Go on and suck right up to yo mammy! 'Cause you ain't man enough to do sompin' 'bout it yoself!"

Reuben mocked him, making the sucking noises again. This was too much for Henry. He flung himself toward Reuben, swinging wildly. His left fist caught nothing but air. His right fist connected with Reuben's forearm but was turned harmlessly aside.

Reuben then forcefully grabbed Henry by the shirt and lifted him off the ground. For an instant, Henry hung suspended like a puppet, and then Reuben threw him to the dirt where he landed like a heap of dirty laundry.

Henry rolled with pain, but he stopped when Reuben knelt beside him and whispered into his ear. "You fight like a scared white boy. Now I's gonna give you a beat-down you ain't never gonna foget."

Curled up, Henry waited for the rain of blows that was sure to fall on him. But after a few seconds, muscles tense with expectation, nothing happened. Abruptly, everything went pitch dark.

Reuben had hooded the lantern.

In the darkness, Henry heard him grope about for the mason jar. Then the inky outline of Reuben's figure knelt over Henry once more and whispered, "You lucky dis time, boy. But you still got a beatin' comin'. Don't you foget."

And with that, Reuben disappeared into the night.

Henry could not believe it. He had prepared himself to endure Reuben's assault, but the thrashing never came. What could have scared him off? Bewildered, Henry scrambled to his knees. As far as his eyes penetrated the darkness, he saw no sign of Reuben.

Thinking that his night had been filled with enough adventures, Henry was about to turn back toward the big house. However, out of the corner of his eye, he became aware of a light twinkling from the river.

It's Reuben, comin' to finish me off, he thought to himself. But then, after a moment's consideration, he realized that the light could not possibly belong to Reuben. Sure enough, it was a lantern. But it was coming from the deep water, and it was gliding upriver from the southeast.

It was a boat.

For an instant, Henry again feared bummers. But he had never heard of Sherman's raiders attacking by boat. He pressed his body against the barn and crouched low. As the boat drew nearer, he could hear the oars' muted dipping and the hushed words of the men on board.

This is what run him off, thought Henry. *He din't want to be spotted.*

Minutes ticked by as the boat glided past Henry's place of concealment. He poked his head around the corner to watch the vessel disappear upriver, but much to his surprise the boat slowed and carved out a turn toward port. One of the men leaped onto Stratmore's dock and helped guide the boat in. Lashings were made. An anchor was dropped.

Henry was so engrossed in watching the boat's activity that he did not even notice another lantern bobbing its way across the property. The bearer of this light was coming from the big house, and Henry knew it could only be one person.

Henry observed with curiosity as Templeton strode onto the dock and greeted the men on the boat. Words were exchanged, but Henry was too far away to make out what was being said. After a brief discussion, the men traversed the dock, stepped onto the soggy ground, and turned toward the storehouse.

Oak trees framed the area that Henry watched, their dangling strands of Spanish moss like black ribbons that snaked and shifted in the breeze. To Henry, the men appeared to move as shadow puppets upon a wall, the wavering lantern light distorting and exaggerating their shapes.

A voice in Henry's mind told him to stay put. It warned him that whatever he was witnessing was none of his business. He should sneak back into the house while Templeton was outside, scamper up to Robert's room, and toss the covers over his head. That was the voice of reason.

But another voice, a more insistent one, urged Henry to find out what was going on. A boat coming to Stratmore in the dead of night. Templeton himself making a secret meeting. It was all too irresistible, and Henry moved closer to try to discover what was afoot.

Gathered at the entrance to the storehouse, the men's backs were turned toward Henry. Undetected, he stole through the darkness and took cover behind an old tree stump that rotted near the water's edge. The pungent aroma of decomposing wood invaded his nostrils as he peered over the rim of decaying bark.

Closer now, the men were more defined. The lanterns provided enough light for Henry to see Templeton remove the key from around his neck and unlock the storehouse door. The men disappeared into the opening, causing a rectangular shaft of light to spill forth from the narrow doorway and make a shape upon the grass outside.

After some time, the men emerged. One walked closely with Templeton while the other two carried objects in their hands. They were dressed in civilian clothes.

"You've got some quality merchandise here, Templeton," said the man walking next to him. Henry noticed immediately that he spoke with a Yankee accent. "These items will fetch a fair price in New York."

"I've no doubt that they will, Mr. Hathaway," replied Templeton with a drawl that was slow but gentile. "I trust that your contact in Savannah has procured a boat?"

"Certainly," returned Mr. Hathaway. "And now that I've seen your inventory, I'm quite sure that it is worth the risk of running the blockade. I'll be sure to show him these items…" here he gestured toward the objects held by the men on the boat "…as a sample of the finery that you're able to acquire."

From his place behind the stump, Henry looked at the men on the dock and gasped. Even in the weak light, he could make out what they held in their hands: the astral lamp from Brewer's place and the box of table silver from Magnolia Acres.

"My wife," continued Hathaway, "will be most delighted to add these pieces to her collection. What is your price?"

Templeton eyed the Northern gentleman for a moment, as if making a final, unspoken determination that he was worthy of his trust. With a deep breath that signaled his satisfaction, he said, "Thirty dollars…in Northern currency."

"Not Confederate?" Hathaway queried with a touch of surprise.

"No. This is an investment in my future. I fear Confederate currency will soon be worthless."

"Very well," replied Hathaway. He produced a pocketbook and proceeded to count the bills. Arriving at the proper amount, he handed the money over to Templeton.

"It's a pleasure doing business with a gentleman such as yourself," remarked the Northerner. "It's a pity that so many of my associates up North think the South is no longer capable of civilized business dealings."

"Well," returned Templeton, "their ignorance creates a greater opportunity for us, now doesn't it?"

"Indeed!" laughed Hathaway. "Quite true. I will display these items to my associate as a showing of your willingness to act in good faith. You can expect me to return in three days. I am interested in purchasing the entire lot."

"I am delighted," said Templeton as he extended his hand.

Hathaway took it and said, "As am I. I have every confidence that this will be a profitable venture for both of us."

With that, Hathaway turned and strode up the dock. As he stepped in, his men loaded the valuables and cast off. Then, as quietly as they had arrived, they glided down the river until they were out of sight.

Henry sank behind the rotten stump, struggling to come to terms with what he had just witnessed. He imagined Mrs. Graves' eyes probing him with the same searching look she had cast upon him when he had given her his word of honor. She had trusted him, just as he had trusted Mr. Templeton. Now her table silver was on its way down the river, soon to adorn the table of a wealthy Northerner. She had been betrayed. Henry clenched his fists and eyed Templeton over the jagged edges of bark. They had both been betrayed.

Angry as he was, Henry knew that he could not remain. Templeton's wrath would know no boundary if he discovered that Henry had been spying. The man stayed for a while on the dock, watching Hathaway's boat sail away. Now he turned and strode toward the storehouse to shut the door and secure it with the lock.

With Templeton's back turned, Henry took a chance. He slipped from behind the stump and stole across the lawn as quietly as he could. If he could make it to the big house, he could sneak up the servants' staircase and back into Robert's bedroom before Templeton even finished locking up. Running blindly through the darkness, he had almost made it to the kitchen yard when his left foot caught a root. With a startled yelp, Henry sprawled face-down on the ground and skidded to a halt. Holding his breath, he hugged the nighttime wet grass and prayed that his mishap would go unnoticed.

He lay motionless for eternal seconds. He desperately wanted to glance backward to see if Templeton had heard him, but he resisted the temptation to make even the slightest movement. He almost thought he was in the clear when he heard slow, measured strides coming toward him. An edge of lantern light advanced across his legs and torso, then bathed him fully. The footsteps stopped. Henry saw boot toes just inches away, but still he lay face down. He drew his arms up to his head, but he was exposed like a frightened turtle without a shell.

Suddenly he felt the collar of his shirt being grasped, and he was gruffly brought to his feet. Thick, strong hands grabbed his shoulders and spun him around while a crooked finger lifted his chin. Mr. Templeton's glare held him with a force all its own.

Even in the darkness, the man's eyes seemed to be on fire. His lips were pulled flat against his teeth, and the muscles in his cheeks knotted as he clenched his jaw. Still, for some time he did not speak. His eyes were branding irons that bored holes through Henry.

At length, his jaw relaxed enough to speak. When his voice came, it was eerily calm. "It is a late hour for you to be out walking on my property."

The night air had chilled enough that his breath produced puffs of steam.

"Perhaps you will explain to me what you are doing." It was a command, not a question.

Henry's chin shook uncontrollably. He looked down and away, but again Templeton jabbed a crooked finger and forced him to look up.

"You will look at me when you speak. I'm waiting."

Henry stammered. He felt his eyes fill with hot tears, and Templeton's face swam before him. The man towered over him, his total authority smashing down with so much unseen force and weight that Henry felt as if he were being crushed. A tear overflowed his eyelid and rolled down his cheek. A spasm in his gut forced short, quick breaths.

"I…I's jist…I din't mean no…"

A sharp, backhanded slap across Henry's face cut short his attempt to speak.

"Don't blubber at me! When I ask you to speak, do it!"

Templeton's knuckles bit Henry's skin like teeth, the sting then fading into hot numbness. The force of the blow turned his face away, but this time Henry himself snapped it back and met Mr. Templeton's glare.

"I couldn't sleep," he managed. "I's jist out fer a walk is all."

"Oh, I see," replied Templeton. "And just what did you see while you were on your stroll?"

Henry forced the words out. "I seen what you give to them Yanks."

"Did you, now?"

Henry nodded slowly. "Yer a liar."

Another backhanded slap bit Henry, but he did not allow it to silence him. "You said we was pertectin' them valuables from the thieving Yanks! You toll Mrs. Graves we was keepin' it safe! An' then you go an' sell it! Yer a filthy liar!"

Henry braced himself for another slap, but this time Templeton reached under his overcoat and pulled out a pistol. He leveled it at Henry and said, "If you call me a liar again, I'll put a bullet in you right here and now." Then he added with a snicker, "No one would even notice you were gone."

The rage in Templeton's eyes told Henry that he was mad enough to really do it, so he bit his lip.

"What you so crudely call deceit," said Templeton, still brandishing the gun, "I call business. This is a business opportunity. Nothing more, nothing less."

"Ain't no business when you go robbin' yer neighbors."

"Shut that mouth of yours before you say something you won't live to take back, boy!"

Then, with less of an edge, Templeton mused. "Ahh...you can't see it now. You're too young and naïve. What do you think this war is about, boy? Slavery? Some would like us to think so. But what is slavery about, after all? I'll tell you what it's about. It's about money. And power. It's business. This war is about business.

Soon as that first shot was fired, it became every man for himself. A man does what he must to survive, including me. And I just so happen to be a business man."

His voice sharpened again, and he focused more intently than ever on Henry. "This war nearly ruined me, but now the spoils are going to set me back on my feet. And you...you little wet-behind-the-ears orphan boy...you're going to keep helping me do it."

Henry shook his head. "It ain't right."

Templeton lowered the pistol and once again grabbed Henry by the shirt collar. With one arm, he lifted Henry to his tip-toes and pulled him within an inch of his face.

"Maybe you've forgotten, boy. I know all about you. I know why you were drifting across the countryside. You yourself told me every detail."

He dropped his voice to a harsh whisper. "I know what happened at Allatoona Pass. I know about the men who died there because you deserted under fire. Their blood is on your hands. If you don't do as I say, then I take you to the nearest Confederate encampment and turn you in. Then you know what comes after that, boy?"

Henry blinked and swallowed hard.

"They'll either hang you from a tree or put you in front of a firing squad."

Templeton pulled him closer still. The key that he wore around his neck, the key to the storehouse, slipped out and dangled between the two of them. For an instant, Henry watched it swing ponderously upon its chain.

"And if you think you're just going to run away and leave me high and dry, well, you'd better think again. Those men you saw with Mr. Hathaway are former slave hunters. I'd turn them loose on you, or else I'd hunt you down and kill you myself."

Once again Templeton flaunted the pistol. "Don't think I wouldn't do it. Because you see, now you know my secret. And I can't have that information being spread around, now can I, boy?"

Henry's mouth had gone completely dry. He swallowed again and shook his head.

"There now," said Templeton as he released his grip and returned Henry flat-footed to the ground. "Maybe now you're beginning to see reason. Do we have an understanding?"

Against every fiber of righteousness within him, Henry nodded.

"Good," replied Templeton. "I assume you overheard the arrangement that I have with Mr. Hathaway?"

Again, Henry nodded. His tongue was still too dry to speak.

"Then you know that a flatboat is arriving in three days' time. I want to greatly increase my inventory before it arrives. This means that you will be very busy. I think I have been perfectly clear about what will happen if you fail me, have I not?"

Finally, Henry was able to make words again. "You have."

Templeton eyed him and waited expectantly.

"You have made yerself clear, sir."

Templeton nodded. "I'm glad we understand one another. Now, go get some rest. Tomorrow will be a long day."

Henry turned and started toward the big house, but he was stopped by more words from Templeton.

"Oh no, my boy. I am not in the habit of rewarding insubordination. From now on, you will be sleeping over there." With his pistol, he motioned toward the stables.

Henry's shoulders slumped, but he marched off obediently. Mr. Templeton watched the boy until the stable door slammed shut behind him. Then the man returned the pistol to its holster, picked up his lantern, and made his way into the big house.

The slamming stable door startled Gal, and she pitched her head curiously to see who might be visiting her at this time of night. Henry went to her and immediately let out a half-hearted laugh in spite of everything and said to himself, "Well, this is where I wanted to be anyway."

His weak attempt at humor did little to bring him comfort. As he stroked her mane, his cheeks smarted from the slaps he had sustained. Nettling him even more was the sting of betrayal. He had been lied to. Duped. And now he was being forced to do something he knew was not right. He had no choice. He was under Templeton's thumb.

So much for trust.

So much for honor.

He kissed Gal goodnight and lay down in the empty stall next to hers. Yet just as he was drifting off, he became vaguely aware of the sound of crying. As before, the baby's cries rose and fell upon the chilly night breeze. Trying to listen more carefully this time, he felt a strange sense of sympathy. He wondered if that baby had anyone to hold it and rock it gently through its troubling time. Henry hoped that it did, for he knew what it was like, not having anybody. And he did not wish that kind of emptiness on anyone else in the world.

It seemed to Henry only a matter of minutes before the clanking stable door woke him. Curled up between two mildewing bales of hay, he heard Gal's stamping and pawing in the stall next to him. He rubbed his bleary eyes, yawned prodigiously, and swiped feebly at the bits of straw dangling from his clothes.

Commanding footsteps thudded down the stable's center aisle and stopped just outside of Henry's stall. Through a gap in the wooden slats he recognized Templeton's boots, triggering unwelcome memories from last night's encounter.

The stall door opened, and there stood Templeton with his hands on his hips. Morning sunshine filtered weakly from the outside, illuminating his imposing figure. He shuffled his feet with impatience, sending up a flurry of dust and flakes made visible in the diffused light. Still lying on the uneven floor, Henry looked up at him, a mouse cowering in the corner knowing full well that Templeton, if he chose to, could crush him with one stomp of his boot.

"Get up, boy. Saddle Gallivanter and hitch up that Yankee wagon. Meet me at the lane."

His words were short and direct, and then he was gone.

Henry lingered in the hay a few minutes more, still foggy from lack of sleep. His head hurt. His thoughts were clouded. His stomach begged for some of Violet's biscuits and gravy, though he doubted that he would taste breakfast of any kind this morning.

Finally, with his joints protesting every movement, Henry rolled onto his side and pulled himself to his feet. His nose was full of black dust, and three quick sneezes shook him. Wiping with his sleeve, he moaned and straightened his aching back.

How badly he wanted to collapse back into the hay and sleep the day away! But he knew it would be an awful mistake to keep Templeton waiting. He fished his hat from among the scattered strands of straw and slapped it against his knee to dust it off. He sneezed again. Then, hat on head, he set to the business of saddling Gal and hitching up the cart.

Much like Henry, Gal was in no mood for another day of excitement. Usually docile, she stubbornly resisted Henry's attempts to saddle her. Even after the cart was attached, he had to haul on the reins with all of his might to coax her even one step forward. Not that he blamed her. He knew she was exhausted from yesterday's action. Still, for her own good, he had to prod her forward. Noble as she was, Gal's simple view of the world did not take into account the single-minded designs of her owner, nor did she fear the consequences, as Henry did, that would surely befall them if they were not punctual.

By the time Henry led Gal around the big house to the oak-lined lane, he saw Templeton waiting for them. He appeared to be agitated at Henry's tardiness, but something else grabbed Henry's attention. Templeton was not alone. Reuben stood next to him, arms folded across his chest, eyes riveted on Henry.

Henry led Gal alongside Templeton and Reuben, and he pulled her up. She rolled her eyes and tossed her head as if still complaining about being up at this ridiculous hour. Henry did not fully understand the meaning of Reuben's presence, though he felt the full weight of the black boy's glare bearing down on him.

Templeton broke the silence. "It's about time," he muttered, eyeing Henry. "Now listen to me closely. I've heard rumor that the Yankees are on the move again. It seems that Kilpatrick is preparing to make a thrust north through Waynesboro. They'll gain the Brier Creek Bridge if they can, and it's likely they'll burn it. Wheeler is in a position to block them, but God only knows if he can hold them off."

Henry felt a flutter in his stomach. Brier Creek was not very far from Stratmore.

"If the Yanks get across Brier Creek, I have no doubt the bummers will hit Hanley Hall. That most resplendent home is owned by Mr. William Hanley, and I'm certain that there are innumerable valuables within. At all costs, you must get there before the Yankees do."

Henry nodded to signal that he understood. He was painfully aware that Reuben had never taken his eyes off of him.

"At news of Sherman's approach, Mr. Hanley fled to South Carolina, and he left everything behind. You should have no shortage of items from which to choose. This must be a profitable venture. I've made assurances to Mr. Hathaway, and I have no intention of disappointing him.

"I want this to be the largest acquisition yet. Therefore, I am sending along an extra pair of hands. Reuben will accompany you on this mission."

Henry's heart plummeted. How was he supposed to cooperate with that slave who planned to beat him down at the first chance he got?

Sensing his apprehension, Templeton added, "He is, of course, under your charge. If he disobeys you or attempts to run away, shoot him."

To Henry's utter disbelief, Templeton parted his overcoat and revealed a gun belt holding twin revolvers. He drew one of them, stepped forward, and laid the heavy gun in Henry's hands. Henry turned it over and ran his fingers along the gleaming barrel. While his thumb traced the outline of the hammer, he looked at Reuben again and saw that the haughty look in his eyes had vanished. He hefted the gun, and then stuck it in his britches. He felt a sense of power and command that he had never known before. The balance had shifted in his favor, and Reuben knew it.

A measure of security now dangled at Henry's side, but it did not fully dispel the uneasiness he felt about riding with Reuben.

Before, when it had just been Henry and Gal, the slow miles of quiet riding had not been so bad. Henry discovered that these times offered freedom to do things that he didn't ordinarily do, like singing or talking out loud to Gal, explaining to her all of his troubles and his views of the world while she listened.

But now, on the road to Hanley Hall, everything was different. Henry sat astride Gal in his usual position, but there was nothing usual about it. Reuben sat behind them in the cart, arms still folded, knees pulled up, glowering at the back of Henry's head. As before, Henry felt the weight of that stare, and it was most unnerving. It made him stiff, apprehensive, and deeply self-conscious. Henry twisted repeatedly in the saddle to make sure Reuben was not trying anything underhanded, so much so that Reuben finally said, "Quit yo squirmin', white boy. I ain't goin' nowhar."

Henry did not respond to this. Though he twisted less frequently, he kept his hand on the revolver.

He had considered trading places, but he could not bring himself to turn over Gal's reins to that slave boy. He resigned himself to plodding forward, making the best of it. Besides, the threat of bummers would occupy him soon enough. Aside from Reuben's lone comment, there was no conversation between them. The jostling cart, the clip-clop of Gal's hooves, and the occasional cry of a passing bird provided the only background for their journey. Henry was grateful for these small distractions because without them, the tension-filled silence would have become unbearable.

They traveled southeast on the road that Templeton had instructed. From what the man had told him, Henry figured Hanley Hall to be about five miles off. As he munched on johnny-cakes, the only food that Templeton had provided the boys,

Henry grew increasingly worried about Sherman's bummers. Brier Creek was not far to the south, and beyond the creek lay Waynesboro. Something inside Henry told him that the unfortunate little town would witness its share of battle today, and he wanted no part of it.

Still chewing on johnnycake and scanning the road for any sign of Yankee activity, Henry suddenly felt a hitch in Gal's step. The rhythmic clip-clop that had lulled him these many miles fell out of synch, and Henry felt the horse shift her weight underneath him. He leaned to the side and saw that she was favoring her front right leg.

"Stop! Pull 'er up!"

Henry was so startled by Reuben's shout that he nearly tumbled from the saddle.

"Pull up dat hoss, fool!"

In a shaky voice that revealed his concern, Henry called out, "Whoa, Gal!" and pulled back on the reins.

Gal obediently and gratefully obeyed. She rolled her eyes and whinnied loudly, tossing her head more forcefully than usual. Henry rubbed her neck and whispered soothing words, but he noticed that Gal was not putting any weight on her foot.

Like a flash, Reuben was out of the cart. Henry watched out of the corner of his eye as the black boy came up from behind him on Gal's right side. He reached for the revolver and pulled it from his britches.

Reuben, however, did not notice this. He knelt on the ground, examining Gal's hoof. After some moments of careful observation, he rubbed Gal's flank and slowly stood. He turned toward Henry in the saddle, only to find the revolver's barrel staring him in the face.

Reuben froze and studied Henry. The gun was shaking so much that it looked like a cattail in a windstorm. At length, the black boy said, "Put dat thing away a'fore you hurt somebody. This here hoss needs some at'ention."

He turned and sauntered coolly back up the road in the direction from which they had come. Reuben passed right by the wagon and kept on walking. Henry watched him and was beside himself, not knowing what to do. Was this slave boy simply going to walk away from him, leaving him stranded on an injured horse? Was he just going to sit there and let him do that?

Hastily, Henry clambered down from the saddle. He jogged a few strides after Reuben, and then called out, "Hey! You come on back here!"

Reuben just kept walking.

"Git back here now, you hear!?"

Still, Reuben ignored him.

"Don't you walk away from me!"

This time, Henry raised the revolver. He was about to call out one more warning when Reuben stopped, leaned down, and picked up something from the dusty road. Then, to Henry's astonishment, Reuben turned and began walking back toward him. With the gun still raised, Henry watched in confusion as Reuben strode right past him on his way back toward Gal.

"Tolja to put that thing down," Reuben muttered as he brushed past Henry.

Henry turned, this time lowering the weapon to his side. He watched as Reuben rubbed Gal's neck soothingly and then once again knelt down by her hoof. He could not help being struck by the tenderness with which Reuben attended to Gal.

Not willing to let his guard down completely, Henry approached Reuben and said, "What you think you doin'?"

Reuben was silent for so long that Henry thought he was still ignoring him. But then Reuben looked up and replied, "I's trying to fix up dis hoss, as long as you don't haul off and shoot me first."

Henry watched how deftly and gently Reuben examined Gal's hoof, how soothingly he stroked her and spoke to her as he did so. Henry looked into Gal's eye and saw that she was completely calm as she permitted this slave boy to work on her. Her placidity eased his own tension, and he slightly lowered his dander.

"What's wrong with her?"

"Threw a shoe," replied Reuben. "I seen it from back thar in that cart. Luckly it din't go far, and the nails ain't lost."

Henry now saw that the horseshoe and a couple of nails lay on the ground by Reuben's knee. These were the items he had picked up on the road.

"Still," continued Reuben, "they's sompin' else wrong here."

Down on one knee, he lifted Gal's leg and examined it again. This time, Henry moved in closer to see. A slight crack had developed in the hoof, and a tiny pebble had lodged in the crack.

"See dat?" said Reuben. "Dat's why she be limpin'. You hold her steady while I pry out dat pebble."

Henry straightened, grabbed the reins, and petted Gal's neck while Reuben went to work. Gal flinched only slightly as Reuben used one of the nails to pry the pebble free.

"There," said Reuben with a touch of satisfaction. "Now we's just got to shoe her. Problem is, we ain't got no hammer."

Reuben cast his eyes about, and then locked his gaze on the revolver that Henry still clutched in his right hand.

"The butt o' that gun would work just fine, I reckon."

Henry was incredulous. Did this black slave think that he was just going to hand the gun over?

"You ain't gettin' this gun."

"Well," said Reuben, "then I guess we ain't got much choice but to set here and let them Yanks come git us."

With that he stood up, walked back to the cart and sat down on the ground with his back leaning up against the wagon wheel. He pulled his hat down over his eyes and made like he was taking a nap.

"Yep," he muttered, "You stay on the lookout an' tell me when old Papa Abe is a-comin' to set me free. Meantime, I's gonna git some rest."

Henry just stood in the middle of the road, not believing what was happening. He had never shoed a horse before in his life, and he didn't even know how to begin. There was no one else on the road, no houses for miles around. On the other hand, he couldn't just give the gun to Reuben. Could he?

A few more minutes passed. Reuben forced out a snoring sound. Henry realized that he didn't have much of a choice. He walked over to where Reuben lounged and said, "Alright. Put the shoe back on my horse."

Reuben poked up his hat and looked at Henry.

"Give me dat gun."

Henry hesitated, not really sure that he wanted to do it, but then held out the gun anyway. It was only after Reuben snatched it away from him that he realized he had made a dreadful mistake. He had not taken the bullets out.

"Well now," smirked Reuben as he stood up. "You jist handed me a loaded gun, boy! Yessir, a black man with a loaded gun! Dat's the white folks' most worst nightmare!"

Henry's face drained of color. Sometimes he could not believe his own stupidity. Reuben pointed the gun at him, and Henry put his hands in the air.

"Aww, come on now, boy. Put them hands down. I ain't gowin' to hurt you. You got my word o' honor."

Having said this, Reuben opened the cylinder and emptied the bullets from all six chambers. Then he snapped the cylinder shut and held out the handful of bullets to Henry.

"Don't want dis to go off whiles I's hammerin'."

Not fully knowing what to make of this, Henry took the bullets and pocketed them.

"Now," said Reuben, "let's fix dat hoss."

The two boys walked up to Gal who, despite the discomfort of having lost a shoe, seemed to be enjoying this short respite. Henry held her reins while Reuben went back to work. He held the horseshoe in place. Using the butt of the revolver as a makeshift hammer, he pounded in the nails that he had managed to recover. It was not a perfect shoeing, but it was adequate given the circumstances. When it was finished, he stood up.

"Where'd you learn to do that?" Henry asked.

"My pappy. He was a blacksmiff used to work fo' Massa Temp'ton. Taught me a lot o' things. Here's yo gun back."

He handed the revolver back to Henry, butt end first.

Henry accepted it and said, "Much obliged."

"Tolja I was a man o' my word," said Reuben. "What's yo name, white boy?"

"Henry."

"I's Reuben."

"I know. I heard your name a'fore from Templeton."

"He don't like me much, do he?"

"Naw."

"Well, don't matter none."

Reuben made like he was going back to his place in the cart, but then he stopped and turned around.

"Hey, Henry. They's one mo' thing."

"What?"

Reuben took two steps toward him, then reared back and coldcocked him in the face.

Henry was laid out on the road like a rag doll. He moaned and rolled in the dirt, his hand up to his jaw where Reuben's fist had landed.

"Aww! What was that for?"

"Well," said Reuben, "that's fo' callin' me a runaway slave. I tolja I was gonna beat you down fo' dat. After all…" he smiled proudly, "…I's a man o' my word."

Reuben stepped forward. Still with a sly grin on his face, he extended a hand to help Henry up.

Henry lay in the middle of the road looking up at him. Was this black boy crazy? Maybe. But at least he was honest…so far.

"Fair enuff," said Henry. He accepted the slave boy's hand, and Reuben pulled him up.

"Now, how far to dat there plantation house?"

"About five mile, I reckon," managed Henry, massaging his jaw.

"Well, den let's move on and git dis over with." Reuben climbed into the cart.

Henry nodded, but before saddling up he pulled the bullets out of his pocket. He flipped open the cylinder, slid each bullet back into a chamber, and then tucked the revolver back into his britches.

"Jist fer pertection," he said in reply to Reuben's look.

"Fair enuff," Reuben replied.

Then Henry mounted Gal and rode once more toward Hanley Hall Plantation.

Among the Southern gentry, Hanley Hall was regarded as one of the finest plantation homes in Georgia. Nestled near a wooded valley, a curtain of trees parted to reveal the majestic big house seated on a hillside like a king on his throne, encircled by a bevy of smaller outbuildings that knelt around it in humble deference. Double hung windows, ever watchful eyes, peered down in every direction and gazed upon the nine hundred acres of cleared land where cotton reigned supreme. The manicured grounds and seemingly endless rows of slave quarters hinted at the affluent lifestyle that Mr. William Hanley and his family enjoyed.

But if the king on his hilltop throne once knew days of wealth and prosperity, those days had evaporated like the morning dew on the fields. The watchful windows were now lidded by shutters locked and nailed into place. Weeds ran riot in the lawns, making slow advances on all fronts. And not a single person, slave or free, could be found on any square foot of all those nine hundred acres. They had all fled in the face of another enemy who was inexorably closing in from all directions. The plantation already had been strangled, even before Sherman's noose had tightened completely. Indeed, if it could somehow look upon itself in its state of abandonment, Hanley Hall would not have even recognized itself.

It was late morning when Henry, Reuben, and Gal rode into the wooded valley which formed the property's western boundary. While the early morning had featured a touch of sunshine, by now the blue skies had been crowded out by a gray blanket. Under the trees the dimness was thicker still, and Henry felt as if the day had gone from morning to twilight in a few short hours.

Long ago, a horse path had been cut through the valley, and it was this that Gal now followed. Yet when she reached the end of the path, at the point where it emerged from the trees and opened up, Henry reined her to a halt.

Reuben crawled to the front of the cart and got to his knees. From there, he could see Hanley Hall proudly perched on the hilltop. Henry shifted in the saddle and gazed at it, too. "Thar she is."

"Ain't dat sompin." Reuben let out a low whistle.

They were silent a few minutes more until Reuben spoke again. "Ain't we gonna ride on up thar?"

"Naw," said Henry. "Not yet. First we go up on foot to make sure they ain't nobody around. Easier to sneak up thar on foot, case somebody is watchin'. When we's good an' sure it's all clear, then we bring up the cart and clean her out."

"What we do wit dis hoss in the meantime?"

"We'll tie up Gal in these here trees. She'll be good and hidden till we need her."

"Awright den. Let's git movin'."

Henry dismounted and led Gal a short distance back up the path to a place where he could bring her in among the trees. The thicket provided enough cover that someone passing by would not know she was there if they weren't specifically looking for her.

With Gal and the cart concealed, the boys proceeded on foot. Emerging from the tree line, they had to cross an expanse of cotton field before they could climb the hill on which the house was situated. Fortunately for them, the field was over-grown with brush and provided plenty of cover. Hunched low, they trudged up the hillside and came to a place where the field gave way to the front lawn. From here, they would have to continue with less cover.

"You sure dat house is empty?" asked Reuben with concern.

"Templeton said it would be."

"And you sure you done dis kind o' thing before?"

"Yeah," responded Henry. "Couple of times."

That statement was true enough, but deep inside Henry felt that it was much different this time. At Rose Hill and Magnolia Acres, he had believed he was carrying out an act of patriotism. Now, he knew he was just a common thief.

The boys slipped from the brush and stole across the lawn, bouncing from tree to tree for cover, eventually arriving at the front verandah. Neither boy had seen a glimpse of anyone or heard a peep of noise except their own.

Henry went to the front door. Not surprisingly, it was boarded up and chained with a thick padlock.

Reuben imitated a gun with his fingers and whispered to Henry, "Shoot dat lock off."

Henry shook his head no. "Too much noise." Then, when he remembered how noisy it was to break a window, that reasoning seemed silly.

"Let's look 'round the back of the house. Mebby they's a different door open."

They slipped around the back and examined the servants' entrance. This door, too, was boarded up, but there was no lock on it. Then, without warning, Reuben dashed away. Henry wanted to shout after him, but he did not risk the noise. In spite of himself, his hand strayed to the revolver.

Reuben disappeared into one of the outbuildings. Several minutes later, he emerged and dashed back to where Henry waited by the servants' door. He held a pry bar in his hand.

"Thought mebbe we could use dis."

"How'd you know that was in there?"

Reuben shrugged, "Din't. But most white folk keep tools o' some kind in they barns. Jist happened to find dis one here."

Slave or not, Henry had to admit that Reuben was resourceful.

"Good thinkin'." Henry took the bar from Reuben and applied it to the wooden boards. Despite some nails that squealed in protest, the wood came free without any trouble. Henry slid the bar into the back pocket of his overalls.

Reuben then lowered a sturdy shoulder and bashed against the door. It swung open with little resistance.

Henry nodded at Reuben. So far, there was no sign of anyone. Together they crossed the threshold to discover what waited for them inside.

It is ironic that when invading a person's privacy, the one doing the invading often seeks his own privacy in which to do so. There is a great deal of checking to make sure no one is around. There are countless rationalizations as to why it's not really the wrong thing to do, or why it is ultimately someone else's fault. But above all, there is a quest for solitude and secrecy. And perhaps most observably, at the moment when the act is committed, there is quietness. A holding of one's breath. A suspension of conversation. Attempts to make all movements so imperceptible that they go unnoticed. It is at these moments, when one has sufficiently convinced himself that no one is looking, that one feels most at ease about crossing lines that one knows ought not to be crossed.

So it was not surprising, then, that neither Henry nor Reuben uttered a sound once they stepped inside Hanley Hall. They each took short breaths and let the air out slowly, as if the very sound of their respiration would bring Mr. Hanley…or possibly even Yankee bummers…bursting forth from some unnoticed hiding place. They stepped lightly and touched nothing as they skulked first through the pantry, then the sitting room, and then the dining room.

Convinced that the first floor was vacant, they continued to quietly canvass the house by ascending the stairs to the second floor. To Henry, this was the most agonizing moment, for he could not put out of his mind the image of some member of the Hanley family who had stayed behind to protect the home, and who was now waiting to ambush them at the top of the stairs. It was a needless worry, as it turned out. The upstairs hallway was empty.

From there, the boys split up and checked all of the bedrooms as well as the upstairs parlor. They met back in the hallway. Now totally convinced that the house was abandoned, they felt at ease to breathe normally and talk again.

"Templeton was right," observed Henry. "Ain't nobody here."

"Or even been here fer a spell, from the look of it," added Reuben. Then, shattering the house's veil of quietness, he exclaimed, "Sweet Mother of Moses! Jist look at dis place!"

He dashed into a bedroom and spun around with his arms outstretched. "Dis one room right here bigger den de cabin I lives in wit my whole family! And dis finery!" he exclaimed while gesturing to the four-posted bed, the paintings on the walls, the silken drapes, and the handsome pieces of furniture. "I ain't never seen so many fine tings all in one place at de same time!"

Raised as a field slave, Reuben had never been permitted to enter the big house at Stratmore.

Wide-eyed, he turned to Henry and said, "How we gonna get all dis in dat leedle cart we brung?"

Henry could not help but smile. "We ain't. We jist need to go through this whole place and take the most valuable things that we kin carry, them things what Templeton kin sell fer a high price."

Again the reality of what he was doing was brought home to him, and he nearly choked on his own words.

"I seen plenty o' thangs downstair," said Reuben.

It was very true. Mr. Hanley had fled leaving a veritable treasure trove behind. Countless pieces made of silver and gold, fine glassware, clothing, jewelry, artwork, even bottles of whiskey were all there for the taking.

"Okay," said Henry. "Now we know it's all clear, you run down and git Gal. Bring her up wit da wagon."

Reuben stood there with a dumbfounded expression, looking Henry over.

"What?"

"You mean you's jist gonna let me run off, outta yo sight, all by myself? You ain't gonna foller after me wit dat gun?"

It had not even occurred to Henry that he had just offered Reuben the perfect chance to escape. He felt stupid for not even realizing it.

"Well, don't make no sense for the both of us to do it. Promise to come back? On your word o' honor?"

"Sure," said Reuben. "You got my word o' honor." Then, with a smile that flashed yellow teeth, he dashed down the stairs and was gone.

Henry began gathering together all of the upstairs items worthy of being taken. He started in the master bedroom. Rummaging through a wardrobe, he collected silver and pearl cufflinks, a cravat, and a new pair of black leather riding boots. Passing through an archway, he crossed into an adjoining chamber that must have been Mrs. Hanley's dressing room.

It was in here that he collected his first major find of the day. At the bottom of one of her numerous wardrobes, hiding beneath a carelessly, or perhaps purposely, wadded cotton blouse, was Mrs. Hanley's jewelry box. Henry withheld his excitement until lifting the lid, for he surmised that Mrs. Hanley had taken the jewels with her and that the box was empty. However, when he undid the leather strap and creaked the lid upward, he was pleased to discover that his suspicions were wrong.

The box was loaded. Necklaces, bracelets, and rings made from gold, silver, ivory, and other precious materials that Henry did not even recognize all glittered up at him. He smiled back at the winking jewels, more out of admiration than approval of what would eventually become of them. He thought about Mrs. Graves' tableware and wondered if some of these pretty items would end up being worn by the same Northern woman who ate with poor Mrs. Graves' silver.

But he could not think about that right now. He had a job to do. Snapping the lid shut and fastening the leather strap, he rooted through the remainder of the wardrobes. Thinking that some men might pay handsomely to acquire gifts for their ladies, he took two gowns and a cotton print dress.

By now Henry had compiled a heap of items in the middle of the dressing room floor. As he struggled to gather everything into his arms, he heard footsteps echoing from the wooden floor downstairs.

Good, he thought to himself. *Reuben's back with Gal. That was mighty quick.*

Then he hollered out loud, "Reuben! Up here! Come help me carry this here load!"

As soon as the words were out of his mouth, the footsteps below halted. There was a moment of hanging silence, and then the unmistakable crack of a rifle ripped through the house, the startling sound amplified within the hallways.

The jewelry box slipped from Henry's fingers and hit the floor, sending its contents scattering in every direction with a shower of sparkles.

Henry was too paralyzed to move. He heard shouts now, men's voices, coming from the front of the house. Their words were blotted out by a series of heavy bangs, *clunk!...clunk!... clunk!,* against the front door. The final clunk was higher pitched and faded into splinters as the front door gave way.

Now the shouting voices were raucous and booming.

"Hey! How'd Sanders get in here?"

"There was a door open in the back, you idiot!"

"You mean we blasted that front door for nothing?"

Still frozen to his spot, Henry realized the awful reality. *Oh dear Gawd,* he thought. *The bummers are here!*

A voice from below, louder and more commanding than the others, boomed and brought a momentary order to the growing din. "Quiet!...Quiet now!...Shut yer mouths! I thought I heard a voice."

"Jist now?"

"Right before you blasted the door."

"Where from, sir?"

"Upstairs."

Henry began to shake uncontrollably. Full-scale panic was setting in. He could not move. He could not reason.

He was freezing.

The room began to spin around him in synch with a voice in his head that whispered over and over, "The Yanks are here. They're gonna git me. The Yanks are here. I'm gonna die."

"If there's someone here, we'll find him, sir!"

A slight pause.

"I reckon so."

Then, louder. "This place is a jackpot, boys! Clean her out!"

The tumult that followed drowned out the voice in Henry's head. He blinked, fighting to overcome the initial shock that had seized him, and for the first time he fully comprehended what was happening.

There was jostling and a clatter of boots on the stairway, heavy steps thundering upward like a hundred pounding hammers.

Henry still did not move a muscle. With the jewels scattered all about him and the dresses and boots heaped at his feet, he stood utterly terrified. Then, a sense of urgency welled up inside of him.

Do something! Don't just stand here like a turnip waiting to be skewered!

He scanned the room quickly, and his eyes fell upon something he had not noticed before. In the corner of the dressing room, a closet had been built into the wall. Unlike the freestanding wardrobes, it had a sliding door.

Henry dashed toward it.

The clomping boots grew louder.

He yanked on the door and it slid open, revealing a narrow enclave in which uncountable dresses hung from a rod. There was nowhere else to go. He slipped inside and slid the door shut behind him just as the bummers topped the steps.

Suddenly engulfed in darkness, Henry felt for the back of the closet. It was not difficult to find; the space was only four feet deep. However, stumbling and lurching with starched dresses in his face, Henry discovered that the closet ran about six feet parallel to the outward wall. He squirmed and maneuvered until he could go no farther. Then he turned. His back to the wall, he slid down and tried to sit on the floor.

Something rigid poked him and stopped him from sitting all the way down. The pry bar! He had forgotten that he had slipped it into his back pocket!

Bummers were now in Mrs. Hanley's dressing room, exactly where Henry had been only seconds before. Henry heard them through the thin wall, shouting loudly and scrabbling across the floor for the jewelry. The wardrobe doors were banging open and closed. It would not be long before one of them discovered the narrow closet and slid it open.

An idea hit him. Awkwardly, he reached behind himself and pulled the pry bar from his back pocket. Then, feeling in the dark, he ran his fingers down the floor groove along which the closet door slid. Then, tightly as he could, he wedged the pry bar between the edge of the sliding door and the wall.

He was not a moment too soon. He heard a bummer yank on the closet door from the outside and curse loudly.

"This door's stuck!"

"Move! Let me try," said another.

Again there was a mighty pull. The bracing pry bar bit into the wooden edge, but it did not give way.

"Arrgg!" shouted the bummer. Then, in a fit of anger, he slammed the butt of his rifle through the closet door. Light seeped through the hole he had made. The bummer reached through with his hand, and his fingers closed on one of the dresses.

He quickly withdrew his arm.

"Nothin' in there but a bunch of dresses!" Henry heard him say through the wall. "If you wanna beat that wall down just for a dress, be my guest. Might look good on you!"

"Shut up!" retorted his companion. "C'mon. I bet there's plenty more loot downstairs."

As gruffly and abruptly as they had come in, the bummers were gone from the dressing room.

Henry breathed a bit easier, but he dared not move from his hiding place. He listened to their bawdy behavior as they moved through the other parts of the house, mostly downstairs now. He could just picture the broken doors, strewn belongings, and overturned furniture littering each room that they ransacked. Gradually the sounds dissipated. A bugle call sounded, probably to gather the troops. Henry figured that the hungry pack of locusts was now outside the house, preparing to swarm on toward the next unfortunate home.

Still, he did not move. He waited, giving them plenty of time to be far away before he emerged. The activity had died down so much that he guessed they were moving on, until the sound of breaking glass shattered that thought.

The Yankees were breaking out the windows. One after another, the glass panes popped, cracked, and shattered. They all seemed to be smashing at once.

"Why are they bustin' all the windows after they's already been in the house?" Henry wondered aloud to himself.

The answer hit him with an entirely new wave of terror.

"Oh, my sweet Jesus!" he gasped.

Reuben jogged down the hillside and through the languishing cotton field, still amazed at all of the valuables he had seen in the big house. He located the horse path and followed it into the wooded valley and found the thicket in which Gal had been tethered. She acknowledged his arrival with a casual toss of the head and nonchalant swish of her tail, and then she went back to pulling up the sparse clumps of grass.

Reuben knelt down and checked that the wagon was securely fastened. He was about to straighten and untie Gal when the sound of voices came riding on the air. He stooped low in the thicket, listening intently to be sure of what he heard.

The voices clarified themselves as they drew nearer, and now they were accompanied by the clapping of hooves. Carefully, Reuben reached for Gal's reins and pulled downward so that she could not raise her head and give them away.

In moments, a band of men on foot rounded a bend in the path and passed by the place where Reuben and Gal huddled behind the screen of trees and foliage. Through the growth, Reuben thought he counted five or six men walking. A mounted rider followed them at a slight distance. He saw that all of them were armed, for the rifles slung on their shoulders poked upward and bobbed in rhythm with their steps. Their uniforms, if they could be called that, were dirty, torn, and disheveled, but even so, Reuben could tell that at one time they had been a dark navy blue.

Men in blue. These were the Yankee soldiers he had heard so much about. This was the great army from the North, the army that brought with it freedom for all those in bondage. How brightly his pappy would smile if he could see this moment! It was the first time Reuben had ever laid eyes on the Federal troops, and his own heart swelled upon seeing that all he had been promised, all that he had been told to wait for, all that he had been counting on for lo these many war-weary years, was finally happening. The tiny detachment marched past him, but to Reuben they might as well have been the entire Union Army. They left the taste of liberation in their wake, and he wanted to stand and cheer for them.

His joy was short-lived, however, when his feelings of exuberance conflicted with a dreadful thought. These Yankees were the bummers that Henry had spoken about. They had their sights on the plantation house, and Henry was still inside!

"Oh, dis ain't good," he muttered to himself.

In spite of his alarm, Reuben remained crouched and still. The small group of men passed him by, moved out of the trees, and began their march across the cotton field toward Hanley Hall. He could not be sure how many more men were in the area, and he did not want to risk getting caught. Still, he knew he had to do something.

"You stay right here, hoss," he whispered to Gal. "I's gonna go have a look-see."

Reuben slipped from the weedy growth and came to the path. Trees limited his vision, but he did not see any more men coming. He turned and followed to where the tree line ended, and there he hid behind a wide oak. Peering around the bark, he saw the company that had passed him. They were already coming to the end of the field and climbing the hill toward the house. But more worrisome than this, Reuben saw another group of bummers already at the big house. They must have approached from another direction. A group of them were huddled around the front door. Suddenly a rifle shot split the air, causing Reuben to flinch. After a few moments of battering, the front door gave way and the blue-uniformed men disappeared into the house.

Reuben felt sick inside. Henry had probably already been caught. There was no telling what they would do to him.

What could he do? He had promised Henry that he would return, but going back now meant that he would be captured as well. Besides, after the bummers finished with the house, there would be nothing worthwhile left behind. While his mind churned, Reuben saw more bummers converging on the property from all directions. Busy as ants, they poured in and out of doorways and crisscrossed between outbuildings, hauling with them their new-found prizes, big and small. Reuben did not see Henry in the midst of the melee, but from this distance he could have easily overlooked him. The house that had been a portrait of abandonment was now the hub of ferocious activity.

Well, thought Reuben, *I still has a hoss and wagon. If I's gonna high-tail it outta here, I best get a move on while them Yanks is busy. Sho do feel sorry fo' dat Henry, though. Seemed alright fo' a white boy. Hope them Yanks treat him proper.*

Reuben turned from the oak, about to go mount Gal and ride away, when a bugle call rang out. This piqued his attention enough that he stopped to watch a while longer.

He saw the body of men gather around the mounted trooper. Most of them were laden with items, but Reuben could not make out the details. The mounted trooper must have given an order because about ten of the men detached and spread around the outside of the house. Reuben could tell they were ripping open shutters and breaking open the first story windows. Faintly, he heard the sound of clinking glass.

Then, to his shock, he saw torches being lit. The men hurled them through the broken windows.

"I'll be," Reuben muttered. "They's torching that big ole' place. Dat ought to be a sight!" With that he hurried away to get Gal.

Flames were already licking out of the lower windows as the bummers reassembled and moved out toward the south, leaving Hanley Hall to burn behind them as they marched away.

❖ ❖ ❖

Henry could already feel the heat rising through the floor boards. His heart hammered so hard that he felt it in his temples. Hiding was no good anymore. He had to get out now, even if it meant being captured.

Inside the tiny, cramped space he struggled to his feet. Beating the dresses out of his way, he reached for the sliding door and pulled. It did not budge.

The pry bar! Of course! In his panic he had forgotten about it. Down on his knees, he crawled back to where he had wedged it. Thin trails of smoke now snaked upward through tiny cracks in the floor boards.

Henry pulled at the bar, but it did not move.

He jerked again.

Nothing.

"No!" he shrieked with a terror he had never known before.

He wrapped his shaking hands around the bar and tried again with all his might.

It did not move an inch.

In a spasm of panic and rage he beat on the closet door with his fists. The barrage rattled the door, but nothing more.

The smoke now stung his eyes. The increasingly acrid air made him cough.

In desperation he clawed once more at the pry bar. He leaned backward with all of his body weight, and with a jolt that sent him reeling, the bar finally came free.

Scrambling madly, Henry slid the door completely open. The dressing room was unrecognizable, totally filled with smoke. He was immediately beset with a fit of coughing and sank to the floor. The only shape that he could make out was the brown mass of one of the wardrobes. He needed air!

Henry forced himself to stand. Staggering to the wall, he felt for the window. Upon locating the frame, he picked up

the pry bar and hammered it against the glass, breaking out the entire pane. Gagging, he thrust his head out the window and drew in a few ragged breaths. He looked down and saw that the entire first story was on fire, and the flames were greedily inching higher.

The window offered a view of the same ruined cotton field that he and Reuben had crossed. It seemed like hours and hours ago. Henry considered jumping, but just as he put a foot onto the window frame, he glanced across the field and saw a rider.

"Hey!" he shouted. "Help me!" He didn't care if it was a bummer or even General Sherman himself.

"Help!"

He needed something more to catch the rider's attention. He dashed back to the closet and grabbed a green dress. As he did so, flames erupted in the master bedroom and began spreading.

Henry forced the dress out the window and shook it madly with one arm while waving the other.

"Hey, out there! You gotta help me!"

He was answered by a crash as the four-posted bed in the adjoining room collapsed in flames.

Reuben untied Gal and brought her out of the thicket where she had been hidden. Anxious to watch the fire, Reuben mounted her and rode her forward to the end of the path where the thick oak stood. He halted Gal and sat watching from the saddle as the flames climbed higher.

Black smoke mingled with the overcast sky. Visible through the distant windows, orange and yellow flames danced fiercely.

Then, as his eyes moved from one window to the next, he thought he saw a head poke out from the second story. Reuben immediately sat up straighter and tensed his legs in the stirrups. "Oh mercy! Is they somebody in there?"

It came crashing back to him that when he had last seen him, Henry was on the second floor.

Reuben scrambled down from the saddle. He unhitched the cart, freeing Gal from the burden so she could run faster. Back in the saddle, he said out loud to her, "Mebbe I's seein' things, but I gotta find out. Now git!"

He spurred Gal to a canter across the field, his eyes riveted to that window. He had not gone far when he saw arms flailing about, shaking some kind of green cloth as a signal.

"They is somebody up dar! Git up!"

Reuben kicked Gal to a full gallop. In no time, she was across the field and up the hill. He guided her around back, where they had entered before at the servants' door. Flames poured from it, so hot that Gal shied away.

"C'mon!" Reuben urged her around the opposite end of the house, looking for any place stable enough to make an entry. Gal tore around to the front, but Reuben abruptly pulled her up. *There!* At the corner of the front verandah, there was an out-door staircase that led to the second floor balcony. Fire raged all around it, but it had not collapsed yet. It was his only hope. Reuben jumped from Gal without taking the time to tie her. She turned and streaked away from the awful heat and flames.

Reuben dashed forward, but then recoiled. The heat was more intense than he had imagined. Determined, he tried again. This time he forced his body to move forward even though every fiber inside of him wanted to turn and flee.

Using his shirt to shield his face, he charged up the steps. Two or three of them were burned out, but he leaped over the gaps. Upon reaching the upper balcony, he kept as close as possible to the open air side and moved toward the other end of the big house.

Henry dropped the green dress. He could not shake it anymore.

Overcome with smoke and heat, he sank to the floor. A river of flame advanced from the master bedroom and snaked its way toward him. It was only a matter of time now. His breathing was shallow. His eyes burned and watered so profusely that he had to keep them pinched shut. He made a last feeble attempt to crawl across the floor, but he only managed a few feet.

The hungry flames came ever closer.

The dresses in the closet ignited with a whoosh!

Debris fell from the ceiling.

But Henry was no longer aware of any of this, for he was unconscious.

There was an opening from the balcony to the master bedroom. Reuben looked in and saw that the bed was on fire. A trail of flame zig-zagged across the floor into the adjoining dressing room. The floor seemed solid, but Reuben knew it would not last long. It was now or never. With a burst of speed, he charged into the room and hurdled the barrier of flames with two bounding strides.

His momentum carried him into the dressing room where he tripped over something and sprawled on the floor. He scrambled to his knees, and through the thick smoke he saw an outstretched arm.

"Henry!"

Reuben pulled the white boy closer.

"Kin you hear me?"

Henry's head lolled to the side, eyes closed and jaw slack.

"Awright. C'mon wit me, den."

Reuben hoisted Henry up and over-the-shoulder. The boy's dead weight smarted against the lash wounds on his back. He jumped and stumbled back the way he had come, avoiding most of the flames but getting singed in places.

He staggered headlong onto the balcony, almost losing Henry over the edge. By now, more of the steps were missing. Reuben clambered down, guessing at which ones were sturdy, hopping from one to the next.

When he was five steps from the bottom, the entire stairway collapsed. He crashed in a heap on the verandah and managed to roll toward the lawn, using his own body to shield Henry.

Recovering from the fall, Reuben stood, grabbed Henry under the arms, and dragged him under a tree a safe distance away.

Then, utterly spent and sputtering from the smoke in his lungs, Reuben collapsed on the lawn.

When Henry came to, he found that he was lying under a tree. His eyelids fluttered twice, three times, and then opened fully. For a time, his vision was blurred, a muddled mix-up of shapes and colors. But gradually it swam into focus, and he saw that he was looking up at branches. They were spread apart like so many gnarled fingers, Henry thought; like a great hand looming over him protectively.

He pushed out a breath, and a burning sensation flared in his lungs. His clothing reeked of smoke and made his eyes water, momentarily drowning his sight. He blinked it away. Saline rivulets traveled down his cheeks, a tiny leak that hinted at the oncoming flood.

A loathsome pressure welled up in his gut. Henry tried to hold it back, but then rolled over onto his side and let it all out. Pent up tears escaped in great, bellowing sobs. He cried so hard that his raspy, smoky breathing hardly kept up. He recalled the harrowing images from those moments. The raging flames. The tight closet. Unbreathable smoke. Desperately waving the green dress. But most of all, he remembered being all alone. Alone and scared.

When his sobbing mellowed, it gave way to a calmer, gentler weeping. Tears of gratitude. He wiped his eyes and looked up again at the branches that so reminded him of a protective hand. That was just his imagination, but there was no doubt that someone's saving hand had reached out to him. Just in time.

Henry lay still for a long time while his tears ebbed. He felt better now, quieter inside. From somewhere up in the tree, a bird called as if to get his attention. Sluggishly, he pulled himself into a sitting position and leaned against the tree trunk. There was not a soul around; Reuben was nowhere to be seen.

That slave's run off, Henry thought. *I ain't gonna see him agin.*

Neither was Gal anywhere about, and at this his heart sank further.

Now sitting up, he surveyed what lay before him. The view was so unrecognizable that for a time he did not know where he was. Hanley Hall, yes…but Hanley Hall no longer existed. Flames still thickened and smoke blew from the giant ash heap. Most imposing of all were the two brick chimneys that reared upward in the midst of the remains. The fire had not toppled them; they were now two monuments marking the plot where a proud and grand home had once stood.

Henry stood and walked toward it. The heap still emanated surprising heat, and he could not get too close. All he could think was that his own remains could very easily have been among those ashes.

A noise from behind caused him to turn abruptly. Henry could not believe his own eyes. Reuben was walking toward him, leading Gal up the slope.

"Well! Now you's up an' about!" called Reuben.

"Yeah," wheezed Henry, not knowing how to respond. He struggled to process how this could be. Then he saw Gal swish her tail, and he smiled.

Reuben lashed Gal to the tree and joined Henry near the rubble.

"Mighty big mess, ain't it?"

"Yep."

"I had to go run down dat hoss," continued Reuben. "Got spooked by dem flames. Shame ain't it? 'Bout dat house, I mean."

"Yeah." The wheels turned slowly in Henry's mind. *Head out the window. Choking. Green dress. The rider in the field…*

Henry turned to Reuben. "You?"

"Yeah. I figgered mebbe you was too hot fo' comfort in there."

Henry wasn't sure if it was a joke, but he noticed Reuben's eyes searching him, making sure he was really okay.

Henry shuffled his feet. "I...I ain't got the words..."

"Tolja I was comin' back," said Reuben. Then he quickly added, "Let's git. They's plenty of them Yanks still around."

Henry could not have agreed more.

Reuben swung into the saddle and watched as Henry untied Gal. "Where's dat gun of yourn?"

Henry's hand went to his waist. The revolver was gone. "Must a lost it in the fire," he groaned.

"Massa Temp'ton ain't gonna be pleased 'bout dat."

"Where's the cart?"

"Someplace down in dat cotton field."

"Nope," said Henry, swinging up behind Reuben. "He ain't gonna be pleased 'bout a lot of things."

Reuben spurred Gal, and she bore them back toward the road, down one hill and up another. When they crested the ridge, Reuben reined her to a halt so suddenly that Henry almost toppled from the saddle.

"What? What is it?"

Reuben did not answer. He was looking away to the south-west.

The ridge they were on provided a panoramic view of the valley that spread below. There, in the wide open countryside, was the largest host of men that Henry had ever seen. An entire division of Federal troops marched in file, a great column of men that wound to the southeast toward the town of Alexander. The line of blue was broken periodically by the white canvas-topped medical and supply wagons that rolled along at pace with the countless marching feet. There were thousands of them, and Henry knew that this was only a portion of Sherman's army. The bummers that had hit Hanley Hall must have been foragers sent in search of food.

Even though their distance discounted any real danger, Henry still felt threatened by the sheer size of that force. In his heart he knew that against an army like that, the Confederates had no chance.

"Let's git," said Henry. "Don't wanna get spotted by them. Reuben?"

But Reuben was not listening. He was still looking off at the Yankee troops, a spellbound and faraway look in his eyes.

"What's got you?"

Reuben merely gestured with a nod of his head.

Henry followed his eyes and finally understood. There, at the rear of the Yankee column was a group of people who were not soldiers. Instead of rifles and canteens and haversacks, they carried shovels or rakes or handfuls of belongings. Some towed goats tied to leads, others carried children on their shoulders. Instead of blue uniforms, they wore tattered and torn work clothes. And instead of white skin, theirs was black.

Slaves. Except not slaves anymore. These were the Negroes who had been liberated as Sherman's vast army swept across Georgia. Their masters fled or dead and some of the plantations burned to the ground, thousands of former slaves had become refugees with nowhere to go. So many of them followed in the wake of the Union Army, staying close to their liberators for protection and hoping that they would lead them to a new place that they could call home.

From the saddle, Reuben watched them wistfully. Thousands just like him were finally taking the long-awaited path to freedom. Henry could see in his eyes that he wanted so badly to dash into that valley and join them.

"I don't git it, Reuben. Why don't you go?"

Reuben snapped back, "I tole you once before, I ain't no runaway slave!" Then, more gently, "I don't run."

"But you's had chances. Out in that river. That time back there on that road." Henry swallowed, "When I was trapped in that house…"

"My pappy, now," said Reuben, cutting Henry off, "he got in his head one time that he was gonna run. Got a whole bunch of Temp'ton's slaves to follow 'long. 'Cept my mammy wouldn't go. Said it too dang'ris. She kep me and my sis at home, but my pappy said he was goin' wit us or witout us."

Reuben paused with remembering. "Well, time come and he done it. Whole lot of slaves got away that night, jist like them folk down there. But not my pappy. Temp'ton caught him and shot him dead. Put a bullet in his head."

A single tear ran down the side of Reuben's face.

"Ever since then, it's been me, my sis, and my mammy, and I swore I ain't never gonna run. I ain't scared of Temp'ton. Ain't him that holds me back. But if a fella' gonna run, he's gotta think. Not jist 'bout where he's goin', but what he's leavin' behind. I ain't leavin' them behind."

Then he turned in the saddle and looked at Henry squarely in the eye. "I don't run."

The words reached in and jabbed Henry deep inside, sending up a twinge of shame. For if he looked in the mirror and was honest with himself, he had to admit that running was all he had ever done.

They sat and watched a while longer. In the saddle behind Reuben, Henry saw that the whipping wounds on his back still bled and seeped into his shirt, marking it with striped stains.

"Reuben?"

"Yeah."

"Sompin' else I gotta ask."

"What?"

"Back there on that road, you coulda done a whole lot worse than punch me."

"Yep. I coulda."

"Why din't ya?"

Reuben considered for a minute. "You coulda tole Temp'ton 'bout me bein' in the river, but you din't. You din't go cry to him like I figgered you would. I guess I figgered you wasn't so bad."

He looked off and thought to himself. "Naw, you ain't like Temp'ton. You ain't got the hate."

It was the closest thing to a real compliment that Henry had heard in a long time.

Soon the Federal troops and the Negro refugees that followed them topped a hill and disappeared from view.

Reuben looked down at the ground and sighed deeply. Then, he straightened his back and lifted his chin.

"C'mon, hoss. Let's git."

They kept on in search of the road back to Stratmore. Henry knew they would not be received there warmly, but what choice did he have? Templeton was not a man who made idle threats. If he jumped off Gal right now and ran away, he knew he would be hunted down. One way or another, he had to face the man.

Worrisome as that was, it was no match for the exhaustion that permeated his every inch. Days with little sleep and too many stressful events left Henry so fatigued that he leaned against Reuben, and before they came to the road he was fast asleep in the saddle.

"Henry."

The day had dawned with sunshine, faded to overcast, and was now heavy with thick clouds.

"Hey. Henry."

Persistent breezes had become more vigorous all through the afternoon, and by the middle of the evening, they had transformed fully into a stiff westerly wind. Though the sun had not set yet, it was nowhere to be seen. It had been blotted out long ago by gray clouds that tumbled over one another in their haste across the sky. The gloominess reached out with a damp and chilly touch.

"Henry, wake up. We's at de lane."

Groggily, Henry lifted his head from where it had settled on Reuben's back. His neck was sore from the awkward position in which he had fallen asleep. It took a minute for his head to clear and for him to realize that they were back at Stratmore, approaching the big house.

Gal carried them down the lane, past the oaks that creaked and groaned in the wind. Ahead, through the thickening gloom, Reuben saw lamplight flickering in a window.

Templeton was waiting for them.

The man stepped out the front door and pulled his frock coat tighter around his shoulders. The wind whipped his graying hair into a tangle as he peered critically into the dimness.

Gal sauntered up to him and stopped at a pull from Reuben.

The boys were a terrible mess. Their clothing and arms were coated thickly with soot, their faces streaked where sweat and tears had left tracks through the grime. Both hunched forward in the saddle, weariness evident in their postures and expressions. Reuben's pant legs were singed, Henry's shirt was torn, and neither of them had had a bite to eat since their early morning johnnycake.

A sympathetic person would have looked upon the boys with pity and concern. A sympathetic person would have put all other matters on hold until they had been washed, their wounds tended, their bellies filled.

Templeton was not a sympathetic person.

To Henry's surprise, it was Reuben who spoke first.

"We had some trouble, Massa. Dem Yankee bummas, dey..."

"Shut up!" snapped Templeton. "You don't speak unless you're spoken to!"

Then, to Henry. "You! Get yourself down here!"

Templeton reached forth and pulled Henry bodily off the horse. The poor boy was taken by surprise. His reflexes were sluggish, his sore muscles slow to respond. He hit the ground with a thud, on his knees before the glowering Templeton.

"Where is my merchandise from Hanley Hall?" The words were cold and demanding.

"All gone, sir," managed Henry from his knees.

"Stand up and talk to me like a man!" Templeton savagely grabbed Henry by the collar and jerked him to his feet. "Gone where?"

"Stole by the Yanks, sir."

"All of it?"

"Yes, sir. What weren't stole was burned up."

"Burned?"

"Yes, sir. Them bummers torched the whole place."

"They beat you to it?"

"Well…naw. I mean, we was there before they was…"

"And yet you didn't get anything?"

Reuben tried to help explain. "See, dem bummers, dey…"

"I told you to shut up! Get off my horse and get out of here!"

Reuben stared back, shook his head, and then obeyed. He clambered down from Gal and strode off toward the slave quarters.

Templeton glared after him, and then refocused his icy cold stare on Henry.

"Now. Tell me where my merchandise is."

"I already tole you, sir. We din't git none."

"But you got there before the Yankees?"

"Yeah, but…"

"Then you must have gotten something!"

"Nothin', sir."

"You're lying to me! Where is the cart?"

"It got left behind."

"How stupid do you think I am!? You loaded it up and then hid it, didn't you?"

"Naw, sir! It ain't like that!"

Templeton's prying eyes went to Henry's britches. "Where is the revolver I gave you?"

"Lost in the fire, sir. I was trapped…"

"Enough! Shut your lying mouth! Do you have any idea how much this load is worth to me? Of course not…or maybe you do? That is why you've kept it for yourself and made up this ridiculous story!"

Henry could only shake his head and stare at the ground. At that moment, large drops of rain began pelting them.

"This is not finished," rasped Templeton. "Go and stable my horse, and when I talk to you again, I want the truth."

He turned and stormed into the house. Henry stood in the rain, water splashing off the brim of his hat. Then he turned to Gal.

"C'mon, girl. Let's git you outta the rain."

After all he had been through, the stables were a welcome sight. They were dry, and body heat from the few other animals inside provided a touch of warmth. Henry removed Gal's bridle, took off her saddle, and led her into her stall. There he rubbed her down, wishing that she could somehow return the favor. He fed and watered her, and then just sat for a long time on a bale of hay, resting his head against her flank.

While he sat, the rain began in earnest. He listened to it pelt the roof, watched as puddles formed at the building's leaky corners. A flash of lightning lit the cracks in the walls, and vibration from the thunder shook the wooden slats. The wind blew harder now, catching the stable door and whipping it open. Henry got up, closed it, and wandered back to the stall next to Gal's.

"Better start making up a bed fer myself," he muttered, tossing his hat aside. "I'll be sleepin' here another night, like as much."

Again the stable door jerked open, and with annoyance Henry went to close it a second time. But when he got close, he froze in his tracks. There stood Templeton, his dark figure filling the entire doorframe. The wind and rain blew in around him. A flash of lightning lit him from behind, and Henry gasped.

He was holding a whip.

The man advanced inward a few slow steps. "Now that you've had some time to think," he said, straightening the cords, "I want to know where my merchandise is. And this time, I want the truth."

Henry was cornered. There was no door at the other end of the stables. He retreated several steps, but Templeton continued to approach.

"I already told you the truth!" pleaded Henry.

"Enough of that! Don't make this difficult. Tell me what I want to know."

Over Templeton's shoulder, Henry saw the open stable door banging idly in the wind. It was his only chance. With a rush, he dashed to get around Templeton. The man moved to block him, but Henry wiggled through. He scrambled out the doorway and slammed the door in Templeton's face. He heard the angry man curse above the howling wind.

Henry was outside now. Night had fallen, and rain hammered him in the darkness. He stood for a few seconds in indecision, not knowing which way to turn. His hesitation proved to be costly, for just then he felt a strong hand grip his shoulder from behind.

Templeton pushed Henry to the grass. He rolled onto his back and tried to look up, raising his hands to shield the rain. Another flash of lightning revealed Templeton leering over him, the rain whizzing in gray streaks all around his face and neck.

The whip was raised.

"How dare you!" he hissed like the wind. "Now you'll find out what happens to those who disobey me!"

Henry covered his face and rolled over. The whip bit into his back, across his shoulder blades, with a sting unlike anything he had ever felt before. He let go a scream that rivaled the thunder.

Twice more the cords tore across his back, ripping open his shirt and laying open the skin underneath. The rain did nothing to cool the hot blisters he felt rising. He buried his face into the muddy grass.

Another lash, another scream.

Templeton began to rave above the storm.

"You will NOT lie to me!"

Lash!

"You will NOT disobey me!"

Lash!

"And if you don't bring me what is mine,"

Lash!

"I swear by God I will kill you!"

Lash!

At last Templeton relented, breathing heavily and looking down at Henry's crumpled, unmoving form. Another flash of lightning. Henry's back was red and crisscrossed with stripes. His hands gripped the sod so tightly that his fingers dug in to the knuckles.

Templeton knelt down and whispered into his ear. "That was only eight. Next time, I lay on twice as many."

He then rose and went back into the big house, leaving Henry lying face down in the rain.

Henry did not know how long he lay there, but after a time he sensed someone leaning over him. Fingers reached out and touched his back, and Henry recoiled with a cry.

"Shhh, chile."

Henry did not look up. The raindrops drummed the backs of his ears, plastered his hair flat against his head.

"Worst is over now. I's gonna help you, but you's got to let me."

Again the hands extended and touched his shoulders. Though it hurt, Henry permitted it this time. He felt them slide under his arm pits.

"Think you kin stand?"

Henry nodded, his face still in the grass.

"Okay now. Up we come."

The strong arms lifted, and Henry struggled to his feet. Waves of pain coursed across his back, and his knees buckled. For support, he leaned into the one who had helped him up.

"Dat's right. You just lean on me now."

Henry raised his chin. Squinting through the rain, he saw Violet's soft eyes looking down on him.

"Oh Gaw…it hurts!"

"I know, chile. Believe me, I know. C'mon now."

She draped Henry's left arm around her neck and he continued to lean on her, hugging her tightly for support. They started forward, she with steady and sure steps, he with jerky, staggering limps. In this way, they crossed the property and made for the slave quarters.

The slave quarters were built in two rows facing each other. A dirt path ran down the middle, but the rain had converted it to a muddy smear. Henry's feet slipped and slid beneath him. He leaned harder on Violet.

"Tha's right. Just a bit farther now."

All of the cabins, save one, were empty. They had been abandoned one by one as slaves had made their escapes from Stratmore. Now dark and dilapidated testaments to the lives their former occupants had endured, the cabins crumbled with the passage of time and ceaseless battering of the elements.

Violet turned him off the path toward the one structure that still showed signs of life. It was an uneven saddlebag cabin with a sagging roof, but a light glowed from inside, a sliver of warmth that beat back the stormy night. Henry moved toward it longingly. Suddenly the door was flung open. Reuben stood barefoot on the doorstep, squinting into the darkness.

"Dat, you, mammy? You got him?"

"Yes, I got him, chile. Come hep me now."

Reuben sprang forward and took a position on the other side of Henry, draping his right arm over his shoulder.

"Lordy. Temp'ton done whupped him up good."

Together the mother and her son bore the injured white boy into their home and shut the door behind.

The light came from a fireplace and from a single candle on a table, and at first it was so overwhelming that it hurt Henry's eyes. He moaned and rolled his head back.

"C'mon, let's git him to de bed."

Henry was only vaguely aware as he was ushered to a raised wooden bed at the far end of the cabin. He saw assorted objects…two chairs, cooking utensils, a crib, an old broom…but none of them stuck with him. He felt his shirt being removed, and then he was carefully laid on his stomach atop a mattress of corn husks. Henry turned his face toward the wall.

"Now you just rest, chile."

Willingly, Henry obliged and shut his eyes.

In body and mind, Henry craved rest. But the discomfort from his wounds and the unfamiliarity of his new surroundings kept him fitful in and out of sleep. The cabin was damp, and the corn husks beneath him hinted of mold. His britches were wet and dirty, and they hugged him with a chilly cling. The living space was so cramped that every movement, every whispered word, every nighttime noise seemed amplified. Even when he did manage to drift off for a few moments, Violet came and laid wet cloths on his back, startling him from whatever semblance of sleep he had fallen into.

But most of all, it was the crying that kept him awake. The baby was in the cabin, and from her first outburst Henry recognized the haunting cry as the one he had so often heard. It was no wonder that her sobs resounded across the property; she wailed as if her very world were coming to an end. Yet more frequently as the night wore on, fits of coughing interrupted her howling. It was not just the kind of coughing one would expect from a mere tickle in the throat. It was from the chest and deep, even for a baby, so deep that Henry thought at times it was not possible for such an awful noise to come from one so small. The fits came upon her so hard that Henry heard her struggling for breath, trying to suppress the croup long enough so that she could inhale and fill her little lungs. It was evident that she was very sick, and even in his own miserable state, Henry's heart was moved with pity. All night long she wailed and coughed until the sounds were stamped indelibly in Henry's memory.

The early morning hours came, and with them, an increase of activity in the tiny cabin. Violet was up and about. Henry heard her give instructions to Reuben about changing the cloths on Henry's back and tending to the baby. Then she was out the door, on her way to the big house to prepare breakfast. Henry heard the door rattle closed behind her, and then he drifted away again.

This time he slept more soundly, and it was hours and hours later when he was awakened by the clatter of gourd bowls being stacked on a low, wobbly table in front of the hearth. Gingerly, he turned his head away from the wall and studied the tiny cabin that had only been a blur the night before.

Reuben sat on the beaten earth floor, up close to the table, where he intently peeled potatoes. Near him, on the other side of the table, Violet stoked a cooking fire at a small hearth. In the corner diagonal from where Henry lay, the baby was nestled in a wooden crib. At last she was sleeping quietly, though she wheezed with every breath.

The candle still burned in the center of the table. An iron pot dominated the hearth and was surrounded by sundry wooden cooking utensils. A cloth partition, hiding the outline of another wood slat bed, hung near the baby's crib, and it undulated gently from the slight breeze that blew in from the glassless window. Beneath the window, a wooden bucket sat all by itself. The two chairs were pushed away from the table, banished to a distance while Violet and Reuben worked on supper.

Busy with their preparations, they had not yet noticed that Henry was awake. He was content to lie silently and watch them for a while. It was a welcome distraction from his pain.

Violet drew his attention immediately. Her hands moved with a quickness and efficiency that could only have developed from years of intense kitchen work, performing under the pressure to have meals prepared on time and served to Templeton's satisfaction. In just the short time that Henry observed her, she diced an onion, put water on to boil, and measured out three bowls of rice, all while cleaning and straightening the items around the hearth.

Henry remembered how softly those quick moving fingers had touched him last night, the soothing words she had spoken to him, and the tender way in which she had lifted him and allowed him to lean on her. He thought, too, of the last time he had seen Violet prior to last night, the time in the dining room when he had ordered her to clean up the mess that he had made. Seeing her now, a mother straining to provide for her family under terrible circumstances, and knowing first-hand the kindness and tenderness that she possessed, he deeply regretted having spoken to her that way.

And then there was Reuben. Working more slowly and deliberately than his mother, he peeled the potatoes with no less sense of purpose. Henry wondered if Violet knew the profound responsibility that Reuben felt for his mother and baby sister, if she had ever heard the conviction in his voice, as Henry had, when he swore never to leave them behind. Somehow—even if Reuben had not told her directly—somehow Henry got the impression, watching how she relied on him even as the meal was prepared, that she already knew.

With his potatoes finished, Reuben looked up and passed them to his mother. In doing so, he caught Henry's eye.

"'Bout time you's up. We's put in a whole day's work awready."

Reuben grinned at him playfully, but it was true. Henry could tell by glancing through the open air window that it was dark outside. He had slept away the entire day.

"Hush, now, Reuben. Don't you give Henry a hard time."

Violet rose from her place at the hearth, brushing crumbs from her apron. Then she crossed and sat on the edge of the bed. She looked over Henry's wounds and then put her hand on his forehead.

"How you feelin', chile?"

"Awright," croaked Henry. "Better than I was, leastways."

"Lord, ain't that the truth!" sang Violet. "Last night you was burnin' up. Couldn't hardly stand on yo own two feet."

"Cain't blame him, none," added Reuben. "Temp'ton done whupped him up good."

"That's so," agreed Violet. "Well now, we's about to have a bite to eat. Think you feel well 'nuff to stomach some food, chile?"

Ten minutes ago, Henry had not been hungry at all. But during the time he had watched them and smelled the food they were preparing, his appetite had come back to him with vigor.

"Yes'm. I'd be most obliged."

"Good. Let's see if you can sit up."

Very slowly, Henry put his arms under himself and pushed upward. The skin on his back stretched and smarted, but he awkwardly managed to swing his legs and sit on the bed's edge.

Violet checked his back again. "You still got some bleedin'," she observed. "Better you keep this cloth on you."

She produced a clean, dry cloth and draped it on his back.

Meanwhile, Reuben pulled the two chairs up to the table. He then retrieved the wooden bucket from under the window. Turning it upside down, he scooted it up to the table as well.

"This seat's yourn," he declared, motioning to the bucket. "Got no backside."

Henry nodded in understanding. The last thing he wanted to do was lean back on anything. He knew that Reuben had been through this kind of thing before and related to his pain.

For the first time in twenty-four hours, Henry stood on his own. He walked over to the fireplace to warm himself and to see what was cooking. Potato and onion soup bubbled in the iron pot, and rice waited in the gourd bowls. Famished as he was, it might as well have been a steak dinner.

"It gonna be mighty tender fo' a few days," said Reuben, referring to Henry's back. "But once dat bleedin' stops, it should heal up awright."

"Yeah," said Henry. The boys looked at each other, suddenly at a loss for something to talk about. "Uh," started Reuben, "I, uh, checked on dat hoss today. Put a new shoe on 'er hoof. Done it proper dis time. She's awright."

Henry was grateful that he was so concerned about Gal. "Good," he said. "That's good."

Then Henry looked at the crib and went quietly over to it. There, tucked snuggly in a blanket, was the cutest little baby he had ever seen.

"Dat's my baby sis," announced Reuben. "Clarissa."

"She's perty," said Henry, "but she sure makes a lot of noise." Henry watched her sleeping and noticed that she had a runny nose and that her face was flushed, as with fever.

"She's sick," said Reuben with a kind of tremor in his voice that Henry had never heard before.

He looked at Reuben and then Violet, and he could tell by their expressions that he had struck a nerve. He had not meant to be callous about her crying.

"Sorry."

"It's the whoopin' cough," said Violet. "She's had it goin' on two weeks now, and she ain't gettin' no better." Her voice, too, was shaky and strained.

Violet crossed the room and stood with Henry near the crib. She reached down and folded back one of the blankets. Henry was startled and took a step back.

There, attached to the baby's leg, was a slimy leech.

"We been tryin' to get the bad blood out, but it ain't been helpin'," explained Violet. "Reuben, how long 'dis one been on?"

"Since we been makin' supper," he replied.

Violet nodded. She reached down, pinched the leech, and pulled it off of Clarissa's tiny leg. The poor baby stirred but did not awaken.

Violet discarded the leech out the open window. Henry had heard that leeches were used on sick people to draw out the illness-causing bad blood or to reduce swelling, but he had never seen it done before. It was unnerving to him, and he suddenly imagined them clinging to his own back.

Violet noticed his worried expression and seemed to read his mind. "Don't worry, chile. I din't use none of them suckers on you."

As she said this, she gestured to a shelf above the crib. There sat a lidded mason jar with three more of the slimy beasts in water awaiting their turn.

Henry looked at Reuben, who was now busy dishing out the soup. *That's why he was in the river*, Henry thought to himself. Now knowing the real reason, he was ashamed that he had assumed Reuben was running that night.

"C'mon, now," said Violet after tucking Clarissa in again. "Let's eat before dis one wakes up."

They clustered around the table and began. The hot soup drove the chill from Henry; the rice and potatoes filled him with much needed sustenance. Even before he was finished, he was feeling much better.

There was no conversation while they ate, but afterward, while Violet heated up some coffee over the fire, she asked Henry, "Tell me, how did a boy like you come to be at a place like this?"

Henry hesitated to answer. There was much about his life that shamed him, and he did not like to talk about it. But seeing Violet's soft eyes upon him, he somehow felt that maybe she would listen with understanding.

And so he told. He told about his own mama's death and the time he had spent living with his aunt and uncle. He described life at the orphanage and how much he had hated it. He related how he had run away and joined the Confederate Army. Shamefully, he explained what happened at Allatoona

Pass. Then came the tales of his wanderings and how he had met Mr. Templeton.

"Guess ya'll know the rest," he concluded.

Violet poured the coffee and then gave him a hug, taking care about his back. "You been through a lot, chile."

It had been ages since anyone had hugged him. He didn't know how to react, but it felt good.

Then, in a sudden rush, he said, "Miss Violet, I'm sorry."

"What for, chile?"

The words tumbled out before he could plan them. "That time in the dining room, when I broke that glass an' spoke that way to you...I shouldn't have done it. I'm gosh awful sorry."

Violet nodded. "Alright. Course, I knew all along it wasn't really you. No, sir. It was that man Templeton. He has a hateful 'ffect on people. But thank you, jist the same."

Henry took a breath and felt a small weight come off of his chest.

"Speakin' of Temp'ton," said Reuben, "He was hotter'n a hornet today lookin' fer you. Threatened to beat me down, but I din't tell him nothin'. I guess he figgers you run off someplace."

"You mean he don't know I'm out here?"

"Naw. But it won't be long. He'll find out 'ventually."

"What we gonna do?" asked Violet.

"Don't know, but when dat Hath'way shows up agin and Temp'ton ain't got his finery to sell, he's gonna take it out on us."

Henry almost suggested that they run, but he knew that Violet would not risk traveling with the sick baby, and he already knew Reuben's feelings about leaving his mother and sister.

"We's in a bind, fo' sho'," observed Reuben as he sipped his coffee.

"Well," sighed Violet. "We got a little time to think on it, anyway. Good rest will help. Henry, you sleepin' on that same bed agin tonight?"

Henry was caught off guard. He looked up from his coffee with a reluctance that he knew was not well concealed. Both Reuben and Violet picked up on it right away.

Last night had been different. He had been brought here under circumstances that were beyond his control. But now that he had a choice ...

"I was thinkin' I'd be gittin' on back to the stable tonight."

He knew as soon as he said it that they were offended. Violet tried to hide it. Reuben did not.

He blinked slowly and just looked at Henry. "What?"

"I think...I think the stables be jist fine."

Now Reuben's jaw clenched. "Oh, you think the stables be jist fine. Well, lissin to dat, now. I guess they be plenty better than sleepin' in some dirty slave cabin, right?"

Violet motioned with a hand. "Reuben, please..."

"Naw, mama! I wanna hear dis! We sticks our necks out bringin' the white boy here. We patch him up, he eats our food, but then he think he a little too good to stay here wit us? Do I got dat 'bout right?"

Henry was dismayed by Reuben's swelling anger. He could not reply.

"Don't matter dat some crazy man after you! Naw, you rather go sleep in his barn den spend another night wit da slaves. Do I got that right, Henry?"

Reuben was standing now, hands on hips, leaning over Henry.

"What you think? Dat he gonna let you back in dat nice big house? Dat you gonna get a soft bed again?"

Reuben shook his head and paced away. Then, facing Henry again, he went on.

"See, you still think you sompin' different. After all that's happin'd, you still think you ain't like us. Well tell me, boy, how exactly is you different?"

Henry was speechless.

"Reuben, hush now!" Another plea from Violet.

"How exactly is you different? Why you work for no pay? Why you break into dat fancy house when you know'd it was stealin'? 'Cause Temp'ton told you to.

"Why you come back here when you had nothin' for him? 'Cause you know he got the secret 'bout what you done.

"Why don't you git up right now and run away from him? 'Cause you know he hunt you down like a dog.

"You know what dat makes you, boy? Dat makes you a slave. He got you right under his thumb, and you ain't nothin' but his slave."

Ruben shook his head. "You cain't even see it, even now dat you got them lash marks 'cross your back. Why you think you different? Only difference between you and me is dat you got white skin and I got black. Is dat what bein' a slave is? Lot more to it than jist the color of your skin, boy. When you on yo' hands and knees front of somebody that's got power over yo' head, you a slave. You betta look at yo'self real close, 'cause that's what you is. White skin or not, you every bit as much a slave as me."

He crossed slowly over to the bed that Henry had slept in last night. "Would sleepin' in them stables make you an animal? Naw. Would sleepin' in this cabin make you a slave? Naw. Temp'ton already done that to you, and you didn't even know it."

As Reuben came to the end of his tirade, Clarissa began to stir. Soon she was wailing, and Violet rushed to her. A coughing fit set in, followed by the infant's struggle to regain her breath. Violet scooped her up and rocked her.

"Now look what you done! You gone and woke her!"

Reuben looked regretfully at his mother. "I's sorry 'bout dat, mama." Then looking at Henry, he added, "But I ain't sorry 'bout what I said."

Then he turned and left the cabin.

Henry sat and stared at the flickering candle, feeling very small and wrung out inside. He had not meant to set him off like that and felt as if he bore some responsibility for the outburst.

"Sorry," he whispered to Violet.

"You ain't got to be sorry for nothin'. Once in a while, Reuben gets fired up somethin' awful. Jist let him cool down."

Against the backdrop of Clarissa's crying, Reuben's words sank in.

Was he right?

Henry had many fears in his life, but he had never feared becoming a slave. He was white! White people couldn't become slaves…could they?

It was strange, this idea that his skin color did not automatically protect him from being owned by another. That, after all, was the difference, right?

Templeton did not own him.

Did he?

Eventually, Clarissa calmed, and Violet sat next to Henry.

"You kin go o' you kin stay," she said to him. "You got a place here…if you want it."

Henry acknowledged what she had said. In a rare moment of serenity, Clarissa smiled from beneath the folds of her blanket. He reached out and gently touched her cheek.

Then he turned and walked out the door.

Henry found Reuben sitting on the doorstep. He was tossing rocks into the mud puddles that still remained after the rain.

"Kin I sit beside you?"

"If you want."

Toss. Splat.

Henry sat.

"I din't mean to set you off like that."

"Yeah. Well…"

Toss. Splat.

"I don't really git it…how a white fella… Well, guess I don't see it like you."

"Guess not."

Toss. Splat.

"Still, some of what you said makes sense. Mebbe I'm not a slave, but I ain't exactly free neither."

"Is there a diff'rence?"

Toss. Splat.

"I dunno. Look, all I know is that I ain't never gonna have no peace long as Templeton's got me under his thumb."

"Uh-huh. What you gonna do 'bout dat?"

Toss. Splat.

"I dunno yet. But sompin', Reuben. I gotta do sompin'."

"Yeah. Well, you let me know when you git some big idea."

Toss. Splat.

"What you and your mama done fer me…shoot. Ain't nobody really cared fer me fer so long, I guess I forgot what it felt like. Anyways…what I said 'bout the stable…I din't mean to 'ffend ya."

"Yeah. Well...I guess mebbe I got a quick temper."

"Yeah."

Toss. Splat.

"Still don't change what I said, though. You best take that serious."

"I'll think on it."

They were both silent for a long time, the white boy and the black boy, sitting side by side on the doorstep, both with their feet in the mud and switch marks across their backs.

It was Henry who broke the silence. "Kin we go back in now?"

"Why? You stayin'?"

"If you let me."

Reuben shrugged. "Guess so. All outta rocks, anyway."

It was another sleepless night for Henry. Clarissa bawled all night long, and her coughing fits were getting worse. There were times, at the end of a fit, when several silent seconds passed before she was able to whoop in a breath. Henry knew that during these times, she was not getting any air. It broke his heart to think of what would happen to her if she did not get any help. She needed a doctor. Soon.

In addition to Clarissa's pitiful struggles, Henry's mind could not shut off the conversation with Reuben. He meant it. He had to do something. All night long, face down on the corn husk mattress, he wrestled with it. What could he do?

The moonlight was bright. Shining through the open-air window, it bathed everything beneath it in a soft, silver spotlight. It seemed to draw Henry, somehow whispering to him across the room, "Now. Now is the time."

Finally, in the wee hours, he rose. He found the remains of his tattered shirt in the dark, and he slipped it on in spite of the smarting pain. He hitched up his britches, pulled on his boots, and quietly rummaged until he found the white cloth that Violet had put on his back. Silently as he could, he moved toward the door.

From where he slept on the floor near the hearth, Reuben went up on one arm.

"You runnin?"

"Naw. I'll come back."

"Yeah?"

"Yeah."

And he slipped out the door into the night.

Only the abandoned slave quarters were there to greet Henry, hollow and crumbling forms that hunkered across the muddy, downtrodden path. Silver moonlight trimmed their edges with lines of brilliance, but open windows and doorless entryways were black holes, dark with the memories of hardship endured by those who had lived there for so long.

Henry turned away from these and hurried down the path, one foot or the other occasionally splashing in unseen puddles. He reached the back of the storehouse and pressed up against it, surveying the wide open yard and the big house that lay beyond. No lights in the house, no movement on the grounds. The bright moonlight, which he knew would ultimately be his ally, was for the moment adversarial. There was no good cover in the middle of the back lawn. If Templeton's prying eyes were watching from any of the windows, Henry would be easy to spot.

There was no way around it. He took a deep breath and then dashed madly from behind the storehouse across the back property. He ran without breathing, for fear that even his breath would make too much noise. It was not until he had reached the stable and secured the door behind him that he allowed himself to breathe normally. His back against the jamb, he waited for his eyes to adjust and also listened intently for any sign that he had been spotted.

Everything remained quiet, except for the sounds of Gal's breathing and pawing in her stall. She knew she had a visitor, but in the darkness she was unable to tell who it was.

Henry did not risk a light. Feeling his way along the partition, he entered the stall next to Gal's. On his hands and knees, his fingers traced over rough edges of wood and hay until he at last located his hat in the spot where he had tossed it before

Templeton had burst in on him. Just putting it back on his head made him feel more at ease, more himself.

Now his eyes were adjusted, and Henry moved into Gal's stall. She greeted him with a swish and nuzzle, as if relieved that he was okay following his run-in with the madman. He carefully examined her hoof and saw that Reuben had, indeed, skillfully re-shoed her. Then with motions so familiar to him that they were easily accomplished in the dark, Henry saddled her. She was docile and offered no protest, as if being called upon to ride at odd hours had become so commonplace that she had learned to accept it.

When she was ready, he led her stealthily out the door. Upon emerging from the dark stable, the flood of moonlight seemed extra bright. Clinging to the edges of dark shadows, Henry led Gal at a walk around to the front and down the oak-lined lane. He repeatedly looked over his shoulder, but still no lights appeared in any of the windows.

Lost amid the tangled and moss-draped intersection of overarching branches, it was not long before the house's outline disappeared entirely.

Still, Henry led Gal at a walk. Even at this distance, he was afraid the sound of her canter would give them away.

It was not until they had reached the end of the lane and were on the road that he dared to mount her. Now astride the saddle, Henry took one last glance down the lane, half expecting to see Templeton raving after him with his whip cracking. But there was no one there.

Allowing himself to believe that the master still slept, he directed his attention forward. The road opened up for him, a serene silver strip that narrowed into the night and disappeared around a bend. Gal chuffed and pawed at the ground, as if sensing her rider's desire. Ever since he had come to know her, Henry had yearned to ride Gal all-out, unencumbered by the clumsy cart, with no need for anything other than raw speed. Now, his chance had come.

Henry spurred Gal forward and she responded immediately, first with a lope and then with a full-bore gallop. The speed took his breath away. With sweaty palms he leaned into her and stretched her out. The burst exhilarated him from head to toe. The familiar road zoomed by invisibly, and he placed his trust in her strong body as it lunged and leaned beneath him. He felt as if he were flying through the night. Clouds of dust, silvery and magical in the moonlight, hung in their wake as horse and rider tore away from Stratmore.

Swiftly, Gal ate up the miles that had grumbled past so laboriously when she had been tethered to the cart. She passed the place in the road where she had thrown the shoe. At Henry's urging, she hurried on. She did not know where they were going, but she responded obediently to her trusted rider's commands. He alone had their destination in mind.

Henry, of course, knew full-well that they were taking the road back to Hanley Hall. When the wooded valley loomed ahead of them, a cluster of ink spots closely grouped along the road, he slowed Gal to a trot. He found the horse path without any trouble and turned her down it.

The canopy blocked out the moonlight, and in this suddenly darker section, Gal walked, picking her way carefully. It gave Henry a chance to catch his own breath and readjust himself after the wind-whipping gallop.

They followed the horse path to the big oak, where it opened up to the cotton field. Here Henry turned Gal aside and pranced around in the weeds for a time. He quickly found the Yankee cart lying in the exact spot where Reuben had detached it. Henry marked the location in his memory, and then he turned Gal and spurred her forward once more toward his ultimate goal.

Up the hillside they went, past the charcoal pile that used to be Hanley Hall. Henry purposely turned his face away from it, not wanting to be reminded of the horrors that had taken place there. Even so, from the corner of his eye, he noted that smoke still rose from the rubble in wispy, white trails that reminded him of dancing spirits.

But soon that scene of destruction was behind him, and he pushed on. Now he topped the hill where they had seen the Yankee column, and Gal carried him down into the valley through which those thousands had recently trod. It was not hard to find their trail, beaten as it was by so many marching feet. Clearly visible in the moonlight, the path led Henry away to the south.

He could not tell how long he rode in this direction, but as he splashed across Brier Creek at a shallow spot he noticed that the moonlight was failing. It was being replaced by a band of grayish light low on the eastern horizon. Dawn was nearly upon him.

The new day's first rays had just begun breaking through the treetops when Henry came to a wooded area. Here he dismounted, poked around among the underbrush, and found a sizeable stick. To the end of it he wrapped the white piece of cloth that he had taken from the slave cabin. Remounting, he held the stick upward from the stirrup, the flag end high, and then continued following the Yankee path around the woods. He knew he had to be getting close now, and a knot of apprehension formed in his stomach.

Not ten minutes later, the thing that he had been counting on, yet dreading at the same time, happened to him.

"Halt! Don't go no farther!"

Then, a different voice. "Identify yourself!"

He had found them: the pickets for the Yankee camp.

He reined Gal immediately in response to their command.

"Name's Henry Akinson," he said to the two uniformed men who appeared from behind some trees. Their weapons were leveled at him.

"I ain't lookin' fer no trouble."

A short silence followed as the men approached his horse.

"That's a Southern accent you got, boy. It's our job to give trouble to Southern folks."

"Don't mean no harm. I ain't even got a gun."

They arrived and stood on either side of him. One was tall and lean, the other built like a bulldog.

"Git down from that horse," said the tall Yankee. "Real slow. No funny business, now."

Henry obeyed. He dismounted and stood in the tall grass with the white flag still steady in his hand.

"Good thing you brung that," grunted the bulldog. "Otherwise I'da put a bullet in your gut."

The thin soldier patted him down, pausing momentarily when he noticed the lash marks on Henry's back. He then rustled through Gal's saddlebags.

"It's true," he pronounced to his partner. "He ain't armed."

The bulldog snarled, "What you doin' here, boy?"

"I come to 'quest some medical attention," said Henry.

At this, the two men snickered. "Medical attention, eh?" said the lean one. "For them whip marks on your back?"

Henry shook his head. "Ain't fer me."

"How'd you git them marks, anyway?" questioned the bulldog. "You whupped up worse'n a slave."

"That's my business," shot back Henry. "Now is thar someone I kin talk to 'bout some medical attention?"

"Cool down," said the thin one. "You'll do plenty of talking to our colonel. I'm sure he's gonna be real interested in you." Sarcasm laced his voice. "Now move."

The lean one took Gal's reins and led her while the bulldog put his gun to Henry's back and prodded him forward.

Well, now I done it, thought Henry to himself. *Ain't no backing out now.*

The colonel was grizzled, gaunt-faced, and tough-looking, and being summoned from his tent so early in the morning rankled him. He frowned in front of Henry, still making adjustments to the battered uniform he had hastily put on, while the flaps on the tent from which he had just emerged waved idly behind him. Henry faced him standing up straight; the two sentries who had discovered him flanked him on either side. They saluted their colonel, and after situating his kepi on his head, he returned it.

"What is it?" His voice came somewhere from the depths of his flecked beard. "This better be good."

"Sir," said the lean soldier. "We found this Reb crossing our lines this morning. He surrendered to us, sir."

The colonel eyed the makeshift white flag that Henry still gripped. "I see that. Was he armed?"

"No, sir," rumbled the bulldog.

The colonel now questioned Henry directly. "What's your name, Reb?"

"Henry Akinson, sir."

"You enlisted in the Confederate Army?"

"No, sir." It was true. He wasn't...anymore. Henry didn't see the need to bore the colonel with all the details.

"What business do you have coming into our camp?"

"I come fer medical attention, sir."

The colonel raised an eyebrow. "Oh? What kind?"

"I need medicine. Fer the whoopin' cough. I figgered mebbe ya'll would have sompin' in yer medical wagons."

"Whooping cough, eh? You sound fine to me."

"Ain't fer me, sir. It's fer someone I know. A child, sir."

"Child, eh? Well, I'm right sorry to hear that, boy, but we can't help you. This is a military operation, not some charity hospital."

"But sir, I…"

"Enough, lad," the colonel cut him off. Then, to the guards, he said, "Detain him until tomorrow. I don't think he's lying, but we can't be too careful. He might be a spy for Wheeler. After we move out, you can let him go."

Before Henry could further plead his case, the colonel brusquely turned and ducked back into his tent.

"You heard him," throated the bulldog.

Henry's heart sank. *No medicine. Held until tomorrow…*

"Move it, Reb."

They marched him at gunpoint down a grassy avenue that stretched through the middle of the camp. To Henry's left and right there were rows upon rows of white pup tents, and he realized now that the camp had been pitched in a meadow just outside of Alexander. Off to the southeast, Henry could just make out a few of the town's buildings.

When he had been brought before the colonel, it was so early that the camp was still asleep. Now, as he was marched to the far end of the meadow, he noticed signs of activity stirring all around him. Men tumbled from their tents, stretching and yawning. One man sat shaving near a pan of water and a fragmented mirror propped on a tree stump. A bugle sounded the reveille. Cooking fires were started; the morning coffee put on to boil. Boots were pulled on. Sleepy-voiced, low conversations gradually grew louder. A few of the soldiers even took notice of Henry, nudging and commenting to their companions as he was marched past.

But Henry was led beyond all of this to the far end of the camp where very little activity was afoot. There were no tents here, just some tied up cattle and a hastily dug latrine. The lean one and the bulldog led him to a tree and pushed him up against the jagged bark without any concern for his sore back. Henry sucked in a painful breath between clenched teeth. They proceeded to tie him to the tree, running the rope so that it pinned his arms to his side.

"There," said the thin soldier after the knot had been tightened. "Now you won't go running off to tell Joe Wheeler what we's up to."

"Not that he could stop us anyway," chimed in the bulldog.

They both laughed at this as they led Gal to the makeshift corral, which was nothing more than some deadwood hauled from the woods and propped up to form a low fence. They tied her near the cattle.

"I'm not a spy!" he hollered after them. They stopped long enough to snap his flag in half and toss it into one of the fires. Then they kept walking until they blended into the thousands of men who were now up and milling about the camp.

Hours passed, and Henry's legs began to fall asleep. He stamped and kicked against the tree, partially to relieve his legs but also out of anger and frustration. *Surrender to the Yanks and get tied to a tree! Some plan this turned out to be.* He remembered promising Reuben that he would come back, and he began to wonder when, or if, he would be able to make good on that promise.

He studied the Yankee camp in detail, mostly because he had nothing else to do. He could tell that it was not built for permanence. It had been made in haste and, presumably tomorrow, it would be broken in haste. Sherman's army was not one that lingered. It was one that marched relentlessly onward. This respite outside Alexander was a mere stopover.

Morning turned into afternoon, and all the while a steady stream of men came to use the latrine. Henry quickly discovered that he was downwind of it, another detail for which he must be sure to thank lanky and the bulldog. At least he was able to keep an eye on Gal who, despite the many ogling eyes of men who stopped to admire her, remained tied up near the corral. Henry worried that she would be taken from him, but she seemed to be okay.

An hour passed. An orderly came around and gave him some hardtack to gnaw on, but then walked away without any conversation.

Another hour passed. Henry grew restless. He shifted his shoulders against the ropes, but each time he did the motion sent ripping pain down his back. This was driving him insane! He had to get free, to find someone reasonable to talk to!

Just then, he saw something that froze him. There, waiting in the line to use the latrine, was someone that he recognized.

It was Spiky Beard.

Henry heard Spiky Beard, louder than all the rest, laughing at a vulgar joke someone had told. Henry closed his eyes and prayed that he would not look his way and recognize him.

For a while, it seemed that Henry would get his wish. Spiky Beard was far too entertained by the off-color antics of his companions to notice him. But afterward, when his group was about to walk back into camp, one of them pointed and said, "Look there! Jonny Reb got hisself all tangled to a tree!"

They all looked and guffawed, but Spiky Beard's grin melted into a look of recognition, and then he flushed with anger.

"Hey!" his voice boomed sharply. "I know that little Reb!"

He strode meaningfully toward the tree with his companions in tow.

"Oh Lordy," muttered Henry. "Here he comes."

Spiky Beard stopped a couple of feet in front of Henry, arms crossed and eyes narrowed.

"Yeah. I remember you, you little cuss. You're the one that stole my wagon."

He turned and preached it to his followers. "This little prick stole my wagon when we was back there near Louisville."

Then, back to Henry. "I missed you then," he said, referring to the gunshot. "But this time, you ain't exactly a movin' target."

He pulled back his coat and revealed a holstered revolver.

"I'm…I'm real sorry 'bout all that," stammered Henry.

"Yeah, I bet you're sorry now."

Spiky Beard drew the gun.

"I know where your wagon is at!" Henry blurted out.

"Yer gonna hafta do better than that."

He rocked back the hammer.

Henry was sweating with desperation. "I kin help you fill it with more riches than you'll ever see again in yer lifetime!"

Even as the words were coming out, he couldn't believe what he was saying.

This wild claim was enough to give Spiky Beard pause. "What do you mean?"

Henry took a few ragged breaths. "I know a plantation house, 'bout a fifteen mile ride from here. It ain't been raided yet."

Spiky Beard raised an eyebrow. "Yeah? What's it called?"

"Stratmore."

"How do you know about it?"

"I used ta work fer the man who owns it."

"Must not care fer him much if yer willing to give way his property so easy."

Henry shrugged. "I got a score to settle with him."

"Is that so?" Spiky Beard glanced at his companions, then back to Henry. "Well what if I think yer a liar?"

"Look," said Henry, gesturing with his chin. "That's my horse over there. Ya'll follow me to the cart, and then I'll lead you to the house. If it ain't all jist like I say, you can shoot me dead and take my horse."

Henry spoke with such conviction that it seemed to penetrate Spiky Beard's doubt. The scraggly man was thoughtful.

"What's in it fer you, little Reb?"

"I need some medicine," said Henry. "Need to talk to a doctor. That's why I come here in the first place."

"And yer willing to sell out yer man just for some medicine?"

"Like I said, I got a score to settle."

Again, Spiky Beard eyed him in silence. Then he turned and spoke over his shoulder.

"Anders! You run and git the sawbones."

"You ain't serious, Clem!"

"Run and do it!" shot back Spiky Beard. "We just might have an opportunity on our hands."

Anders darted away and returned some minutes later with a bald man who wore spectacles.

"Clem, what is this all about?"

"Howdy, doc. We got a prisoner here who says he needs some medicine."

The bald man regarded Henry from behind his glasses. "What kind of medicine, son?"

"Fer whoopin' cough," said Henry anxiously. "You got anything fer whoopin' cough?"

The doctor shook his head sadly. "Sorry, son. We ain't got...well, now wait."

"What?" Henry craned his neck forward hopefully.

"Naw," said the doctor, "it ain't much. Just some herbs I brung with me from Atlanta. Some folks have been known to use 'em to treat whooping cough. Maybe works sometimes, I reckon."

"What kind of herbs?"

"Oxeye daisy," replied the doctor.

Spiky Beard, or Clem as he was apparently known, now broke in. "You see doc, this little Reb wants to make a deal. In exchange for them herbs, he's gonna lead us to a plantation house that ain't been touched yet."

"Clem, you can't go! Orders are to stay put!"

"Orders?" retorted Clem. "We bummers got standing orders to clear out any property we kin get to. This unit ain't movin' out till tomorrow. We kin be back by then, can't we, little Reb?"

Henry nodded.

"And we can come back a good deal richer than when we left, maybe even something in it for you," Clem added, eyeing the doctor.

The sawbones shook his head. "It goes against my judgment, but come to my tent. I'll give you what I got, but I ain't going with you to no plantation house."

Clem smiled and holstered his gun. "Well, little Reb. Looks like you and me got a deal." He began to move off with the doctor.

"Ain't you gonna untie me?"

"Patience, boy. Me and my boys will come git you tonight when we're good and ready. In the meantime, don't you go nowhere."

The group laughed raucously at this crude joke as they marched off, and Henry wondered if he had been foolish to pin his hopes to such a desultory bunch. But given his options, which were none, he had to place his confidence in the small chance that they would come through on their end of the deal.

Night fell, and with it so did the temperature. It might have been tolerable if he could have moved around, but in his bonds all Henry could do was shiver. Activity in the camp died down. Campfires winked for a while, but even they were put out before long as the men turned in early in anticipation of the next day's early departure.

There Henry stood against the tree, with each disappearing campfire feeling more and more like he had been hoodwinked into thinking that Spiky Beard was sincere. He hung his head in despair and fatigue and nodded off, his own dead weight straining against the ropes that held him up.

More time passed.

Then, out of the emptiness of the night, he was roused by the sound of hooves.

Riders were approaching. Many riders.

They came forward at a walk and bore no lights so that the lead horse was practically on top of Henry before he could see that it was Clem.

"You ready, little Reb?"

The fatigue was at once ousted by the jolt of excitement that coursed through him.

"Yep. I'm ready."

Clem dismounted and cut the ropes free. Henry rubbed his arms, leaned over and did the same to his legs.

Clem whistled, and from the darkness someone brought forth Gal. Henry patted her neck, and she seemed relieved to see a familiar face.

But before he mounted, Henry turned to Clem.

"Where's the medicine?"

Clem produced a pouch from his inside coat pocket. He held it out and even lit a match so Henry could see. In the sputtering light, Henry read the paper label scrawled in pencil: Oxeye daisy.

Henry reached out to take it, but Clem pulled it back with one hand and shook out the match with the other.

"Not so fast, little Reb. We git our loot; you git your medicine."

Henry watched him tuck it back into his coat pocket.

"Fair 'nuff."

With that, Henry mounted Gal.

"Ride behind me 'till we're through," said Clem.

Henry didn't really know what he meant, but he obeyed. They walked their horses a distance, and Henry could not get over how many there were behind him. Twenty or thirty bummers must have been rounded up for this midnight foray, and they were all mounted. That was different than what he had seen before.

They know they have to be back quick, before sun-up, thought Henry. *They would never make it if they was walking.*

In front of him, Clem stopped. He called out a password, and the nighttime picket answered. Clem and the group proceeded past the unseen sentries. Then he turned to Henry.

"Okay, little Reb. Here's where you take the lead. And don't think about running off, neither. You got a whole company of Feds right on your tail, and we's all armed."

In the nighttime stillness, Henry heard Clem's revolver go to half cock.

"I ain't runnin'," replied Henry. "Ya'll just follow me now."

Through the darkness he led them across the fields and valleys back the way he had come. Some of the men lit torches, and when Henry looked back he saw the flames bounding through the night, sometimes kicking up sparks that arced upward like giant fireflies. The journey back seemed faster than when he had come, and soon they were passing by the remains of Hanley Hall.

They cascaded down the hillside and into the cotton field, to the area where Henry knew the wagon waited amid the weeds. He pulled up and said to Clem, "Have your men search in this spot, and you'll find your wagon."

Five of the men with torches began circling, leaning from their saddles and extending their flames across the overgrown field. Soon one of them barked out, "Here, Clem! Yer wagon's over here! It's in good shape, too!"

One of the bummers fastened the cart to his horse, and as he did so Clem nodded at Henry.

"So far, so good little Reb."

Henry nodded back and smiled grimly at the Yankee. The wagon had established some trust, the first evidence that he was acting in good faith. Now, with it in place, they were ready to roll on.

Henry located the horse path, which they all followed through the valley. Then it was onto the road, and at a brisk clip Gal proudly led the way as the entire company of loot-hungry bummers closed in on Stratmore Plantation.

"Did he say where he was goin'?"

Violet's question hung in the air as she tidied around the hearth. The area needed no cleaning; supper had long since been over, the gourd bowls and wooden utensils were stacked and aligned with precision, and her rags had passed twice over every surface, edge, and corner. It was only out of mounting nervousness and concern that she now fussed about, a relief valve for her growing anxiety.

For his part, Reuben stood at the open-air window leaning forward, arms folded on the ledge, eyes peering into the darkness. His right foot tapped out a slow, even rhythm like a moving clock hand's incessant tick. He tugged at his ear and then, shaking his head, he returned his hand to its resting position.

"Naw, I tole you before, mama. He din't say."

Violet at last put her rags down and wiped her hands on her apron. She sighed and walked over to the corner cradle where Clarissa slept, her breathing slow and ragged. The baby flinched in her sleep, and then her tiny arm slowly resettled upon the blanket. Violet laid her fingers across her rosy cheeks and rested them there for several moments. Clarissa was hot.

"Gettin' chilly out," Reuben said from his post at the window. He reached out and closed the loose, weather-beaten shutters, and then he went to the corner and stood by his mother.

"Her fever down?"

Violet shook her head.

"Well," said Reuben, searching for something positive, "at least she be restin' now. First time all day."

It was an ongoing balancing act between the two of them to satisfy Templeton's demands and to care for the ailing baby.

Reuben tried to be with Clarissa while his mother worked at the big house during meal times. But when they were both put to work at the same time, well, it was then that Reuben neglected his chores for Templeton and stayed with the baby instead, despite the fact that this choice often earned him harsh words or, worse yet, whippings from his master. He had settled in his mind that he could endure all manner of fury from Templeton as long as his sister and mother remained untouched.

Violet put her arm around her son and led him to the low table where they sat down. She looked into his eyes and saw that he was as troubled as she was.

"Reuben," she said gently but firmly, "mebbe he ain't comin' back."

"He said he would, mama."

"I know, chile. I know." She reached out and held his hand. "But you gotta consider…what's here fo' him?"

Reuben looked at her with questions in his eyes.

"I mean, chile, what reason he got to come back here? Now you, you got your baby sista an' me, and don't you think for one second I don't love you wit all my heart for stayin' here wit us. Ain't one day goes by that I don't thank the dear Lord for you."

This brought tears from Reuben.

"But Henry, now…what he got? Seems to me he got more reasons to run than to come back to dis awful place."

"I know," snuffled Reuben. "I jist…I thought…I thought mebbe I…we would be the reason."

Now Violet hugged him and drew him close, her hand patting the back of his head as he cried on her shoulder.

"Oh, chile…I know…I know… But if he wants to run… if he think that's what's best fer him…then you gotta let him go."

She rocked him for a time, until he had his tears under control. Then she gently pulled him off of her shoulder and held him at arm's length, her misty eyes looking into his. There were long moments before she could trust her voice.

"Reuben," she said finally. "Honey...I'm a'feared Henry ain't the only one we gotta think about lettin' go..."

Her voice failed her, and she could only glance at the cradle.

The meaning registered with Reuben, and something inside of him raged against what she implied.

"No! No mama...don't say that..."

He crumbled, relenting to another upwelling of tears.

Violet slowed her breathing enough to find her voice again. "Chile," she said, "she ain't gettin' no better. They's only so much we can do...and she jist...she jist ain't gettin' no better. I'm...I'm a'feared it's only a matter of time now, and we got to be willin' to accept that."

She could not say anymore. She leaned into her son and hugged him as tightly as he clung to her. It seemed they had run out of things to hang on to, so they hung all the more tightly to each other.

Gradually, slowly, they pulled apart. Tears were wiped, and no more words were exchanged as they each struggled in their own way to come to terms with the difficulties that lay ahead. Having seen more years of life, Violet had learned that sometimes things were inevitable, and no amount of praying, pleading, or sobbing would change a thing. It is what it is. Ain't no changin'. Accept it and move on.

She went back to her tidying.

Maybe because of youth, or ignorance, or both, Reuben was not ready to accept anything. He wanted so much to believe there was a way to change things, to somehow overcome that invisible force, whatever it was, that always seemed to snuff out any chance for something good.

He had felt the weight of it pressing down on him his whole life. It had crushed him time and again. Yes, his spirit had rebounded, but that was not enough. It was not enough to pull himself from the mud only to be whipped down again. He wanted more than that.

He wanted to overpower the hand that wielded the whip.

Why?

So that he could become the wielder?

No.

He wanted to break the whip itself.

He wanted to tear it to pieces and fling the fragments where they could never be found.

And then?

And then he wanted to just be. Just live. Just grow. Just do. Just love.

Just be without fear.

But he was afraid.

Because the hand still held the whip.

And he was afraid that one of these days, his spirit would not be able to get back up.

He flopped down on the corn husks and turned his face to the wall.

A dreary silence set in. Reuben closed his eyes and fell into a sleep that was not restful. Violet swished her broom and quietly hummed an old spiritual that her grandmother had taught to her in days long gone. But the humming was hollow and brought no comfort, for Clarissa's ragged breath provided the only accompaniment. Eventually Violet stopped and sat down, laying her weary head on the table top. She was so bone tired. And old. And empty. She closed her eyes.

And in this way, an hour passed.

Wham!

The cabin door burst open, shattering the gloom that had so thickly gathered.

Startled, Violet jumped from the table.

Reuben turned with a jolt and swung his legs over the edge of the bed.

"Henry?" he called out expectantly.

There was no reply, only heavy steps as a man entered the cabin.

Templeton.

The whip was in his hands.

Reuben jumped immediately to his feet.

Violet grabbed her broom handle and stepped in front of the cradle.

"Get out!" snarled Reuben.

"Shut your mouth!" boomed Templeton. He snapped the whip, adding to his words a frightful exclamation mark.

The noise woke Clarissa, and she began wailing and coughing.

"Where is he?" Templeton demanded.

Violet desperately attempted to quiet Clarissa. "W-who, sir?"

"Don't play stupid with me! Where's the white boy? I know you've been hiding him! Where has he gone?"

Reuben stepped forward to take the heat off his mother. "He ain't here. He done run off."

Templeton redirected his icy stare. "To make off with the items that you two stole from me?"

"Ain't no items!"

"Where did he go?"

"I dunno! I jist seen him run."

"I know he ran!" shouted Templeton. "He stole my riches, and then he stole my horse! Nobody steals from me!"

Clarissa wailed louder.

"Shut that brat up!"

Reuben took another step forward. "You don't talk 'bout my sister that way."

Templeton backhanded Reuben across the face and then grabbed him by the collar.

"Let me tell you how it's going to be, slave," he hissed. "Either you tell me where the white boy is and what you've done with my merchandise, or your mama is going to get a beating that she won't recover from."

Reuben matched his glare. "Don't you lay a finger on my mama!"

Templeton gripped him tighter. "Tell me where!"

"I don't know! Ain't no items! It all burned! All you gots left is locked in dat storehouse!"

"Lies!"

Templeton flung Reuben across the room. He hit his head on the edge of the slat bed and rolled to the floor, unconscious.

Violet tried to rush to him, but Templeton blocked her way.

"Now, woman," he said, flaunting the whip, "you have one more chance. Where is my merchandise?"

Violet stared him down, long years of bitter resentment bubbling to the surface. Then in a snap, she took the broom handle and whacked him across the face. She caught him in the eye, causing him to stagger backward and flounder, temporarily unable to see.

Violet seized her chance. She grabbed Clarissa from the cradle and squeezed out the doorway as Templeton cursed and felt across the floor for his whip.

She fled into the night with the baby wailing in her arms, running but not knowing where. She hurried down the path between the abandoned slave quarters and past the trees that grew around the long-empty overseer's house. From there she hustled past the storehouse and dock. She made for the stables, but she had no plan for when she got there.

Templeton was close behind her now. He had recovered from his knock, and being much faster than she, he had closed the distance rapidly. Even above Clarissa's siren, she could hear his boots thumping and his breath rasping.

Then his heavy hand clasped upon her left shoulder. He pulled back with a force that at once sent her spinning and crashing to the ground. She landed on her back, clutching poor Clarissa tightly to her chest. There, lying in the middle of the back yard, she looked up to see Templeton looming over her.

He uncoiled the whip and snapped it once above his head. "Now I'm going to whip both of you to pieces," he snarled.

Violet closed her eyes, clutched the screaming child to her bosom, and waited for the first lash to fall.

It never came.

She opened her eyes.

She heard Templeton curse and saw him take a step backward. He dropped the whip and stared open-mouthed at the big house.

He cursed again. "What ... what the devil is happening?"

Down on the ground, Violet turned her head to see.

Lights were moving from window to window.

Henry sat tall in the saddle, riding the crest of the vengeful wave that was about to come crashing down on Stratmore. He could not help but feel elevated by the power personified in the thirty armed riders who followed him down the oak-filled lane. He heard them check their weapons and speak gruffly to one another. He saw the torches' fierce glow make silhouettes of the drooping Spanish moss as the house came into view. In their eagerness, some of the riders now pulled even with Henry, even slightly ahead of him. This pack of wolves was hungry, and no force—not even Templeton—was going to hold them back. For once, Henry was on top. This time, he had the upper hand.

They came to the verandah and pulled up, the rumble of hooves that had rolled unbroken for fifteen miles now fell conspicuously silent. Horses whinnied and chuffed. More torches were ignited. Thirty pairs of eyes, round with anticipation, ogled the stately house.

From amid his companions, Clem searched out Henry. "Well, well, little Reb. You weren't pulling my leg."

Henry nodded back to him. "It's all yours."

Clem stood up in his stirrups and waved his hat. "You heard him, boys! Let's clean her out!"

A great shout went up. Some of the men dismounted, and like water breaking through a floodgate, they crashed through the front door and poured inside. Henry saw their torches through the windows, darting from room to room as they smelled out treasures with an acute sense that only the truest of bummers had developed. In just moments, torchlight was visible on every floor of the house. Toppling furniture and slamming doors made the window panes rattle.

The remainder of the men stayed on their steeds and rode around the house, heading for the outbuildings that awaited them in the back yard. Clem led this group, and Henry rode closely behind him.

Templeton watched in disbelief as the torch lights swarmed through his beloved home. He heard shouts now, men's voices calling out raucously from inside. The walls shuddered with tramping and thudding and crashing. A window burst from the second story, sending shards of glass raining down into the kitchen yard. A torch-bearing figure appeared in the opening, let out a triumphant howl, and was gone again.

Violet did not miss her chance. While Templeton stood staring at the house, overcome by the bedlam erupting in front of him, she picked herself and Clarissa off the ground and ran back toward the slave quarters where she found safety among some trees. Clarissa's wailing, loud as it was, was now challenged by the destructive clamor in and around the plantation house. Violet settled herself between diverging branches and watched the scene unfold.

Templeton appeared to have recovered from his shock and boiled anew with rage. He strode toward the house, as if intending to go inside and personally throttle each one of the invaders. But just as he made his move, a group of riders swept around the house and into the back property, weapons drawn and torches held high.

Clem noticed Templeton advancing, and he put his horse between him and the house. Henry was not so bold and held Gal back, in the trees near the privies.

"Get out of my way!" Templeton roared up at the spiky bearded rider.

"Sir," said Clem coolly, "I'm going to have to ask you to step away from the house."

"Step away? This is my property! Get out of here!"

The mounted bummer stood his ground and spoke again, this time with an edge. "This here is military activity. If you value your safety, you best back off. Now."

Templeton glared up at him, wild-eyed and haggard. "You blue-bellied Yankees!" he flamed. "This is no military activity! This is stealing private property! Nobody steals from me! Nobody!"

Templeton pulled back his frock coat and went for the revolver that was tucked in its holster. But before he even got a finger on the handle, Clem fired a single shot.

The report echoed across the property, causing everyone to freeze and look. Templeton sank slowly to his knees, his face contorted in a horrified expression. The dark stain on his white shirt grew ever larger as blood seeped from the bullet hole.

Clem took aim again, but held his fire. He could see that one bullet was enough.

With a last attempt at words that came out only as a guttural croak, Lewis Templeton collapsed face down on the grass and died.

Clem holstered his gun. The bummers resumed their activity as if nothing had happened, and in seconds it was as loud and tawdry as ever.

Astride Gal, Henry ventured from his place near the privies. Still not quite believing what he had just seen, he guided his horse next to Clem's and looked down at Templeton's lifeless form.

Clem narrowed his eyes. "Did that settle yer score?"

Henry nodded one time. "It's a good start."

Then he dismounted and stood over Templeton's body. All the intimidation was gone. All the hate that had emanated from the man vanished into the air like the puff of pistol smoke. He was nothing more than a heap of cold flesh, on his way back to where he had come from. Kneeling down, Henry reached out and yanked the chain from around the dead man's neck. The key fell into his palm, and Henry held the shiny object up in the torchlight.

"Follow me," he said to Clem.

Hiding within the trees, Violet was startled by a hand on her shoulder. For an instant, she feared that one of the bawdy soldiers had found her, but great was her relief when she turned around and saw Reuben.

"Mama? You all right, mama?"

"Reuben—oh, my dear Reuben!"

With one arm she hugged him, pressing his cheek to hers. "Yes, I had a fright, but I's awright." She noticed the welt on his head and touched it gingerly. "Oh, my. Are you okay, chile?"

"Knocked me silly fer a spell, but I's awright. What's going on, mama? What's happening?"

"Bummers, Reuben. Yankee bummers is looting the house."

He drew in a breath. "Well, I'll be…"

"Reuben."

"What, mama?"

"They killed Massa Templeton."

Reuben stared back at her in disbelief. "What? You sure?"

She nodded gravely. "I stood here and seen it done with my own eyes."

"Praise be to Gawd Awmighty!" he shouted. Then, noticing the riders advancing on the storehouse, Reuben caught his breath.

"What is it, chile?"

"Look, mama. That rider ain't no Yankee bummer. Dat's Henry."

Henry dismounted, walked to the storehouse door, and inserted the key. With a twist, the lock snapped open obediently. He pushed the door wide and looked at Clem.

"Take all you want."

Clem touched the brim of his hat. "Much obliged, little Reb."

In a flash, he and his companions were down from their horses and inside, piling their arms full of all that remained of Templeton's trove.

Henry did not watch. He walked over to a tree and sank to the ground underneath it. The enormity of all that was unfolding overwhelmed him. For some reason, he thought of the dead soldier from the cavalry clash, the one who had died with gold coins unknowingly in his hand. He surveyed the madness all around him, grown men scrambling around like wild pigs, loading their haversacks and pockets, even their socks, with loot that they desired, it seemed, more than their own salvation.

He, Henry, had unleashed this.

Was it all worth killing for?

He looked at Templeton's body, a distant and dark shape.

Was it worth dying for?

He was jarred from his thoughts by approaching footsteps. He looked up to see Reuben and Violet peering down at him. Having worn herself out, Clarissa was asleep in her mother's arms.

Reuben shook his head at him. "I'll be."

Henry nodded up. "Tolja I come back."

Violet was about to say something, but then she sucked in her breath and exclaimed, "Oh, my dear sweet Jesus! Look at that!"

The boys looked and saw that the bummers were setting the house on fire, hurling their torches through broken windows. Unwanted memories came back to Henry, and he squirmed as he saw the flames lick higher. Right before their eyes, the walls went up in sheets of orange and yellow, casting an intense light and heat upon them, even from the distance at which they watched.

Words were pointless. They just silently watched as the once mighty Stratmore was consumed.

They were so enthralled by the flames that no one noticed the flatboat that had appeared on the river. It was not easy to spot, for it showed no lights and it remained at a distance. It floated near the shore for a while, the men upon its deck observing all of the mayhem. After a time, two shadowy figures leapt from the deck onto the grassy shore and slipped toward the property, blending into the night. A third man remained on the boat and kept it near the shore, though he allowed it to drift further downriver and out of view.

As the flames grew higher, the bummers' activity began to lessen. They had loaded the cart fully and had packed their saddlebags to the point of breaking. Now they remounted and gathered themselves for the return ride.

Clem guided his horse to the tree where Henry sat. The spiky bearded man gazed at him, and then took notice of Reuben and Violet. Upon seeing Clarissa, a look of understanding flashed across his face. He reached into his inner pocket and pulled out the bag of oxeye daisy. He tossed it down from the saddle, and Henry caught it.

"So long, little Reb."

He jabbed the spurs into his horse, and with brazen shouts that carried above the thundering hooves, the Yankee bummers disappeared into the night.

The days and weeks that followed were slow and quiet, a time for all of them to grasp how significantly everything had changed and to begin facing the question that was on each of their minds: where do we go from here?

The unwelcome task of burying Mr. Templeton fell to Henry and Reuben. They faced it the very next day after the raid, for they both knew that the longer they waited, the more gruesome the body would become. There was a family plot on the property where Mrs. Templeton was already buried, and it was next to her that the boys scraped out a narrow trench. They then dragged the man across the lawn and pushed him in face down, for neither of them had any desire to see his face again, even in death.

Henry picked up the revolver that Templeton had attempted to draw in his last moments. From the make and design, he saw that it was the partner to the one that had been lost in the fire at Hanley Hall. A check of the cylinder revealed six bullets waiting patiently for their time to come. Henry snapped the cylinder shut and tucked the gun into his britches.

Reuben stumbled upon the whip. It lay coiled in the grass where Templeton had dropped it. He held it in his hands and looked at it a long time, recalling the times when those cords had ripped into his flesh. Then, pushing those images out of his mind, he took it to the plot and tossed it into the open grave. It landed, black and snakelike, across the dead man's back. Then they filled the trench with dirt and walked away.

No marker was placed.

Neither of them said any words.

Violet had started Clarissa on the medicine the very minute that Henry had explained to her what it was. Over the hearth, she boiled the oxeye daisy in water and spooned it to the baby in small doses. For the first couple of days, it did not seem to make any difference. But then, on the third day, her coughing fits became less violent. She was able to breathe without rattling. And each time Violet gave her a spoonful, she whispered in her ear, "My sweet chile, you got Mister Henry to thank fo' dis."

Reuben and Henry spent their days roaming about the property, gathering anything that would be useful back at the cabin. Henry frequently looked in on Gal, making sure that she was well fed and had plenty of water. He did not ride her much during these days, for the poor girl had been worked hard and deserved a good rest.

They spent the evenings together in the cabin, talking, swapping stories, laughing in ways they had felt reluctant to before. Henry described his experience in the Yankee camp and explained why Clem, Spiky Beard, had at first been so angry that he almost shot Henry. Reuben told his mother about the long line of Negro refugees they had seen from the hilltop, and they all speculated on where those people were now, and where they might eventually end up.

And every time they talked about those refugees, it was followed by a predictable and thoughtful silence, each one of them more fully realizing they had to leave Stratmore.

The big house was a total loss, to say nothing of the fact that most of Violet's food supplies had been stored in the pantry or kitchen yard and had been destroyed by the fire. The better part of winter lay ahead, and they did not have enough to make it through. Clarissa was now clearly on the mend and would soon be able to travel. They needed to find someplace with food stores and better shelter.

True as all that was, there remained a deeper and perhaps more compelling reason. The chapter in their lives that had been Stratmore Plantation was now finished. For Henry, that chapter had been brief. For Violet, Reuben, and little Clarissa, it was all they had ever known. But for all of them, it had now ended, and it was time to move on.

They began laying plans. The old rowboat was still moored to the dock, still bobbing along with the current as if unaware that anything around it had changed. Reuben proposed that they use it to float down the river to Savannah where they could connect with other refugees. From there, well, it was hard to say. Maybe they could find passage north.

The others agreed that the river was the fastest and easiest route with Clarissa, and so they began gathering provisions for the trip. The rowboat was tiny and would not allow them to take much, but there were some essentials that they cached in the storehouse until it was time.

Through it all, an unspoken question loomed and grew bigger by the day. How many would make the trip? Three or four? None of them had yet found the nerve to ask or decided the manner in which to bring it up.

Two days before they were set to leave, Henry and Reuben carried some blankets to the storehouse and placed them in a corner with some of the other items they had stockpiled: a lantern, matches, a crate of potatoes, some dried meat, a pot that Violet could use for cooking along the way. Reuben turned to leave, but Henry was drawn by an object near the back that he had not noticed before. He walked toward it, further into the dim and earthy room.

"What you doin?" Reuben asked.

Henry did not reply. He knelt down and picked up the object. He crouched still, looking at it and tracing his fingers over it.

Reuben came up behind him and looked curiously over his shoulder.

"What dat?"

Henry now straightened and showed it to him.

"It's a vase."

"A what?"

"A vase. Fer holdin' flowers 'n such."

"Huh." Reuben touched it. "It's smooth."

"Yeah," said Henry. "Made outta ivory."

Even in the dim storeroom it had a lightness that set it apart from the shadows.

"I took this from Mrs. Graves," said Henry.

"Dem bummers din't take it?"

Henry shook his head. "Must not of seen it. Or din't want it."

He looked around. Of all the goods that he had collected for Templeton, this was the only one not taken.

"What you gonna do wit it?" asked Reuben.

Henry stared off into nowhere. "I ain't sure yet," he muttered.

That night at supper, the ivory vase sat in the middle of the table. In spite of the rough treatment it had received, it was still clean and white, and the flickering candlelight played upon its graceful curves.

It was a quiet meal. Breathing free and clear, Clarissa snuggled and slept soundly. She had not coughed for days. They slurped their soup against her rhythmic breathing. Deep in thought, Henry never took his eyes from the vase.

The meal ended. Violet poured the coffee.

Henry took a sip and finally looked up.

Chapter Twenty-Three

"I gotta take it back."

They both looked at him.

"What, chile?"

"That vase," Henry nodded. "I gotta take it back to Mrs. Graves. It ain't right fer it to stay here."

Violet looked knowingly at Reuben, and he back at her. It seemed to them that the question had just been answered, without ever having been asked.

"Alright, chile. If you feel dat's what you got to do."

Early the next day, Reuben helped Henry saddle Gal. It had been weeks since the raid, and the air was decidedly colder. Gal, however, was well rested and seemed eager to be taken out.

When she was ready, the boys walked her into the yard. Violet was there waiting with Clarissa in her arms. She stepped forward and dropped some warm biscuits into one of the saddlebags.

"You ride careful now, chile."

"I will."

The vase, wrapped in a cloth, was slipped into the other saddlebag, and Henry swung up. He looked down and regarded Reuben who stood on the grass and held the reins.

"We pushin' off tomorra."

"I know," said Henry. He looked at Reuben softly in the eyes. "Good luck to you."

Reuben swallowed hard. A tear escaped down his cheek. He extended his hand, and Henry shook it firmly.

"Good luck to you too, Henry."

Then he handed over the reins and stepped back.

Henry spurred Gal softly, and she started forward.

"Henry!" Violet called out to him in a voice shaky with emotion. "I won't never fo'get what you done fo' my little girl!"

Henry waved back at her, but right at that moment he found that he could not speak.

And so they stood and watched as Gal carried him around the ruins, down the lane, and out of sight.

It was midmorning when Gal reached Brier Creek Bridge. She clip-clopped easily up the road, seemingly daydreaming more than paying attention to where she was going, and she might have walked right over the edge if Henry had permitted it. It took three strong tugs before she stopped. She pulled her neck up and looked about, wondering why her rider had interrupted their crisp morning walk. Then she put her nose to the ground and realized that the road in front of them ended abruptly. She whinnied loudly, as if laughing at her own absent-mindedness.

Henry replied with a low whistle of amazement. "Well now, Gal. Would you look at that?"

Brier Creek Bridge was gone. The dirt road they had been traveling was cut short, severed entirely where the bridge planks ought to have begun. There was no extension at all, just a sheer drop down the steep embankment to the creek below.

Near the water line and on the opposite bank, Henry saw signs of what had happened. Downstream, the blackened remains of trusses were wedged against large rocks, pinned there by the current. Dark pilings stuck up from the water like the jagged ends of broken pencils. On both banks, the weedy undergrowth was scorched down to the bare earth.

"Geez," snarled Henry. "Why them Yanks gotta go and burn every durn thing?"

His irritation compounded the unsettling feeling that had weighed upon him ever since he had left Stratmore. Usually a morning ride with Gal made everything right with the world, but not on this day. And it was no secret what was eating him inside. The departure from Reuben, Violet, and Clarissa had been much harder for him than he had imagined it would be. He had wrestled with it the whole morning, ceaselessly going over his reasons and rationalizing to himself why it was, in the end, the best thing. But he had only succeeded in making himself more upset, so much so that having to find another place to cross Brier Creek made him bristle more than he otherwise might have.

Grumbling something more about the Yanks and their dadgum torches, he turned Gal off the road and trotted her westward to a place where the bank was not so steep and there weren't as many rocks. She carried him across the shallows where the water was just above her hooves, then she lunged strongly up the overgrown opposite bank. When the ground leveled out, he directed her back to the road.

On this shore, he regarded the bridge from the reverse angle. Two blackened boards jutted out like arms stretching for what could no longer be reached on the opposite side.

Disconnected.

Henry sighed and climbed down from the saddle. He pulled Violet's biscuits from the saddlebag, sat down on a rock, and began munching them while Gal browsed the tall grass along the lonely dirt road.

"It's all fer the best," he said out loud to her, his mouth full of biscuit. "I mean, they's nice folks an' all, but…"

He knew the issue but somehow had trouble saying it out loud.

Gal pulled up her head to chew and looked him directly in the eye. With just a glance she forced him to be honest with himself.

"I know," he admitted. "But Gal," he said more impassioned now as he made his defense, "it just wouldn't of worked out. I mean on down the road. How 'bout when we met up with them ref'gees? What then? I ain't no…ref'gee. I jist…I ain't like them."

He chewed down another bite and scuffed the dirt with his foot. "I ain't meanin' nothin' bad. Shoot, Reuben, he saved my life an' Violet, well, she treated me like she was my mama."

Gal rolled her eyes and shook her head as if to say, *This is your argument for leaving?*

"But it ain't that simple!" he persisted. "They's more to it than that. I...I don't fit. Do I gotta have more of a reason?"

He looked back at Gal, who now seemed to have forgotten all about him and his struggle and had gone back to her browsing.

"How come you make me think but never give me no answers?" he said to her chidingly, but then became very pensive and sat that way for a long time.

Eventually he finished the biscuits, realizing with the final swallow that they were the last of Violet's cooking that he would ever taste. But he pushed that aside, retrieved Gal, and mounted up.

"Okay, girl. Let's git on to Magnolia Acres...if it's still there."

If the plantation had been hit, as he suspected it had, the chances were slim that Mrs. Graves would still be there. Deep down, Henry did want very much to return the vase. He had given his word, and he felt sure it was the right thing to do. But even deeper inside, he knew that this journey was really not about the vase or Mrs. Graves. Those were merely excuses. And grappling with that knowledge, he was inwardly troubled by his own motives.

Once again he spurred Gal on, leaving behind a burned bridge and moving forward with the disturbing feeling that he was pulling away from something that did not want to be let go.

He continued on through Waynesboro, taking note of the battle scars that had been freshly inflicted on that poor town since the last time he had come this way. He stopped briefly to allow Gal a drink from the trough, and while he waited for her a few locals passed by and inquired about his travels. From them, Henry learned that men from Wheeler's command, brave-hearted Texas and Tennessee boys, had made a stand against Kilpatrick's cavalry a few weeks back, right in the middle of town. It wasn't enough to hold, though, and the Federals had broken through and burned bridges north of town. Henry nodded and remarked how he had just come past Brier Creek. The locals told of how the Yankees had moved on to Alexander, and from there had moved out toward Savannah. The latest news, which was a couple days old, reported they were getting close to that port city and preparing for a siege.

Gal finished her drink. The locals bade him well and moved on, their expressions grooved with the sadness of knowing that another of their proud cities was about to fall to Sherman. Henry turned and rode out of town, noting as he did so that the stars and bars of the Confederacy no longer flew over Waynesboro.

Outside of town, the country opened up before him once again, and another stretch of miles slid past. It was a clear day, and though the sun had climbed as high as it would get, the air remained chilly. Here and there, Henry recognized small landmarks which assured him that he was on the correct path: a familiar tree, a fence row, a pile of rocks along the road. But then Gal brought him around a bend and the most telling of all landmarks came into view. Henry had not prepared himself for it, and the sight jarred him.

He had come upon the site where the cavalry clash had occurred. The hillside from which the Yankees had swooped down onto the road, where Henry himself had been caught in the onslaught, loomed off to his right. The last time he had seen it, it had been covered with the bodies of dead and wounded men. Spiky Beard…Clem…and his men had just set to the grizzly task of digging graves. Now, the entire hillside was dotted with slats of wood sticking upward, marking the final resting places of the men who had fallen there.

Henry reined Gal to the slowest of walks, for this was a place to be passed quietly and with respect. Finally, when she had brought him abreast of the slope, he dismounted and tethered her.

Henry walked through the weedy ditch and up the grassy incline. Soon he was among the gravesites, surrounded by mounds of earth and the silent wooden markers that spoke volumes. He noticed that a few of them were carved with names, but most were not. He wondered which mound of earth covered the dead soldier he remembered. He wondered what his name was.

Henry was surprised, and moved, that the Yanks in the burial detail had taken the time to bury the Confederate dead as well. Out of respect, he removed his hat.

There was no order to the graves. The men had all apparently been hastily buried where they had fallen. It was strange then, as Henry walked among them, that aside from the few markers carved with names, he could never be sure if he was looking at the grave of a Reb or the grave of a Yank. At this point, he supposed, the sides didn't matter so much. They were all men, and sooner or later all men share the same fate, no matter which side they claimed to support while they were alive.

Henry wandered until he stood at the place where he had fallen after the Yankee saber split his hat. He fingered the sliced brim and wondered, what if it had been different? What if that saber had found its mark? What if he had died that day and had been buried on this very spot? How would the grave diggers have regarded him?

As a Reb?

As a Yank?

His own quick, obvious answer was that he was for the Confederacy. He was a Southern boy, had joined the Confederate Army, and had marched with them into battle.

But then he gave it more thought and realized that his own actions muddied the question. He had deserted the very army to which he claimed to belong. He had stolen from his countrymen and played a part in those goods being shipped North. He had allied himself with Yankee bummers and permitted them to seize and destroy Southern property.

None of these things were deniable.

And he called himself a Reb?

Well, maybe. But on the other hand, maybe sides aren't always so easy to figure. Maybe the things folks call themselves aren't quite as clear as they want them to be.

Yank or Reb?

He thought of what Reuben had said the night he got so angry.

Black or white?

He looked again at the graves all around.

In the end, does it really matter?

He shrugged and muttered to himself, "I reckon when ya look at sompin' a different way, ya doesn't always see the same picture."

He whispered something close to a prayer, and with a deep sigh, he put his hat back on. Then he wandered back down the hill, untied Gal, and continued on his way.

The remainder of the ride to Magnolia Acres seemed to take longer than he remembered. Like a lingering fog, the somber images from the graveyard hung with him and even seemed to affect Gal's spirit as well, for the usual lightness in her step was absent. She plodded forward, pounding out a slow rhythm that was as heavy as the thoughts that burdened him.

Lost in his own musing, he gazed at Gal's mane with eyes that looked but did not really see. The splayed strands of hair wisped outward in a hundred different ways, a mixture of cream and brown, blown without pattern by unseen, ever-changing currents. He reached forward and stroked the softness, a habit that brought him comfort. On one end the hairs were haphazard, waving loosely without direction. But on the other end, deeper and beneath the skin, on the end that Henry could not see from the surface, each and every strand was rooted in its place. Of those thousands that intersected and entangled themselves with each other, each sprouted upward from a place where it belonged.

Henry believed he was resolute in his decision to leave, but the more miles he put behind him the more he felt his resolution weaken. His rationalizations were no longer quite so clear. There was something there, nagging at the outermost edges of his thoughts that would not leave him alone. He could not put his finger on it, and the more he tried, the more it eluded him.

He stroked Gal's mane again and again, and the long slender hairs slipped through his fingers.

It was a relief, finally, when the oak-lined corridor leading to Magnolia Acres came into view. It was a distraction, a respite from his emotional wrestling match, and he turned his attention to what lay before him.

The lane was exactly as he remembered it, the same number of stately trees, each of them robed in flowing mossy garments. But beyond them, in the space where a once proud façade looked out upon the lane, there was now nothing but an empty gap of sky.

Henry came to the end of the lane and stopped. He was saddened, but not at all surprised to find Magnolia Acres in ruins. The dark smoke he had seen after departing from Mrs. Graves had been an ominous sign, and the Yankee's ensuing treatment of Hanley Hall and Stratmore gave him little reason to believe that they had shown any mercy here.

Gal nosed about the charred remains of the big house, wreckage that was now beaten, smeared, and strewn by the weather weeks removed from the actual burning.

Henry surveyed the mess as well, a sight that was becoming all too familiar to him. He nudged Gal and rode slowly around the perimeter of the foundation. There did not seem to be anyone around, and a palpable quietness hung over the entire property. A streaked wooden chair with two legs burned off sat alone and askew in an open area that might once have been the parlor. Fragments of glass made opaque by the smoke and flames littered the ground, and Henry reined Gal to sidestep them. One small section of a stairway still stood, seven steps up that led to nothing.

The scene was disquieting, but different than what he had experienced before. As much as the inferno at Hanley Hall had been one of horror and the blaze at Stratmore had been one of vengeance, the burned-out rubble here bespoke distress. It whispered of a family displaced, a mother with two hungry children, a lifetime of memories scorched with burn marks.

Beneath two crisscrossing black timbers, Henry spotted a trunk. Without knowing why, he dismounted and walked toward it.

Debris shifted, crackled, and crunched under his feet. Ashes and soot that had been settled now stirred up again with each step, forming a dirty cloud around his knees. Henry reached the place where the trunk was wedged and kicked at the sides of it. Charred wood flaked off and the boards pulled away from the iron corners, but they did not collapse entirely.

Henry was taken with an urge to know what lay inside. Grabbing hold of one of the beams that lay overtop, he pushed until it and its companion slipped off the trunk and fell loudly amidst the rest of the rubble. Instantly more dust and ash rose up and turned everything hazy.

Henry knelt in front of the trunk and ran his hands, now made black by the soot, over the arched top. He saw that the fire had eaten out a hole in the backside and that the hinges were missing. Gripping the lid's edges, he pulled upward. At first it resisted him, but then it came loose so suddenly that it sent him reeling backward.

Henry set the charred lid aside, crept curiously back to the open trunk, and peered inside.

What he found there touched him unexpectedly. Square blocks with letters on them. A wooden locomotive engine with attaching cars. A skipping rope. Dolls.

This had been the children's toy chest. The items at the top of the heap had been scorched by the fire, some destroyed entirely. But those buried deeper were reasonably intact.

Henry reached in and pulled out the train engine. He turned it over and over, just looking at it. The soot on his hands smudged the wood.

Henry never had many toys of his own, but this piece reminded him of a toy train from his aunt and uncle's house that had been his favorite. He remembered spending hours hooking up the cars, laying out the tracks, making the sound of the whistle and the chugging engine.

He closed his eyes and pictured the memory.

It wasn't that long ago, yet it was ages ago.

What he had been through, the things he had seen since then, made him long for the days when life was simple and there were no hard decisions. But then again, maybe it had never been simple. In those days, he just hadn't yet seen life for what it truly was.

He opened his eyes again.

An entire trunk full of toys. There was a time when Henry would have been jealous. Why should these kids have so much when he himself had so little? But it was pity, not jealousy, that he now felt for those children. Their innocent view of the world was probably now in shambles every bit as much as the ashes under his feet. Having faced horror before they were ready inside, they were forced to grow up too quickly. And Henry pitied them, for he knew exactly how that felt.

He gently placed the train back into the toy chest and replaced the cover as best he could. Then he wiped his hands on his britches and walked slowly back to Gal.

"Well, girl," he said, taking a long look around, "they's long gone for sure. No surprise, I reckon. Ain't even sure why we come here at all."

He swung up and sighed. During the ride here, he at least believed he had some purpose. Now the notion of finding Mrs. Graves seemed foolish.

"Where to from here, girl?"

Gal responded with a shake of her head.

"Don't know, huh? Well, that makes two of us. C'mon. Let's git to wherever we's gonna git to."

With a motion more perfunctory than purposeful, he directed Gal back around the big house ruins and started down the lane. He headed toward the road without having any idea what direction he would take when he got there. The all-seeing but unspeaking oaks watched him move by, just the latest member of a parade that they had been observing for a hundred years.

He was halfway down the lane, deliberating on which way to turn, when he thought he heard a rustling behind him. He slowed Gal and looked over his shoulder, but he saw nothing. Then he moved on again, chalking it up to his imagination.

But he had not gone another twenty feet when *crack!* The sound of a snapping twig from behind him shattered the silence. There was no mistaking it this time, and a wave of alarm rippled through him. He pulled back hard on Gal's reins and yanked her to the left. She whinnied, went up on her hind legs, and spun around. Henry already had the revolver drawn and pointed to the side of the lane from which the sound had come.

At first, he saw nothing. The trees were stoic as ever, their moss swaying with the slight breeze. Then a stronger breath of wind pushed more forcefully and brought out from behind one of the oaks a flash of color that caught Henry's eye.

It was the hemline of a woman's dress.

Henry kept the revolver trained on the tree. He had learned the hard way to never take any chances. He spurred Gal a step closer and called out, "I see ya! Come on out from behind there!"

The figure behind the tree made no move to come out, but again the breeze caught her dress and Henry saw the fabric flutter.

"I said come on out."

A set of fingers apprehensively appeared and rested against the bark. Then, very slowly, a portion of the woman's face slid into view. First her bonnet, then her forehead, and finally her eyes peered from behind the tree.

"Don't shoot!" she called out.

"I won't," returned Henry, though he did not lower the gun. "Come all the way outta there."

She hesitated, but then did as Henry asked. A couple timid steps brought her fully out from the tree and into the lane, her frightened eyes never leaving Henry or the barrel of his gun. She was in her fifties, Henry guessed, with a thin face that was at this moment rather pale. Her eyes were green and her skin speckled with freckles of the type that darken in the summertime. A lock of light brown hair strayed from her bonnet and divided her forehead. Her eyes were narrowed, making lines across the skin at the corners. Another breeze billowed her dress, and she pulled her arms about her midsection as if chilled.

"I don't mean no harm," said Henry trying to sound reassuring, but he realized the pointed gun did not lend his words any credence. He lowered the weapon.

This gave the woman an ounce of relief, but he now saw a look of dark suspicion come across her eyes.

"What are you doing here?" she demanded.

"Nothin'," replied Henry.

"Nothin'?" She almost mocked the way he said it. "Don't you 'nothin' me, boy! You don't go snooping around what's left of that house if you're just doing nothing."

Her voice was quickly losing fear and taking on the tone of a scolding mother.

"Now you tell me straight, boy. What are you doing here?"

Henry thought about raising the gun again, telling her to go mind her own business, but he resisted the temptation. After all, it was a fair question and he did not have anything to hide.

"I'm lookin' fer someone."

The woman crossed her arms tighter and took a step forward.

"You're a liar."

"I am not!"

"Yes, you are. If you were looking for a person, you would not have been rummaging through property that does not belong to you."

She nodded at him in a knowing way. "That's right. I was watching you the entire time. You're just another scavenger looking for something to steal!"

Now Henry grew agitated. She had no right to accuse him of such a thing.

"You're dead wrong, ma'am. I told you I was lookin' fer someone. 'Sides, I din't take nothin', did I?"

She glared at him a moment, and then put her arms akimbo. "Alright then. Suppose you tell me the name of the person you're looking for?"

Henry replied without hesitation. "Mrs. Graves."

The woman showed a trace of surprise at his answer and the confidence with which he said it, but she quickly shielded this with another scowl.

"She doesn't live here anymore."

Henry nodded. "I figured. That's why I was just leavin'."

"Well. You just be on your way then."

"Yes ma'am. That's what I'm aimin' to do."

Henry stuck the gun back in his britches and was about to turn Gal back up the lane when the woman suddenly approached so closely that Gal almost bumped into her. Henry stopped what he was doing and looked down at her. There was a searching look in her eyes, a curiosity.

"Just...just what do you want with Mrs. Graves?"

"Why?" returned Henry. "You know where I can find her?"

She hesitated. "It depends on what you want with her."

Henry studied her more carefully. She obviously knew more than she was letting on. He decided to draw out what information he could.

"I have sompin' as belongs to her. I'm tryin' to return it."

"Really?" she replied sarcastically. "What possession of hers could you possibly have?"

Henry was getting tired of being talked to this way and wanted very badly to make her change her tone. He reached into the saddlebag and pulled out the vase.

"This."

The recognition on her face was instant, and this time there was no hiding it.

"Oh!… Oh, my. What a pretty vase."

"You recognize it, don't ya?"

She bit her bottom lip and grudgingly nodded.

"And you know Mrs. Graves, don't you?"

She nodded again. "I'm her sister. Come on. I'll take you to her."

Henry put the vase back into the saddlebag.

"It's this way." The woman motioned back toward the big house.

Henry turned Gal and walked her slowly while the woman came alongside. By now the sun was sinking swiftly, and the evening air grew ever cooler. The woman had no shawl and rubbed her arms for warmth.

"My name's Fannie Cooper," she offered. "I live in Waynesboro. I came out to be with Amelia after I heard what happened. Brought some clothing, food and supplies and the like. My husband now, he's off fighting the war and, well, it didn't make any sense staying away when I knew that Amelia needed me…" Her voice trailed off at the memory of it all.

When she didn't say anything more, Henry introduced himself.

"Henry Akinson."

Her face lit up at the name. "You're the boy, the one who works for Mr. Templeton?"

Henry nodded.

"Amelia told me about you. Said you came on an errand to keep some of her valuables safe."

He nodded again.

"Well! Now it makes some sense! She's going to be glad to see you. Lord knows we haven't had much good news around here for a long while."

She paused for a short time and then continued. "I'm sorry I was hard on you back there. We've had plenty of scavengers come through here after the Yankees left. Think they can pick through and take anything that's left, they do. Well, this is still private property, even if it isn't what it used to be."

By now they had skirted the big house and were making their way across the back portion of the property. Henry was surprised to see that they angled toward the slave quarters.

"After the burning," Fannie continued, "Amelia and the children needed somewhere to stay. I tried to convince her to move back to town with me, but she refused to leave her property. Stubborn woman. So she took up here, in the overseer's house, and I said I'd stay with her as long as she needed the company."

She gestured with her arm up ahead, and now Henry saw it. Near the slave quarters but sitting apart from them was a small cabin. It was far from impressive, but neither was it ramshackle like the slave shacks that stood nearby. It was one of the few outbuildings that the bummers had left untouched. Henry noted that a thin trail of smoke rose from the chimney.

Henry tied Gal to a nearby tree, and then he and Fannie walked to the front door. She opened it and called through the entryway.

"Amelia! There is someone here to see you."

The cabin was not spacious. Over Fannie's shoulder, Henry saw that there was one main room with a cooking hearth and two adjoining rooms, which he presumed to be bedrooms. There was no second story or a loft, but there were wooden floors and glass panes in the windows.

Mrs. Graves appeared from one of the bedrooms, her two children in tow, hanging shyly behind their mother. Henry recognized her of course, but at the same time it was not the Mrs. Graves that he remembered. The feisty, defiant look was gone from her eyes and was replaced by one of tired resignation. She wore a battered dress that looked as if it had seen much action between washings. Her hair was wound into a bun, and a coverless book dangled from her left hand. Henry guessed that she had been giving a lesson to her children.

He removed his hat and shuffled his feet, trying not to let his expression betray his surprise at how run-down she looked. It seemed as if she had aged ten years in a month.

Fannie stepped further into the room, allowing Henry space to come fully inside.

"Amelia," she said, "I'm sure you recognize Henry Akinson. I found him on the property looking for you."

Recognition and a glimmer of hope washed across her face. "Why, yes! Of course I recognize him! Mr. Templeton's boy."

Henry nodded at her. "Ma'am."

Mrs. Graves handed the book to her daughter, took a step closer to him and brought her hands together in a hopeful clasp.

"You've come to return my valuables?"

Henry started to reply, but Mrs. Graves cut him off.

"Oh, Fannie! Isn't it wonderful? It's the perfect Christmas gift!"

"Well, actu'lly ma'am, I…uh…Christmas?"

The women and children were incredulous.

"Well of course, boy!" responded Mrs. Graves. "Didn't you even know that this is Christmas Eve?"

Henry was shocked. He truly had no idea. Violet and Reuben had kept no calendar, and with all of his activities, the past days and weeks had all run together such that he didn't even know the day of the week, let alone that it was Christmas Eve.

He glanced at the hearth and noticed two patched stockings hanging expectantly from the mantle. He felt stupid for not knowing but also amazed that an entire month had passed since last he had known the date.

"Shucks…uh…no, ma'am. I…I din't even know."

The two children giggled quietly at his clumsy answer.

"Well, for heaven's sake! Where have you been, boy? Mr. Templeton is a man of detail. Surely he keeps a calendar!"

Henry fidgeted with his hat. "Well, actu'lly ma'am…Mr. Templeton is dead."

Fannie closed her eyes and crossed herself. Mrs. Graves gasped and put a hand to her mouth.

"How awful."

Henry thought that if she knew the whole truth, if she knew where her table silver was right now and how it had got there, she might think otherwise about the man's death. But he did not see any need to get into all of that.

"Yes, ma'am. Some weeks back. Yankee bummers burned Stratmore jist like they done here to you. They done shot him dead."

The children hung their heads. The flash of hope that had briefly lightened Mrs. Graves' face was replaced by a hollowness that seemingly had become the expression she now wore most frequently.

Henry could see that the poor woman had endured more than her fair share of heartache, and he was reluctant to tell her the rest. Even so, there was no way around it.

"Ma'am…them bummers, they took everything they was… includin' all them fine things you give me to keep safe. I done gave you my word to pertect it, but I couldn't do nothin' 'bout it. I...I'm most gosh awful sorry, ma'am."

Mrs. Graves moved to the table in front of the hearth and eased herself down. For long moments, she stared at an invisible spot on the floor. Fannie crossed to her and put a hand on her shoulder.

"So that's it then," said Mrs. Graves at length. "Now they've taken everything. All this time I held out hope that something would survive. Well. That was a foolish thing to believe in."

"Now Amelia," consoled Fannie. "Not everything."

She looked across at Henry.

"That's rightly so, ma'am. Not everything."

He dashed out the door and retrieved the ivory vase from his saddlebag. When he came back inside, he held it gently out to Mrs. Graves.

"This is yourn. It's the only thing them Yanks din't take. I come to give it back to ya."

Mrs. Graves reached out and took the vase with two trembling hands. One of her tears splashed down and formed a rounded droplet atop the snow white ivory.

"This is it," she quietly sobbed. "The one thing that I have left."

She clutched it to her bosom and cried with her eyes tight shut. The children ran to her and consoled her with hugs. Henry stood there and watched awkwardly, not knowing what to do or say.

Finally Mrs. Graves composed herself and placed the vase in the middle of the table. She wiped her eyes with her apron.

"Thank you," she said to Henry. "You brought back what you could, and you kept your word as a Southerner."

At that moment, Henry felt a hundred times bigger than he had ever felt working for Templeton.

"Yes, ma'am," he nodded and smiled back at her. "Yer welcome."

They insisted that he stay for supper, and Henry was only too happy to oblige. The children ran off and found some holly growing on the back property line. They picked some sprigs and put them in the ivory vase. Fannie and Amelia got busy at the hearth and soon pulled together a meal of soup and bread. When they gathered around the table, Mrs. Graves insisted that they join hands and say a prayer.

She closed her eyes and said, "For what we are about to receive, may the Lord make us truly thankful. And even though these are not the best of times, we still thank you, Lord, for your son Jesus. Amen."

"Amen," they all chorused.

Still they did not let go their hands. Mrs. Graves opened her eyes and continued.

"I was wrong," she said, "about what I said earlier. Those Yankees did not take everything, and this vase is not the last thing I have left. I have my beautiful children, and I have a loving sister who cares so much that she came here to be with me during this difficult time. When you have folks like that around you...well...then nothing else really matters so much."

"Well said, Amelia," added Fannie.

They let go hands and Amelia began ladling the soup. When she put the bowl in front of Henry, she asked, "What about you, Henry? Do you have any folks?"

Immediately his mind flashed on Violet, Reuben, and little Clarissa. He wondered how they were spending Christmas Eve. Did they know what day it was?

"I...uh..."

The children looked at him with wide, round eyes.

He swallowed.

"I...had some."

She cut a piece of bread and gave it to him. "Well," she said. "If you're lucky enough to get folks in your life, maybe it's best to hang onto them."

Then she ladled soup to the others and did not say anything more about it.

Though simple, the meal was filling and through it all the mood became more festive. They sang Christmas carols, enjoyed a sugar cake that Fannie had prepared, and even popped corn over the fire. The children strung some of the popped kernels on a thread and hung them up as decorations. Then, when the hour grew late, they went off to bed sharing their hopes of what Father Christmas would bring to them.

After the children were in bed, the women stayed up later and talked with Henry in front of the fireplace. Mostly the conversation was about Sherman and how long Savannah might be able to hold out before it fell. All the while, Mrs. Graves finished sewing together two simple dolls that she then put inside the children's stockings.

The women then retired to the other bedroom, and Henry was given a place to sleep on the floor in front of the hearth.

It had been a day of many different emotions, and Henry found it difficult to rest. As he lay there looking up at the stockings, an idea came to him. He quietly arose and lit a lantern with an ember from the fire. Then he was out the door and into the chilly night. Across the lawn he hustled, pausing just long enough to look in on Gal. Soon he was at the ruins, and in the darkness he located the remains of the toy chest.

Many of the toys were too badly damaged, and with the lantern in his hand he could only carry a few items. Still, he managed to retrieve the train engine and an attaching car, some wooden blocks, and the skipping rope.

Henry crept back into the house and blew out the lantern. The low, red fire still provided enough light for him to see, and he stuffed the toys into the stockings. He stepped back, regarded the now bulging socks, and smiled. He had become quite skilled at sneaking in and out of houses with things that did not belong to him, but this time it was different. This time, it felt good. And when he lay down again in front of the slowly fading fire, this time his mind was more at peace. His last flickering thought before sleep was that maybe, just maybe, he had done something to restore some of their innocence—and maybe some of his own.

Henry woke early, very early, to joyous shouts. The children tumbled out of their bedroom and nearly trampled him as they ran to their stockings. The ruckus brought the women from their bedroom, but it all melted into hushed amazement when the children pulled the toys from the stockings. They, as well as Mrs. Graves, were astounded.

"Mama! Look! These belong to us!"

"They were lost in the fire, but Father Christmas brought them back!"

"And look! New dolls too!"

Mrs. Graves did not know what to say and looked at Fannie. Fannie, for her part, smiled knowingly at Henry. He beamed as he watched the children's utter joy, and his soul had not felt so good in a long, long time.

Henry joined them for breakfast, and then declared that he had to be on his way. He hugged the children, the two women as well, and thanked them for their hospitality.

When he was ready to go, Mrs. Graves joined him at the door.

"Henry, are you certain that you have somewhere to go?"

He put on his hat and nodded to her. "Yes, ma'am. I have an idea where I need to be."

Satisfied with this answer, she let him pass.

The weather outside was clear but very chilly. Henry greeted Gal with long strokes and ran his fingers through her mane.

"Merry Christmas, girl!" he whispered in her ear.

Then he climbed into the saddle, waved to the four watching from the cabin's door, and rode off toward the lane.

He had to laugh at himself as he went. *Did I really fergit Christmas? Lord, sometimes I'm sitch an idiot.*

But then, more seriously, he realized that if he had not happened upon Fannie, he would have spent Christmas alone. Not only that, it would have come and gone without his knowledge. And what about next Christmas? And the year after that? Did he want to spend those alone as well? Or spend them wandering among strangers?

He came to the end of the lane. Gal stopped and waited for a signal from her rider. To the left or to the right?

Henry reached down and patted her strong neck. "C'mon, girl. Let's go find our folks."

Then he flicked the reins and spurred her on the road back to Stratmore.

Chapter Twenty-Six – Departure

"Reuben."

The boy felt the gentle hand on his shoulder, but he pulled his knees closer to his stomach and pushed his face deeper into the corn husk mattress. It was chilly inside the cabin and so early in the morning that not even a hint of sunlight filtered through the cracks in the wooden shutter above his bed.

Violet stood over her sleeping son, reluctant to wake him but knowing that they needed an early start. Again she touched him and called his name, this time more loudly.

"Reuben. C'mon chile. It time to be gettin' up."

He moaned and rolled over. Violet moved away from the bedside and busied herself at the hearth, getting the morning cook fire hot. The sounds of her bustling were enough to coax Reuben's mind out of slumber. He yawned and stretched until the tattered blanket slid off of him. Then he swung his legs over the bed's edge and sat for a few moments rubbing his eyes.

The room brightened as Violet stoked the fire to life. She crossed to the bed. Sitting down on the edge beside her son, she hugged him close to herself.

"Merry Christmas, Reuben."

He leaned in, her soft cheek against his, and hugged her back.

"It tiday?"

"Roundabout, the way I reckon," she nodded gently.

"Merry Christmas, mama."

She rocked him slightly, almost like she did when he was small. "This is a blessed day for us, chile. More than normal."

"Yes, ma'am."

She rocked some more. "I know we got to move on. I want to move on. But I don't mind tellin' you I'm scared just the same."

"Don't worry none, mama. I be dere wit you, no matter what come."

She hugged him tighter. "I know it, chile. Oh honey, you know I know it."

They held close for a while, and then Reuben pulled away.

"I best be off to the dock, git dat boat loaded an' ready."

Violet nodded in reply. "I'm fixin' to make breakfast. It be ready when you come back."

She kissed him on the forehead and went back to her cooking. Reuben pulled a shirt on, strapped up his britches, and slid his feet into falling-apart shoes. But before leaving the cabin, he slipped quietly over to the crib. Clarissa slept peacefully, her steady breaths coming in little puffs. He reached out and touched her tiny nose.

"Merry Christmas, little sis."

Violet saw this and smiled at what a precious Christmas gift she had already received. Several weeks ago, she would not have thought it possible.

"C'mon now," she said. "Git a move on. I want you back fo' a hot breakfast. Gonna be a long day."

"Awright, mama."

Reuben touched his sister once more, flipped his hat onto his head, and was out the door.

❖ ❖ ❖

It was still dark outside as Reuben found his way to the storehouse. He opened the door and began toting to the dock all the items they had stockpiled. From there, he packed them into the old rowboat, taking care to balance the load. When he was finished, there remained only enough room for him and Violet to sit on the benches and space enough below for their feet. It would be a cramped journey for sure, but he did not care. He felt he could endure any amount of discomfort if it meant that he could get away from this place.

Just as he finished packing, the sun broke over the eastern horizon. Reuben stood on the dock and took it in. It shone from the direction they would be traveling, and it made the water sparkle as if it were the beacon of freedom itself. Hope stirred inside of him, hope for the future into which he was about to move. But at the same time he felt a profound loneliness, and he wished that Henry were there to share the moment with him.

Funny. Of the million times he had dreamed of departing this place, he had never imagined being sad about leaving anything, or anyone, behind. Yet here he stood, feeling exactly that way.

He looked away from the rising sun, across the ruined big house, toward the lane. But of course no one was there. Nor would there be. He knew that.

He sighed as he stepped off the dock and headed toward the cabin. It wasn't fair, he thought as he walked, that even life's most long-awaited and joyous moments could sometimes be tinged with sadness.

❖ ❖ ❖

Back at the cabin, breakfast was ready. Reuben ate biscuits and drank his coffee while Violet fed Clarissa.

"Boat all ready to go?"

"Yes, ma'am."

"I gots a few more things I wants you to carry down."

Reuben shook his head. "Ain't no room, mama. Only jist enuff fer the three of us da way it is."

Violet looked at him pleadingly. "Not even a few more thangs?"

"Naw. Not 'less you wanna send us to da bottom of da river."

"No," chuckled Violet. "Don't wanna do no such thing."

Reuben finished eating and wrapped up extra biscuits to eat on the way. Violet bundled Clarissa tightly to protect her against the chilly air and then cradled her in her arms.

The cook fire was put out. The window was shuttered. The candles were extinguished. And all at once, the finality hit them. This was the last time they would leave the place that they for so long had called home.

"Lots o' memories here," observed Violet as they stood close together near the threshold. "Some I'll treasure fo'eva, others I wish I could fo'get. Oh my, my...I never thought I would see dis day. Well. We just gotta trust that the hand of the Lord will deliver us to some new place that we kin call home."

"He will, mama."

She nodded and wiped a tear from her cheek. "C'mon. We got one more goodbye to say."

Then she turned and stepped outside. Reuben followed and shut the door behind him.

They did not go directly to the dock. Instead, the three of them walked through the slave quarters to a lonely plot of land that lay beyond. Here, a host of weather-beaten wooden crosses marked the final resting places for the poor slaves who did not live long enough to feel the touch of freedom's finger. Violet and Reuben weaved among them, not speaking but each of them recalling the faces and voices of those who were buried here. At length, they came to one of the most recent graves, the one most personal to them.

"Your daddy," said Violet, "he would'a' loved to see dis day."

Reuben did not reply. He stared sternly at the cross.

"I know you think hard 'bout him sometimes, but your daddy was a good man. He just wanted to be free so bad he

212

couldn't stay around and wait for it to come to him. I know he's somewhar smilin' at us today, and I know he's so, so proud of you."

She knelt down. Clarissa wiggled an arm free, reached with her tiny hand and touched the cross.

And then Violet began to sing.

> Hurry on, my weary soul
> I heard from heaven today
> Hurry on, my weary soul
> I heard from heaven today
>
> A baby born in Bethlehem
> I heard from heaven today
> A baby born in Bethlehem
> I heard from heaven today
>
> My sin is forgiven and my soul set free
> I heard from heaven today
> My sin is forgiven and my soul set free
> I heard from heaven today
>
> The trumpet sounds in the other bright land
> I heard from heaven today
> The trumpet sounds in the other bright land
> I heard from heaven today
>
> My name is called and I must go
> I heard from heaven today
> My name is called and I must go
> I heard from heaven today

"Merry Christmas, Mac. And goodbye."

They came to the dock, and Reuben helped his mother into the boat. Once she was situated, he handed Clarissa to her. Then he busied himself with untying the rope. Through it all, he looked toward the lane a half dozen times.

"Reuben," said Violet softly. "You know de choice he made."

"I...I know mama."

"Leave it be, son. C'mon now. Let's move on."

Reuben nodded and fought away the temptation to look again. He unfastened the rope, clambered into the rocking boat, and gripped the oars. With short, careful strokes he backed the boat away from the dock and toward the middle of the river.

The current caught them and swung them around. Now Reuben leaned in and hauled harder on the oars, making broad, deep strokes that moved them briskly and kept them straight in the water. And off to their right, Stratmore Plantation began to slide away, dropping back further and further, until it was behind them entirely.

The Savannah River was abandoned and quiet, a glinting dark green ribbon that wound its lonely course southeast. For many years before the war, the steady flow had faithfully shouldered the loads of Southern agriculture; cotton, rice, and indigo shipped to the port city and away to distant markets; iron and slaves imported from across the great expanse, sent up the river and delivered to the plantation owners. In those days it was a bustling lifeline, but no longer. While its water flowed as freely as ever, the war had reduced its traffic to a mere trickle. So as Reuben, Violet, and Clarissa set out, there were no steamboats, flatboats, or barges to compete with their little rowboat. Just miles and miles of quietly moving water.

As the rowboat drifted along, the sun climbed higher but did little to warm the cool air. They moved downstream, and Reuben was glad for the fact that he did not have to battle the current. It was enough work to keep the boat straight and to avoid debris, activity that kept him warm and moving. Violet, on the other hand, was chilled by the insistent breeze. As one accustomed to moving about all day, it was not long before she became restless sitting on the hard bench, holding still in the cramped space. To occupy her mind, she chatted with Reuben or hummed old tunes that she remembered from childhood.

Clarissa was cooperative enough. Though she had been awake when they embarked, the boat's undulating motion had soon lulled her to sleep.

And so the morning passed quietly and uneventfully. The winter had dulled the countryside with various shades of brown, and they watched it slip by peacefully to their right and left. The only real activity came when Reuben was forced to maneuver the boat around a tree that had, some time ago, fallen into the river. Its bare branches, piercing the surface like long fingers that strained the current, threatened to capsize the boat if it should happen to wedge against them. But Reuben deftly avoided the hazard, and they floated on.

Not long after they passed the tree, Clarissa began to fuss. Reuben's stomach was growling loudly, and Violet desperately needed to stretch her legs. Reuben spotted a sandy shoal on the southern shore and guided the boat to it. He scrambled out when the bow ground against the sand and pulled the rowboat far enough onto the tiny beach to prevent its drifting away. Then he offered a hand and helped his mother out.

She groaned at the stiffness. "Oh, Lordy! I been sittin' too long."

Reuben just shook his head. "Best git used to it, mama. We got us a long way to go."

"Mercy!" she exclaimed as she stretched. "How far you think we come?"

"Hard to figure. Eight or ten mile, mebbe."

"Well, we git back to floatin' soon enough. Need to walk a bit an' feed the darlin' baby girl. You eat some of them biscuits we put in. I been hearin' yo stomach for the past hour."

The site where they had stopped was a pleasant place. The shoal, sandy near the water's edge, became gradually more rocky until it merged fully with the bank which itself was a grassy, gradual hillside spotted with trees and boulders. Upstream of where the boat had been beached, an enormous tree angled itself toward the water, one of its sturdy branches jutting over the rocky area. A log, which might have fallen from the tree long ago, lay embedded in the sand. To the downstream side, tall grasses rubbed against one another. Reuben imagined how inviting this place would be on a hot summer day. Even now in the chilly breeze, he found it peaceful and comfortable.

He retrieved the sack which held the biscuits, sat down on the log, and popped one into his mouth. After walking up and down the shore a few times, Violet sat next to him and prepared to feed Clarissa.

Reuben had the second biscuit halfway into his mouth when he looked up and noticed a movement on the river. It was to his right and hard to be sure about through the swaying grasses. He bit off a piece, chewed slowly, and stood up to get a better look.

There was no mistaking it now. As it emerged from behind the weedy screen, a flatboat became fully visible. It was moving upstream, tracking along the opposite shore.

He did not know why, but the boat gave Reuben a bad feeling inside. They had gone the entire morning without seeing another vessel, and that had been just fine with him. He knew there were still plenty of people around who would not take kindly to a Negro family traveling on their own.

He turned to his mother. "Mama. Look dere."

Hearing the worry in Reuben's voice, she raised her eyes and saw it. "Just another boat, Reuben. You din't think we'd sail all the way to Savannah without seeing anyone else, did ya? They'll likely pass us by."

She had intended to calm him, and for a while it looked as if she was right. The flatboat hugged the opposite shore and stayed its course. But then, shadowy figures of two men on the deck came near to each other. One of them gestured toward the shoal. And in another minute, the flatboat began carving out a turn and crossing to the southern shore.

Chapter Twenty-Six

Now Reuben paced back and forth. "I don't like this, mama."

"Be still, chile. We ain't got no reason to be afeared of them. They's probably taking a break, no different than us."

Reuben did not buy it. "Plenty of places they could of laid up over dere. Why dey gotta cross? I'm tellin' you, mama. I don't like it."

By this time the flatboat was more than halfway across. The men aboard were easily visible. Two of them poled the boat along. The other stood near the bow, arms crossed, watching them.

"Get in the boat, mama."

"What? I ain't even fed Clarissa yet. I..."

Then Violet looked again at the approaching boat, at the silhouetted image of the man with the folded arms, and a feeling of foreboding washed over her as well. Like Reuben, she could not explain where it came from. Perhaps it was a sense of inner warning, heightened by years of violence, fear, and intimidation. Whatever it was, it was seldom mistaken.

The flatboat came closer.

"You're right, Reuben. I don't like it neither. Let's move on."

She gathered up Clarissa while he scooped the remains of the biscuits. Hurriedly, they crossed to the sandy part of the shoal and Reuben tossed the sack into the rowboat.

He glanced up. The flatboat was nearly upon them. It was so close that he could see the eyes of the man with the crossed arms. They were not friendly.

Reuben turned and helped Violet step in. Her weight tilted the unsteady boat and she nearly lost her balance. Reuben had to reach out clumsily and catch her.

"Ahoy there!"

The man at the bow called out to them. His voice was rough, laced with a trace of sarcasm.

Reuben raised an arm to acknowledge that he had heard, but he said nothing in reply. Instead, he quickly settled Violet into her seat. Clarissa, still hungry and now upset by the tension in her mother's arms, began to cry. Violet tried desperately to hush her.

"Reuben! Hurry!" she hissed through clenched teeth.

The flatboat reached the shallows. Reuben heard it grind against the sandbar even as he struggled to push the rowboat away from the very same.

All three men jumped off, splashing into water up to their ankles. Reuben felt them approaching.

"Quick, Reuben!"

He gave the rowboat one more hard shove and felt it slide from the sand. He was about to scramble in when a heavy hand came down upon his shoulder. He noticed only that it was white.

He tried another push, but the boat did not move. He looked up. The other two men clutched the sides and held it fast. They were white, too. Guns dangled at their sides.

Reuben looked at his mother. Her eyes were tightly shut, and she rocked the wailing Clarissa with short, choppy movements.

"Well now," said the man who grasped him. "Nice day for a boat ride, isn't it?"

Again the biting sarcasm. He spoke with a strange kind of accent that Reuben did not recognize. He spun the boy around and looked him in the eye. Reuben struggled against him.

"You get yo hands offn' me!"

The white man laughed. He was surprisingly strong and held Reuben firmly in place. He wore a dark blue cloak and a brown leather hat. His black beard was neatly trimmed, angled at the point where it blended with his sideburns. His eyes were black as well and were filled with the same haughty look that Reuben had so often seen in Templeton. They burned into him.

"I can tell that you don't recognize me, but we recognize you. Don't we, boys?"

He looked across to his companions. They both nodded and smiled grimly.

"Oh yes, we're well aware of who you are. But allow me to introduce myself. My name is Hathaway, and we're all going to sit down and have a little talk."

The crisp morning was not even fully mature when Henry rode down the lane to Stratmore. He had pushed Gal hard all the way and had not made any stops. Now, as he rounded the burned-out ruins and made for the dock, he slowed her to a walk and allowed her to catch her breath. He could see that the rowboat was gone, as he expected it would be. He had given them no indication that they should wait for him. Quite the opposite.

Just to be certain, he trotted over to the slave quarters. The cabin was shut tight. There was no sign of anyone.

He rubbed Gal on the neck. "Okay, girl. We missed 'em. But that's awright, 'cause they's only one place they kin be. On that there river."

Henry walked her back to the dock area and allowed her to drink.

"Tha's right. Drink up, girl, 'cause you an' me got some country ridin' to do."

Gal lifted her head, signaling that she had drunk her fill. He reined her to the right and spurred her forward.

"Ain't no tellin' how far ahead they is, but if we keep this here river to our left, we'll spot 'em by and by. C'mon girl! Git up now!"

The strong horse responded willfully and bounded away through the thicket that grew along the southern bank.

Reuben and Violet were seated on the log, she with the baby in her arms. Their hands were bound, and the two burly men who had stopped the rowboat now stood behind them ready to pounce on even the slightest move that they should make. Hathaway paced in front of them, clearly irritated by Clarissa's bawling. At length, Violet was able to calm her, though she had no luck trying to calm herself. Hathaway stopped and faced them. The corner of his left eye twitched. A revolver peeked from underneath his cloak.

"Now. Let me tell you something more about myself," he began. He sighed and looked away to the sky, as if recalling a story.

"I am a business man, a man of profit. I make my home in New York, but recently it has become profitable for me to have dealings here in the South, festering swampland that it is. But it is not without its opportunities. I'm sure I don't need to tell the likes of you that it has become increasingly dangerous here, but I calculated my reward to be worth the risk. In fact, not long ago I struck a deal with a Mr. Lewis Templeton."

He saw the flash of recognition in their eyes.

"Yes, that's right. Your owner. Or shall I say, former owner?"

Reuben squinted hard at him.

"Yes, boy. I know that he's dead. I know far more than you realize. You see, we were there that night, my men and I, and we saw what happened."

In spite of herself, Violet gasped.

"Does that surprise you, woman?" He chuckled. "I know what you must be thinking. 'How could they have been there? We didn't see them.' Do you know what these men behind you used to do for a living? They were slave hunters. So you see, they are quite adept at remaining unseen. It's a pity those days are behind us—such a waste of good talent."

Reuben made a move to stand up to him but was instantly slammed back onto the log.

Hathaway continued as if nothing had happened. "But I digress. That night, after the Yankees left, my men scouted the property and reported back to me. They saw Templeton's body, they confirmed that the treasure was gone, and they saw you. You and some other boy."

Reuben's mind whirled. *Henry.*

"I din't see no boat o' yours," Reuben hissed back.

Hathaway shook his head. "Idiot. Did you think I would sail right up to the dock? The last thing I needed was a company of Federal troops burning my flatboat. No, I know when to keep my distance. Sometimes information is more powerful than bravado. You see, I am an educated man. For the considerable risks that I take, it is important to know all the facts. For instance, I've become quite a student of the troop movements. I know that Sherman's men were camped in Alexander. They were set to move out toward Savannah the very next day. Stratmore was not in their path. There was no reason for that many Yankee riders to range so far out of their way, unless…"

Here he trailed off and stared at Reuben directly in the eye. "Unless they were tipped off."

Reuben heard the implication loud and clear. "I ain't never talked to no Yankee in all my life."

"No? It seems that the bluecoats have befriended your kind. The slaves follow them around like lost puppies. Are you suggesting that your people, even you yourself, would not jump at the chance to get revenge? My associates have filled me with stories about what lengths devious slaves will go to in order to strike back at their masters. Poison their soup. Loosen the axles on their carriages. Murder them in their sleep. Or even possibly—if they have the opportunity—bring a whole army crashing down upon them."

At this, Reuben erupted and leaped to his feet. "You shut yo mouth! We din't have nothin' to do wit any of that!"

It took both burly men to force him back down.

Hathaway probed him with his eyes. "Maybe you didn't. But someone did. Am I right?"

Reuben steamed, but said nothing. He broke off eye contact.

"I thought so," he said. Then he leaned in and whispered fiercely into Reuben's ear. "Now you get this straight. I don't care about Templeton, and I sure don't care about you slaves. But when those Yankees brought down Stratmore, it cost me a great deal of money. For that, someone is going to pay. The only question is who. If it wasn't you, then just tell me who it was. Then you can go your merry way and my men will hunt down the cuss who did this to me."

The man's face was so close that Reuben felt the scratch of his beard. He heard his own mother just a few feet away, whimpering like the little girl that she clutched in her arms.

Henry.

All he had to do was say Henry's name, and all of this would stop.

"Was it that other boy?"

Reuben pursed his lips together and said nothing.

"Boy, if you love your mother and sister you better speak up!"

Reuben closed his eyes. The weight of the man behind pressed down on him, but far heavier was the consequence of his choice. Sweat stood out on his forehead. His hands shook uncontrollably. His mouth was so dry that he could hardly swallow, but he forced it down and then ran his tongue over his lips.

He opened his eyes, looked straight at Hathaway and said, "I ain't got nothin' to say to you."

Hathaway stared back at him with an icy glare. "Then you're going to pay the full price."

He straightened and nodded to his henchmen.

"Boys, hang 'em all."

Gal carefully picked her way through the weeds and briars that flourished along the uppermost ridge. To her left, the ground sloped steeply down to the water's edge, dangerous footing that Henry made certain she avoided. They had picked up the remains of an old trail a while back and had made good time, but still Henry had not seen any sign of the rowboat. Sitting high in the saddle, he had a good view of the river and he scanned it repeatedly, looking away only to make sure Gal was keeping to the safe, high ground. Occasionally stands of trees blocked his view, and he had to strain and stand up in the stirrups to see around them. So far, a fallen tree with branches poking through the water was the only object that he had noted.

Presently they came to a place where the bank sloped more gently. The area before them opened into a clearing with shorter grass that was punctuated with occasional trees and boulders. Henry was about to spur Gal ahead when suddenly a shrill scream knifed through the chilly air. It sent a shiver down his back and caused Gal to prick up her ears. The troubling sound had come from the water's edge and was very close.

He leaned forward in the saddle and listened harder. The scream had not fully faded before it was joined by the unmistakable wailing of a baby.

"Clarissa!"

There was no doubt in his mind. By now, he could recognize that cry from any distance.

"I think we found 'em, Gal! But good Lord, what's happnin' down thar?"

Though he could hear the cries of distress, he still could not see anyone. He kicked Gal into a trot and rode into the clearing, angling slightly down the slope. The view opened up.

Reuben and Violet were struggling mightily against two large men who were dragging them toward a massive tree. A third man, who appeared to have jumped off the edge of a nearby flatboat, ran toward the others. He had ropes in his hands. These he tossed over a large branch that jutted over the shoal. Henry focused on the dangling ropes and gasped.

The ends were looped into nooses.

Clarissa, who had apparently been torn from her mother's arms, lay on the ground off to the side, wailing at the top of her lungs and kicking her little legs into the air.

He heard Reuben cursing and shouting at the man who wrestled with him, saw him writhing and shaking his head ferociously. Violet twisted and turned from the strong arms that held her, bending her entire body in Clarissa's direction, craning her neck and chin outward toward her baby. Words that were almost unintelligible blended with her sobs.

"Don't you do this! Don't you lay a hand on my baby!"

The men, too, made a commotion. They grunted with their efforts, shouted hoarse orders to one another, cursed the woman and boy and told them to shut their mouths.

The man who had put up the ropes ran to a log that lay across the sand. He half dragged, half rolled it until it was positioned under the ropes. The others forced Reuben and Violet to stand on the log. They snugged the nooses around their necks.

Still Henry sat and watched.

Oh my Gaw...Oh my dear Gaw...

He was frozen. Unable to move.

It was all happening so fast.

Two of the men knelt down, ready to roll the log out from under their feet.

At that moment, Gal whinnied loudly and went up on her hind legs, nearly toppling Henry from the saddle.

The startled men jumped to their feet and looked up the bank. They instinctively drew their guns.

"Up there!"

Henry's mind was muddled dissonance. He heard the sharp *crack! crack! crack!* as all three of them fired. He listened to the bullets whiz past his head, one of them ricocheting off of a tree behind him. And he caught Reuben's distant, disconnected voice hoarse upon the air.

"Henry! Please! Oh, Gaw! Please!"

Suddenly everything around him slowed and muted. He saw puffs of smoke as the men fired again, Clarissa's little feet kicking, Reuben's lips and jaw line working as he formed his words, but there was no sound anymore.

He felt the reins fall from his hands.

A numbness crept over him.

Translucent, lurid images wavered before his eyes.

He saw the men pinned down in the ravine.

The voices in his head started talking again.

They're all gonna die!

He saw the saber slashing his hat.

Move it!

He saw the flames of Hanley Hall.

You gotta help me!

He saw Templeton's cracking whip.

I swear by God I will kill you!

He saw the white face of the dead Yank.

In the end, does it really matter?

And then slowly pushing aside all the rest, he saw Reuben's face again.

Jaw set.

Eyes intense.

Staring squarely back at Henry.

"I don't run."

Henry shook himself. He blinked hard, sat up straighter. Like a locomotive engine rushing outward from some faraway tunnel, the pandemonium roared back to his ears. His limbs tensed with feeling. His eyes sharpened and focused.

He felt Gal sidestepping underneath him as the bullets flew, sensed her energy building, ready to explode.

With one hand he reached down and gathered the reins.

With the other he drew the revolver.

I don't run. I don't run.

"No," he said out loud to himself. "Not this time!"

He leaned forward and kicked Gal hard. She lunged down the slope, galloping headlong into the spray of bullets.

Startled by the sudden charge, one of the men kicked at the log. Once…twice…

Now a new voice spoke in Henry's head, one that he had not heard for a long, long time.

His uncle.

Exhale … aim … squeeze.

Henry aimed and squeezed off a shot. The man kicking the log threw his arms in the air and then slumped to the sand and lay motionless.

Gal now charged so forcefully down the bank that the two remaining men retreated a few steps toward the water's edge.

Henry fired twice more and missed. One of the men emptied his revolver and, crawling across the sand, went for his companion's gun. Henry dropped him with a shot to the head.

Now only one man remained. His dark blue cloak fluttered as he turned and ran for the flatboat.

Chapter Twenty-Nine

Henry took aim and squeezed. His shot went wide and plunked in the river.

He had only one chance left.

Gal leaped the jagged rocks and landed on the sand. She held steady while Henry leveled the gun.

On the boat deck, the man scrambled for a shotgun and started turning.

Exhale...aim...squeeze.

Hathaway dropped the gun and doubled over, clutching at his midsection. He staggered forward, leaned toward the tiller for support, then collapsed over the edge and splashed face down in the shallows.

Henry lowered the revolver and took a deep breath. He was weak and shaky all over, but Clarissa's crying reminded him that the job was not yet done.

He climbed, or more so fell, from the saddle and floundered toward the log. There he removed the nooses from Reuben and Violet. Pulling a knife from the belt of one of the dead men, he cut their hands free.

The moment her hands were loose, Violet rushed to Clarissa, scooped her up from the sand, and squeezed her to her bosom like she would never let go.

Henry was faint and leaned on Reuben, who grabbed him in an embrace. They held each other up as he repeated over and over again, "You come back. You come back to us. Oh thank Gaw you come back."

Then the boys staggered over to Violet and hugged her from each side, and all four of them hung on to one another.

It was a long time before any of them could speak. The sounds of their crying gradually dissipated, and even little Clarissa, back in the security of her mother's arms, settled down. It was strange, Henry thought, how silence returned so quickly after such a violent explosion of action and emotion.

The cold breeze bore down on them, more chillingly now that their bodies were sweaty. The rowboat, still stuck on the sand but turned askew by the current, bumped idly against a rock. All about them, the sand was gashed and imprinted with the signs of their struggle.

It was Violet who finally found her voice. She shifted Clarissa to her left arm, and with her right she wrapped Henry around his shoulders, drew him to herself, and kissed him on the forehead.

"Oh, Henry…Henry…You's just like an angel watchin' over us."

He had no words to say in reply and simply returned the hug.

Visibly shaken, she sighed deeply and spoke in a quaking voice that quickly gave way to fresh tears.

"Boys, I can't…I can't go no further."

Reuben stroked her back in an attempt to comfort her.

"Mama, what you mean?"

She sniffled and wiped beneath her eye with a bent finger. She heard the concern in his voice and knew what he was afraid she might be trying to say.

"Now, don't git me wrong, chile. We ain't never goin' back there. Put your mind at rest 'bout that. But all this here,…" she gestured with her arm toward the carnage, "I need some time. Jist need some time."

"Sure, mama. Sure. We lay up here t'night. Git some rest an' start fresh in da mornin'."

Violet flicked a terrified eye toward the bodies on the sand.

"I cain't get no rest with…them…"

"We move 'em out," Reuben hurried to assure her. "Henry an' me, we move 'em out."

She pinched her eyes, but nodded. "Awright, chile. Awright. Let me set, now. Let me set. Jist need some time…"

Henry and Reuben rolled the log back to its original place. Violet sat down, her back to the bodies. Clarissa began fussing again, and as Violet rested and fed her, she hummed softly and looked away, into space, constructing a mental wall between herself and what she had just been through.

Gal had wandered off the beach, back up the slope to find grass. It seemed that she, too, needed some time to herself. Henry went to her, rubbed her neck and ran his hands through her mane.

"Thank you, girl. Thank you," he whispered in her ear. And then he left her and went back to the task at hand.

They recovered Hathaway's body before it floated away. They dragged him and the other two to a place that was shielded by tall grass, beyond the tree. With no shovel, they piled stones atop the bodies until they were covered completely.

"Thought you was never comin' back," said Reuben as they put the final stones in place.

Henry stood and wiped the dust and dirt from his hands. "Yeah. Well, I thought so, too."

"What changed yo' mind?"

Henry looked away to the sky, thinking. "Figured I was runnin'. Runnin' from sompin' I most always was wishin' I had."

"What's dat?"

"Folks. Folks to call my own."

"Yeah? Well…you find 'em here?"

"Reckon so."

Reuben reached out and shook his hand. "Yep. I reckon so."

That night they built a fire on the beach and huddled around it. Once the sun had set, the temperature plummeted and now they drew as near as they could to the flames. The biscuits were gone, but they gnawed on strips of dried meat.

The burning logs shifted and crackled. Reuben, his eyes bright in the firelight, leaned in and spoke.

"Henry."

"Yeah?"

"What you done today, and what you done fer my sister…I ain't got no words."

Henry nodded. He wished he could somehow explain to Reuben just how much he had done for him.

"But Henry."

"Yeah?"

"It ain't never gonna stop."

Violet stared away into the flames. She knew what her son was saying. It was a reality that she had accepted long ago.

"What ain't gonna stop?" Henry asked.

"This. What happen'd today."

Henry was confused. "I ain't sure I foller yer meanin'."

Reuben tossed a twig into the fire. "They's always gonna be someone agin' us, Henry. Mebbe not always like today, huntin' us down with guns a'blazin. Mebbe not always like Temp'ton.

But they's always gonna be folk tryin' to keep us down. Always gonna be some who got the hate."

Henry shook his head. "Ain't no slaves sittin' round this fire."

Reuben smiled weakly at this. "True 'nuff. But even if we ain't slaves no more, it don't make all the rest of it dis'ppear. It don't wipe the black off'n my skin. Kind of freedom we got, they ain't gonna be no milk an' honey."

He sighed. "What I's tryin' to say, Henry, is dat our road from here ain't gonna be easy. Now we all," he pointed with a stick to his mother and Clarissa, "we's gotta take it. Ain't no other choice but to go back, an' we ain't goin' back."

Now he directed the stick at Henry. "But you…well…they's other roads that you kin take. Mebbe ones that ain't so hard."

Henry stared back at him through the flames.

Violet closed her eyes and nodded once, knowingly.

"You jist…think on it," said Reuben. Then he lay down in the sand and closed his eyes.

Henry lay back as well, but his eyes remained open for a long time. He thought he had settled on his path, but Reuben's words caused him to reconsider. Being with them made him a target, and choosing a different way might very well spare him many hardships. He hadn't thought of that.

Was it worth it?

Were they worth it?

❖ ❖ ❖

With the first light of dawn, Violet opened her eyes. Reuben lay curled up in the same place where he had bedded down, but Henry's place was empty.

She sat up quickly and looked about. There was no sign of him.

Now Reuben's eyes opened as well. Mother and son looked at each other wistfully.

"Mornin'!" came a voice from the flatboat. "Thought mebbe they was some supplies left on here we all could use."

They snapped their heads around and looked. From the boat deck, Henry grinned back at them.

"Reckon we ought to git an early start."

Violet smiled broadly and Reuben scrambled to his feet, wiping the sand from his clothes and face. "Yep," he beamed. "Reckon so."

While they did take a few small supplies from the flatboat, they decided against using it to float the rest of the way down the river. As Reuben put it, "All it takes is fer one man to 'cuse us of stealin' it, an' then we's in another pickle."

"But," said Violet, "we ain't got room enough fer Henry in the rowboat."

"I won't be floatin'," said Henry. "I'll be ridin'."

He led Gal up near the shoal and rubbed her affectionately. "If you think I'm leavin' this girl behind, you ain't right in yer head."

Gal whinnied loudly at this, coaxing a laugh even from Violet.

"'Sides," continued Henry, "now we kin go in spells. I'll ride 'long the side while Reuben rows, and then we kin switch off."

And so they were set. Reuben helped Violet get settled with Clarissa, pushed the boat off the sand, and climbed aboard.

Henry swung up and sat high in the saddle. He watched the boat arc outward until the current caught it and sent it on its way.

Gal's hair fluffed in the breeze, and he ran his fingers through her mane.

"Where we goin' girl? What comes next?"

She did not have any more answers than he did, but he did know one thing for sure. No matter where the currents might lead and whatever might happen along the way, this time he was not alone.

Knowing this, he smiled to himself and spurred Gal forward.

Afterword

On December 13, 1864, Sherman's army stormed and successfully took Fort McAllister on the outskirts of Savannah. Confederate forces secretly abandoned the city on the night of December 20, crossing the Savannah River and escaping into South Carolina. By the wee hours of December 21, Federal troops were in Savannah's streets.

On December 22, General Sherman sent a telegraph to President Lincoln: "I beg to present to you as a Christmas gift the city of Savannah, with one hundred fifty heavy guns and plenty of ammunition, also about 25,000 bales of cotton."

Sherman's March to the Sea was complete, but his punishment of the South was not. From Savannah, he turned his army north and marched through the Carolinas and into Virginia. In South Carolina, Sherman's bummers were reportedly even more destructive than they had been in Georgia. Sherman declared that "the devil himself couldn't restrain my men in that state." The city of Columbia was burned during their occupation. Figured in terms of 1865 currency, it is estimated that Sherman's army did $100 million worth of damage.

Thousands of refugees, white and black alike, were scattered in the wake of Sherman's hordes. While some staunch souls, particularly women, remained on their properties, many white Southerners abandoned their homes and fled to nearby cities outside of Sherman's path. Others went to Richmond, Virginia, hoping that the Confederate government would protect them. Still others evacuated to regions as far away as Texas. But when they returned, they found their homes destroyed, their livelihoods ruined, their communities demoralized.

General Sherman was not fond of the African American refugees that followed his army. He felt that they slowed his progress and drained his supplies. But clearly, the government could not ignore the millions of displaced former slaves. Accordingly, the War Department created the Freedman's Bureau on March 3, 1865. More than four million newly freed African Americans benefitted from food, clothing, and medicine that the Bureau provided.

President Andrew Johnson restored ownership of abandoned lands in the South to pardoned white Southerners. Thousands of unemployed former slaves returned to the South and went back to work on plantations as sharecroppers.

Though many of the characters and all of the plantations in this story are fictional, they are placed in the context of real historical events. Between November 26 and December 3, 1864, a number of skirmishes occurred in and around Waynesboro, Georgia, between the Union cavalry commanded by Brigadier General Judson Kilpatrick and the Confederate cavalry commanded by Major General Joseph Wheeler. The Battle of Waynesboro took place on December 4, 1864, and resulted in the burning of wagon and rail bridges north of the town.

The battle of Allatoona Pass, fought on October 5, 1864, occurred as described in the story. Today the railroad cut, trenches, and earthworks are remarkably well preserved. Thanks to the maintenance efforts of the Etowah Valley Historical Society, Red Top Mountain State Park, the Bartow County Government, and the U.S. Army Corps of Engineers, the battlefield is open to the public.

"In Sherman's Path" is a compelling tale of the Civil War, very much recommended reading.

Midwest Book Review

"A wonderful story of how war and peoples' actions can have life-changing effects on one young mans life."

Teresa Gaylard, Children's Librarian, Dayton Metro Library.

"Some people aren't cut out for war, but times may need them any-way....The Civil War story of In Sherman's Path, features Henry who abandons the battles and retreats to a remote plantation in Georgia. But as Sherman's war machine storms through Georgia, Henry realizes that running forever won't save him forever, and it may be down to him to slow down the cruelty of Sherman. It is a compelling tale, very much recommended reading."

Midwest Book Review

"Through vivid description, a well-crafted plot, and a satisfying ending, J.F. Spieles brings to life an ugly time in American history through the eyes of an innocent boy struggling to survive.... In Sherman's Path exposes the roots of prejudice and teaches timeless coming of age lessons of tolerance, trust, and humanity. A must read for any student who thinks one's skin reveals anything about the person beneath it."

Becky Davis: 8th grade language arts teacher.

"Spieles's amazing attention to detail, especially in regards to what life was like for women and children, as well as newly freed slaves, will make Civil War history come alive for students. It is particularly unique that students have an opportunity to view events through the eyes of Southern characters, providing a fabulous opportunity to encourage a discussion about points of view and how history is written. What a great resource!"

Jessica Klinker, Library Media Director,
Immaculate Conception School, Columbus, Ohio